The Red River Boy

J C Wegener

The Red River Boy

Written by J C Wegener.
Published by prosolin.
© Copyright, J C Wegener, 2023. All rights reserved.
Cover designed by 100 Covers.

Chapter 1

Vila Feliz

"Pew, pew, pew, pew," Donato mouthed as he transformed his clasped hands with pointed fore-fingers into a laser gun, replaying the sci-fi television show he watched earlier. He stood on a ladder at the top of a water tank in the park of Vila Feliz, perched on his spaceship. Imaginary aliens crept towards him in the dimming light, as the sun disappeared behind the western hills. He zapped each one out of existence as they showed their alien faces, satisfaction showing on his face with each hit.

The park spread out beside a slowly flowing stream in the village of Vila Feliz, a village like many others in the expanse of the South American countryside. The green grass contrasted with the dusty brown-red streets and multi-colored buildings dotted throughout the rest of the village. A smell of stagnation rose from the bottom of the tank, but Donato ignored the stench. He bent his elbows and raised the laser gun close to his face. A curious smile remained as he scanned the area for any remaining aliens.

"Donato? Donato? Where are you Donato?" his mother, Catina, called from the front door of the family home.

Hidden from view, Donato looked towards his house from his elevated vantage point. He climbed out the tank and negotiated the external ladder to the ground. Dusting off his clothes to remove the grime, he noticed that instead of cleaning his clothes they were becoming increasingly grubby with each swipe of his hands. He frowned, but the disappointment quickly evaporated as he started running home.

"I'm here, Mama," Donato said between gasps as he ran up to her, smiling, the excitement of his adventure still lingering in his mind.

"Where have you been? Supper's ready. You shouldn't be outside in the dark. You could get lost and then how would you find us again? Look at your clothes and hands. Wash up and come to the table. I was hoping they would have lasted the day."

His mother's rebukes buffeted Donato. "Sorry, Mama," he said, hanging his head. He disliked disappointing Mama, and the frown on her face said 'disappointed' to him. The walk of shame to the bathroom accompanied his remorse. Washing his face and hands, he returned to the kitchen and to the table where dinner stood waiting.

Papa sat looking at him with a slight smile, a smile Donato liked. He sensed love behind the smile. Papa looked at Mama. "He's only a boy."

"It's all right for you. You don't have to clean his clothes." Mama's words sounded stern, but her look was anything but when she gazed at Donato. That same sense of love flowed over him.

Papa sighed. "You know Mama doesn't like you playing

in that tank. She wouldn't get so cross if you tried to keep yourself cleaner."

"Sanchez! Don't put ideas in his head." Mama looked at Papa firmly.

Papa laughed. "Catina, you know you look so beautiful when you frown like that."

Mama huffed. "Let's just start supper," she said as she sat.

Papa, still grinning, folded his hands. Mama and Donato did the same. "Heavenly Father, bless this food, for life and health and every good."

"Amen," they all said.

Donato grabbed his knife and fork and started eating hungrily, the smell of the beef and salsa in the burrito making his mouth water as he devoured the food.

"Eat properly," Mama berated. "You need to chew it properly, so you don't choke."

Donato nodded and slowed his chewing.

"I've got tomorrow off," Papa said, taking a break from his eating. "It's supposed to be a pleasant day. How about we have a picnic lunch in the park?"

"Yeah," Donato said, leaning forward as he looked at Papa and then Mama.

Mama smiled. "That would be nice. I might even put on that dress you fancy." Her eyes sparkled.

Papa laughed and wagged his fork at her. "It's a deal."

A loud rumble disturbed their conversation. Mama tensed and looked out the window. "Why do they have to blast when we're having dinner?"

"You know why. They do it at the change of shifts, when everyone's out of the way," Papa said.

"Well, it's very disconcerting."

Conversation escaped them, and they ate the rest of the

meal in silence. Donato finished his supper and took his plate to the sink.

"It's time to have a bath and get ready for bed," Mama said.

Donato nodded. He suddenly realized how tired he was after his busy adventures that afternoon. He ran the bath and took off his clothes. Hopping into the bath, he watched the water splash over him as it rose to halfway and turned off the taps. The warmth of the water soaked into him as he lay there. Knowing Mama would come in soon, he grabbed the soap from the holder and started rubbing the grime from his body and face, dunking his head to shampoo his hair.

Mama came through the door and smiled. "All clean?"

Donato nodded.

"Let's get you dry and off to bed then."

Standing up, Donato carefully hopped out of the bath. Mama held a towel ready and started drying him off, starting with his hair and slowly descending to his feet. She gave him his pyjamas and grabbed a comb, gently pulling the tines through his hair.

"Ouch."

"It's just a knot." She untangled the strands of hair with her finger and continued until his hair sat neat and straight. "Now clean your teeth and off to bed. Papa will come to tuck you in."

"Goodnight, Mama."

"Goodnight." She bent over and kissed him on the cheek. Donato smelled the slight scent of perfume. "We can all have a fun time at our picnic tomorrow."

Donato beamed. "Yeah."

Mama left, and he quickly brushed his teeth. He went to bed and waited for Papa.

"Where's my adventurous little boy?" Papa asked as he came into the room.

Donato grinned. His Papa always teased him with similar remarks each night at bedtime. "I'm in bed."

"That's a good boy. But where's super teddy?" He grabbed the teddy bear at the base of the bed and tucked it in beside Donato. Mama and Papa had bought the teddy bear on one of their shopping trips to El Grieta for his sixth birthday. It was brown, furry all over and soft, with leather soles on the feet, black button eyes and black leather nose. "He'll keep the monsters away."

Donato's smile widened. "There're no monsters."

"Not with super teddy protecting you there aren't. Now say your prayers." Papa sat on the side of the bed and Donato recited the prayer his parents had taught him. Papa rose and leaned over, kissing Donato on the cheek. "Goodnight."

"Goodnight, Papa."

Papa switched off the light and closed the door as Donato closed his eyes.

Chapter 2

Disaster

"Time to report," Jose told Rodriguez over the radio from the Vermelho Mine control room. As field inspector, Rodriguez had to provide regular updates on the dyke system that contained the tailings of the processed ore. He trudged around the dyke wall, feeling lethargic as he negotiated the narrow path. As he inspected the outer face, he saw brown liquid weeping down the steep slope to the trickling watercourse below. He conducted the required measurements and pulled the radio mouthpiece from his belt. "All stable here. Same as last time."

"Roger."

"Coming back in."

"Roger."

As Rodriguez was packing up his instruments to start the long walk back, the dyke wall started shaking. The inspector shifted to keep his balance as the wave passed over him. He grabbed his radio. "Jose, what was that?"

Jose looked at the monitors across his control desk. A light was blinking, signifying a minor earthquake. "Just another tremor, nothing to worry about. Come on in."

"Roger." Rodriguez kept walking but a creaking sound made him turn around. His mouth dropped open in disbelief. The dyke wall was cracking! The seepage had become a steady flow and the wall above bulged until it split open, freeing the trapped tailings corralled behind it. Rodriguez started running away from the fissure as he frantically called the control room. "Jose!" he yelled, panting from fear and effort. "Emergency! The dyke is collapsing. Repeat, the dyke is collapsing!"

Jose pressed the radio button. "What?"

"I'm telling you. The dyke is collapsing."

"Get out of there!"

"That's what I'm..." The radio went dead.

"Rodriguez, are you there? Copy?"

"..."

"Rodriguez...?"

"..."

Sanchez's body warmed as he lay on the picnic rug in the park by the creek, enjoying a much-anticipated picnic with his wife and son on his day off. He lay with his head nestled in Catina's lap, under a cloudless sky, with a slight cooling breeze wafting over him. The lawn, manicured to perfection, extended to the creek and had the smell of fresh cut grass. Catina wore her promised halter dress, the vivid one Sanchez liked. He looked up past the cleavage of her breasts to her face, as she gazed toward Donato in the playground. He felt content.

"Mama, Papa!"

Sanchez turned his head, wondering why Donato wanted their attention.

Donato hung upside down from his knees on one of the horizontal bars, swinging back and forth, his shirt hanging inside out over his shoulders, threatening to come off.

"Be careful," Catina said, raising her voice.

"Ahh, the joys of childhood," Sanchez said.

Catina looked down, love flowing between them. She smiled. "Yes, the joy." She caressed Sanchez's hair, its slight oiliness evident to her touch. Sanchez stroked her cheek in response. She tilted her head to let it rest in his palm and closed her eyes, enjoying the pleasure, like a cat purring.

Sanchez's phone beeped, destroying the moment. He took his phone from his pocket and frowned. "The boss wants me to call him. Says it's urgent."

Catina sighed, disappointed by the interruption. "You better call him then," she said.

"There isn't much reception here. I'd better go up the hill to call him." Sanchez strolled up the mound at the edge of the park, about fifteen metres above creek level, and called.

"Hi Sanchez, good of you to call back. Sorry to disturb you on your day off."

"It's Catina you'll answer to," Sanchez said as he looked over to his wife.

The supervisor, Enrico, laughed. "We've just received an urgent order for... what's that noise?"

"What noise?" Sanchez asked, looking around. "Oh... mercy be..." His eyes widened in terror as he watched a viscous torrent of red mud oozing down the creek bed like a stream of fresh magma towards the park.

"What's happening?" Enrico asked.

Sanchez couldn't answer. The red demon was heading straight for Catina and Donato, who sat and played in its path. Dread held him as he saw the inevitable. Panic froze him in place. He couldn't reach them before the flood engulfed them, and they were too far away to make it to higher ground.

Catina stood, puzzled by the unexpected noise. She saw the wall of red and screamed, turning towards Sanchez, fear in her eyes.

Donato heard the scream and looked at his mother, confused.

Sanchez looked left and right, frantic for a solution to save his family. He seemed out of danger, but certain death flowed towards his loved ones. He spied the corrugated iron water tank close to Catina, the same tank Donato used as a spaceship. The free-standing tank could be easily moved as people regularly drained it to prevent mosquitoes breeding. The tank stood about two metres in diameter and three metres high, with a ladder inside and outside. Sanchez hoped it would dislodge from its concrete base and float on the viscous fluid. "The tank... the tank!" he shouted down to Catina, as the rumble of the expanding mudslide grew louder around them.

Catina realised what Sanchez was telling them to do and cried out to her son. "Donato run... run to the tank!"

The little boy dashed to the tank, stopping just before he collided with it.

His mother was by his side. "Up the ladder. In the tank," she said, puffing from her sprint.

The ladder was rusty and some of the supports were fractured from corrosion, but Donato climbed in with practiced ease.

Catina looked up as he climbed, waving for him to get to the top. She saw him disappear over the edge as she glanced over her shoulder. The approaching front had reached the edge of the park and was steaming towards her.

She climbed, fumbling for a rung in her panic. After a few rungs, her foot slipped, and she lost a shoe, but she didn't stop. Catina reached the top as the vanguard of the attacking torrent prepared for its assault. The engulfing stain wrapped its tentacles around the tank, jolting it to one side. Catina overbalanced at the sudden movement and catapulted towards the opposite side, losing her grip on the ladder. She collided with the wall, falling to the base like a rag doll. The tank jerked and jostled, rocking and rotating as it floated on the evil flood, almost like a trophy for the demon destroyer.

Sanchez looked on, helpless. The cataclysm of oozing destruction shattered houses like matchsticks with the weight of sludge and detritus; cars and uprooted trees bobbed on top of the passing force. The flood peaked about three metres below him. That didn't help the rest of the village, though. He didn't realize he was still holding his phone when Enrico's shouting drew his attention.

"What's happening?" Enrico yelled.

"The flood... a red flood... flowing through village... destroying everything... Catina... Donato... in tank... floating," Sanchez said blankly, as the tank disappeared around a bend. He dropped the phone as his knees buckled and he landed on the ground, curling into a foetal position, screaming.

Chapter 3

Roland

Roland Cavendish, Chief Executive of Zagreus Minerals, was roused from his siesta. He always had one after lunch when he didn't have meetings he couldn't avoid. His desk phone bleated for his attention. Rubbing the remnants of sleep from his eyes, he fumbled for his phone and saw his personal assistant's image on the screen.

"Yes, Laura."

"Sorry to disturb you sir, but Santos from Vermelho Mine is on the line. He says it's urgent."

"Okay, Laura. Put him through." Music replaced Laura's voice for a few seconds before being reconnected. "Santos?"

"Mr Cavendish, I must speak with you. We don't know —" Santos blurted.

"Whoa, whoa, slow down Santos. Take a breath." Roland snapped into focus. Santos usually remained calm under stress.

After a few deep breaths, Santos started again. "Sir, there's been an incident at the mine."

"What sort of incident?"

"The tailings dyke wall has burst."

Perspiration dampened Roland's forehead and his heart hammered as adrenalin spiked in his system. He knew the implications of the news, but prayed it would not confirm his worst fears. "How much escaped?"

A few seconds of silence bridged the gap in conversation. "All of it, Sir."

Roland closed his eyes, hoping to wake up from the nightmare. The tailings dam held 46 billion liters of tailings. He dreaded asking the next question, but knew he had to ask it. "Anyone hurt?"

A longer silence followed before Santos replied, "Nineteen employees are missing... most presumed dead, as they were downstream of the dyke wall..."

Roland waited for Santos to continue. "And?"

"And there are untold civilians missing, Sir. There are many villages along the path. Some are the families of our employees... whole... families..." The tragedy was clear in Santos's agonized voice.

Roland's mouth went dry. He tried moistening it with his tongue but couldn't get any moisture anywhere. His mind raced to develop an action plan. "Okay Santos, I'm on my way to the mine. The media won't be far away, if they haven't already got the story. Just tell them you are assessing the situation, if they contact you. Tell them I am coming, and I'll provide a statement when I arrive. You have that, Santos?"

"Yes, boss."

"I can't fathom what you're going through, but keep calm, and implement the site's disaster plan with the people still there. I'll contact you when I arrive. And may God's mercy be with you... with you all."

Roland slumped back in his chair in disbelief. For several minutes he let the disaster sink into his psyche before raising Laura on the intercom.

"Yes, sir?"

"Please organize transport to Vermelho Mine. I need a private jet for Carlos City, not a commercial flight. And hire me a helicopter at Carlos City airport to take me to the site. Co-ordinate with Felicity at our Carlos City office. I'm going home to pack on the way to the airport. Tell Sid to bring the car around. Forward the arrangements to me when you've made them."

"Yes, sir."

"And... you'll see some confronting images in the media. Pray it isn't as bad as the media is reporting."

Roland packed his briefcase and put his laptop into its protective sleeve. With a quick backward glance over his desk, he caught the elevator down to his waiting limousine.

Sid stood erect, holding the rear door open as Roland slid into the back seat. Checking that Roland and his belongings were inside, he closed the door and walked around to the driver's side, taking his position in the driver's seat. "Where to Mr. Cavendish?"

"My home, and then to the airport."

"Yes, sir."

The vehicle started moving as Roland reached over to the drinks cabinet and pulled out a bottle of scotch. His hands shook as he poured a double shot into the tumbler. Bringing the fiery liquid to his mouth, he took a large gulp and waited for his nerves to settle.

"Are you okay, Sir," Sid asked, looking at Roland through the rear-view mirror. "You look a little pale."

Roland peered in the mirror. "Not really. There's been an incident at Vermelho. It doesn't look good."

"Oh."

Silence filled the air.

"Nothing you haven't been able to sort out in the past, Sir."

"Yeah... hope you're right."

After the side trip home to collect his belonging, Roland made a mental note to call his wife Deborah, who was away at the time. As he took a deep breath, he was overcome by a panic attack and flung open his briefcase, sighing in relief as he saw his passport lay there. His phone chirped. A message from Laura. "Atchison Aviation, Sid. It's in the private operator's terminal."

"Laura has forwarded the directions to my navigation, Sir."

"Oh... Good." *The marvels of modern technology.* He sat back and tried to relax.

Sid switched on the video and tuned to Roland's favourite news channel. Typical news stories broadcast from the unit. Roland remembered he needed to call Deborah, so he muted the video. Several rings went by before Deborah answered.

"Hi honey. I didn't expect a call from you."

"Hi sweetie. Yeah, well, I wish I didn't need to call."

"Why? What's up?"

"I'm going to Carlos City. An incident has occurred at Vermelho Mine, and they need me."

"That sounds serious."

"It is. You'll hear about it on the news before the day's out."

"Anything I can do?"

"Stay calm. Don't talk to the media, keep the daggers at bay, and pray it isn't as bad as the news reports."

"Oh... and what about you?"

14

"I'm coping... I think. I'd better go. We're nearing the airport, so I'll call you later today or tomorrow. I don't know when I'll be back."

"Love you, honey."

"Love you, too."

Roland turned up the volume on the video but didn't pay much attention.

Ten minutes later a Breaking News banner appeared at the top of the video screen with 'Mining Disaster Near Carlos City' below it. A news anchor appeared as Roland focussed on the screen. His body filled with dread.

"In news just in, a mining disaster occurred earlier today at the Vermelho Mine, located two hundred and seventy kilometers from Carlos City. Zagreus Minerals owns the mine. We have a reporter on location, and we will switch over to him for further details."

A man sitting in a helicopter with headphones and a microphone sat in silence, concentrating, as if waiting for his queue. "Yes, Malcolm," the reporter said, raising his voice above the noise. "I am circling above the Vermelho Mine site. I understand that at approximately one-thirteen this afternoon, the dyke wall for the tailings dam on the site collapsed, releasing the entire contents of the dam into the valley below. Details are sketchy, but we have footage of the disaster, which we'll show you now." A red snake appeared on the screen, bursting forth from the dam and weaving its way through the valley to the Plata River, where it stained the water red.

"The dam collapse has released a significant quantity of tailings, producing a potential environmental disaster of unknown magnitude," the reporter said as the doomsday images continued on screen. "We believe the release has destroyed several villages."

"Any reports of casualties?" the anchor asked.

"I understand there have been casualties, but I have received no official reports suggesting numbers at this early stage."

"We will leave you there, Earl. We'll return to you for further developments as they become available."

"Will do, Malcolm. Earl Thompson reporting from Carlos City."

The visual changed back to the studio. "We will keep you updated with developments in that story, as we receive them."

Roland turned it off. His shaking hands reached for the whisky bottle and he downed another shot under Sid's watchful eye.

They reached Atchison Aviation's terminal and, half an hour later, Roland was taxiing to take off for the six-hour flight. He was relieved no media greeted him at the airport and he settled into the flight determined to have an action plan on arrival.

Chapter 4

Donato

As the tank bumped and bounced its way along the cascading deluge of red poison, Donato clamped his eyes shut to block out the nightmare and clung to the ladder for his life. He heard his mother scream with each shudder. He ached to move and find her protective arms, but couldn't let go. The tank, empty except for a thin layer of mud, rolled Donato around the bottom, caking him with dirt. Welts turning into bruises covered his body as he crashed into the tank walls. He cracked his eyes open and looked up to the sky. It rocked back and forth with the rhythm of the tank's motion.

A violent jolt reverberated through the iron shell, as if they hit an object solid and hard. The ladder came loose, and he lost his grip, catapulting him across the vessel. His mother shrieked and then went silent.

The violence subsided, and a gentle rocking resumed. He wondered why his mother had become so quiet. He screamed. His mother sat by the ladder supports with one sightless eye looking at him. A rusted support from the ladder poked out of the other eye. It had pierced her skull and lanced her eye. She died instantly.

"Mama?..."

He sobbed and tried to block out the sight of his dead mother. Donato, alone and helpless, wanted someone to come and save him.

Day transformed into evening and night, and the rocking tank cradled Donato into a tortured sleep.

The sound of birds greeting the day woke him, as dawn transitioned the darkness to light. Donato was again confronted by the horror of his mother, still staring at him with one sightless eye, now becoming milky and sleepy, as the top eyelid drooped. He looked away and cried for his mother. He felt so alone. Thirst and hunger were his only companions as he sat in his open top prison, sobbing and shivering with the lingering chill of the night, the tank drifting on its merry way to wherever.

Flies buzzed around his mother as the day temperature rose. He tried shooing them away, but the numbers proved too many. He wanted to touch his mother, but fear prevented him. The tank smelled putrid, maybe because of the tank's contents, maybe himself, but Donato knew his mother was part of the reason. He had never seen something dead, not that he could remember, anyway. Their dog died a few years ago, but Papa buried it, so he only had a fleeting look before Papa whisked it away. He now knew death, and he didn't like it. It hurt, it hurt so much.

The sky clouded over mid-afternoon and the sound of thunder approached. Flashes of lightning lit the tank as rain started falling. Donato held his tongue out to catch a few drops and cupped his hands to catch whatever he could, his thirst barely satisfied before the rain stopped and the sky cleared again. Donato fell into a bad-tempered brooding

mood, one his parents often rebuked him for. The hopeless-
ness of his predicament crushed him. How could he find his
father? Where on earth would he end up? The tank
continued to bob and revolve. There seemed no end to his
travels in sight.

Day changed into night, and Donato settled into a fitful
sleep until daybreak. His stomach grumbled and
complained and he felt thirsty again, his mouth parched.
Midway through the morning, the bottom of the tank
scraped against something hard. It steadied and came to a
complete stop. The rocking and rotating finally ended. He
had landed somewhere... but where?

Even though the tank gave him protection, he needed
food and water. He had to get out. The ladder teetered from
its mounting support at the top. It needed straightening but
that meant placing it on top of his mother. He was heart-
broken but knew he must escape the tank. Leaning against
the wall and fighting the pain from his cuts and bruises, he
staggered over to the ladder as the stiffness in his joints
eased. He looked at the cadaver that used to be his mother.
"Sorry Mama," he said, as he straightened the ladder. The
end did not reach the bottom of the tank so all the weight
was being supported from the flimsy mountings at the top.
Donato placed his foot on the bottom rung and lifted
himself off the tank floor and onto the ladder. It swung to
the side as the center of gravity changed, causing Donato to
yelp in surprise. He lifted his foot for the next rung when
the ladder support fractured and fell to the bottom of the
tank. He yelled in frustration and pain but rose to his feet
and studied the ladder to find a solution. The ladder rested
halfway up the side of the tank. He needed to get it closer to
the tank rim. He raised the ladder on an angle, resting the
top half a meter from the edge. Donato hoped he could

swing over the top from there. He moved the ladder to the left, bringing it into line with the outside ladder. The ladder felt steady when he placed his weight on it this time, and he scaled it with caution until he reached the top rung. He almost overbalanced but clutched the top lip of the tank to steady himself.

The tank had settled on a sandy beach on a bend in the river. He wondered about the river's name. Donato was overcome with shock when he saw the water stained red as far as he could see. Fish lay upside down in the shallows, gulping for oxygen as they surrendered to death. A thick forest approached the river's edge and the ground rose to a green undulating landscape. Rocky outcrops blemished the otherwise pure verdant scene. A slight breeze wafted past him, cooling him as it flicked at his hair. The scent of flowers and death intertwined.

Donato grunted in frustration as he saw no outside ladder, torn off at some stage in his voyage away from his home. Resigning himself to falling into the river, he lifted himself over the edge of the tank and lowered himself down, falling the two meters into the water, which only just covered his prone body. He jerked his head up and gulped for air. *At least I get a wash*, he thought.

He walked over to the dry river bank, turned and said with sadness, "Bye Mama."

Chapter 5

Sanchez

S anchez lay motionless in a catatonic state, unaware of time. He didn't care since his dear Catina and Donato no longer shared his life. A helicopter flew overhead in the late afternoon, but its significance escaped him. Sometime later, he heard its presence again, and the noise became louder as it hovered overhead. The downdraft of the rotors buffeted him as he watched it descend, coming to a stop twenty meters above him.

A winched rescuer descended on a rope. "Are you injured?"

"No. But my family..." Sanchez collapsed.

"Okay. Let's get you somewhere safe and we can continue from there. Does that sound good?"

Sanchez nodded.

"Okay, I'll put this harness on you and hook this rope onto you. We'll winch you up to the helicopter. I'll be with you to help."

Sanchez nodded again, as he meekly succumbed to the harness. The rescuer signalled to be winched up to the helicopter and Sanchez found himself dangling in mid-air as they rose from the ground.

"You're doing good," the rescuer shouted above the whirring blades. "At the helicopter, they will swing us both up and we'll be safe. We'll take you to a recovery center and register you and you can rest."

Everything was happening too fast for Sanchez. He became disorientated but took deep breaths before settling in for the ride to safety. The landscape flashed past as they flew along, and he wondered how he could move forward in his life. He observed the carnage wrought by the red flood. It looked like a blood-stained tapestry and he shivered as he recalled the wall of destruction coming towards him not so long ago. How many have someone missing? How many others are dead? He stared at the floor and retreated into self-pity. *You never realize how much you take for granted until fate takes it away from you. Taken away? More like ripped out of my life while I watched, feeling helpless. What will life hold for me now? They could have found Catina and Donato and they're waiting for me. That tank was robust. But you saw how it destroyed those houses like paper. How could anything survive that? They must be alive. I have to find them. They'll be there, waiting for me.*

Sanchez noticed they were flying towards El Grieta, a larger urban center upstream of the disaster. He travelled there often with Catina and Donato on shopping trips. They reached the outskirts of the town where the forest turned to suburbia. A large sporting complex lay ahead, where people played football, and other sports. A large pavilion stood on the sports field, and he wondered why it stood there. The helicopter approached the complex, guided by someone waving paddles. The rescuer helped Sanchez out of the cabin to safety where a medic was waiting for him. Moments later, Sanchez watched the helicopter lift off in search of anyone else still alive.

"Are you injured?" the medic asked.

Sanchez shook his head.

"Good, come with me and I'll take you to our admittance section for a check-up and registration."

Sanchez allowed himself to be guided in silence. A few moments later, they entered the pavilion Sanchez saw from the air. It was filled with injured people, medical staff with Red Cross armbands, and other volunteers and helpers, busy trying to help. A mass of people with vacant eyes and mud-stained clothes sat, defeated. Several of them looked up as he entered. But one by one they lowered their heads in disappointment and despair, as they realized he wasn't who they hoped for. Sanchez scrutinized the survivors, hoping to see Catina and Donato, but their absence was a lead weight. The rip in his heart lengthened with the anguish, his head sagged, heavy with grief.

A Red Cross worker was asking him if he was injured. "Do you have any pain?" she asked as she lifted Sanchez's chin.

"No."

She shone a bright light into his eyes. "What is your name?"

"Sanchez Barbosa."

"Good, well Mr Barbosa, there's no concussion and you appear uninjured. You're one of the lucky ones. Please check in at the registration desk. Hope everything goes well." She moved off to her next patient.

One of the lucky ones, Sanchez thought with a note of bitterness. But when he surveyed the crowd, he realized many people were swathed in bandages and dressings. Some even rested on makeshift hospital beds. Maybe he should count himself lucky. He joined the queue at the registration desk and turned his head, hoping Catina and Donato stood behind him, but hope turned to despair.

"Next," a person behind a desk announced.

Sanchez walked over to her.

"Please take a seat," she said. "My name is Maria Diaz, and I have some questions for you. You can eat and rest afterwards."

Sanchez thought she seemed pleasant and had a caring smile.

"What is your name?"

"Sanchez Barbosa."

She wrote the information on a form she had in front of her. "Is that spelled correctly?"

"Yes."

"Where are you from?" she asked, poised to write the response.

"Vila Feliz."

Maria's head jerked up and she stared at Sanchez in disbelief. "You are the first from that village," she mumbled as she wrote. "What were you doing when the incident happened?"

Sanchez looked at the floor, the memory overpowering him. He inhaled and then said, "I was picnicking with my family, but I went to higher ground for a phone call and..."

Maria looked at Sanchez, pity in her eyes. "I'm so sorry," she said as she wrote her notes.

"But they're alive. They must be alive."

She moved her hand to comfort Sanchez. "As I just said, you are the first survivor from Vila Feliz. The flood destroyed it. It's unlikely others survived."

Sanchez became agitated. "But you don't understand.

They climbed into a tank. It floated away. They could still be alive."

Maria's eyes brightened as she realized there was some hope. She pulled her hand away and exclaimed. "You are sure?"

"Yes, yes, I saw it."

"What are their names?"

"Catina is my wife and Donato, my son."

"Such beautiful names."

Sanchez smiled forlornly.

"Can you remember anything else?" She considered what might be useful. "Can you describe the tank? How large is it?"

Sanchez tried to recall the size of the tank. "It's two meters in diameter and three meters high, made of corrugated iron and very rusty, but it holds water."

"Wouldn't the tank be full of water?"

"No, they drain it when it rains but they close it afterward."

Maria scribbled what Sanchez said. "How did they get into the tank?"

"It has a ladder outside the tank... and inside too."

"Anything else?"

Sanchez shook his head as he reached out to grab her forearm. "You must find them. Please..."

"We will do our best, Mr Barbosa. You're the first person to tell us there might be more survivors out there. A rescue team will place your case in a priority list." She placed her free hand on top of Sanchez's as she looked into his eyes. "I hope and pray they find them," she said, with the hint of a tear. "Now go have something to eat and drink and whatever else you need. It's getting dark. You need to rest."

Sanchez headed for the buffet while Maria got a red

pen from her desk and wrote a large red 'R' (for Rescue) on the form. She took it over to the tray for the rescue team and noticed with sadness how few forms rested there.

Sanchez filed past the buffet table, where people served him chicken stew with rice and a bread roll. He sat at the nearest trestle table and soon realized how hungry he was. The food vanished.

He found people who were handing out bedding and blankets and searched for a bed. He found one in the section for unaccompanied men. Tiredness overcame him, but the torment of feeling useless kept him awake. He should be out there doing something, trying to find his family. But he knew his best bet lay with the rescuers finding them.

"Where are you from?" someone next to him asked.

"Ha..." Sanchez said, surprised that someone was talking to him.

"Where are you from?"

"Vila Feliz."

"Oh, I heard they got hit hard."

"Yeah, and you?"

"Vila Rio Ver."

"That's near Rio Plata, isn't it?"

"Yeah."

"You lose anyone?"

"No, I live alone. Lucky, I guess. A lot of others have lost everyone... and you?"

"Wife and son are missing. They could be alive. They were the last time I saw them."

"I hope they are."

"So do I."

Chapter 6

Carlos City

Roland landed in Carlos City just before midnight. Two security officers were waiting for him at the bottom of the stairs when he disembarked.

"Your office has arranged for us to escort you through Customs and keep you away from the media, Mr Cavendish," the taller man said.

Roland followed them to a private entrance of the terminal building where an Immigration Officer stamped his passport and waved him through. "Have a pleasant stay," the officer said.

Roland glanced back to see if the man was making fun of him, but realized he was on automatic pilot and didn't realize what he was saying.

Felicity, the company country manager in Carlos City, met him as he entered the luggage hall. "Good Evening, Mr Cavendish."

"Evening, Felicity. Good of you to meet me."

"It's been a rough day for you, Sir."

"It's been a rough day for everyone."

They retrieved Roland's case and left the airport terminal.

After they got into the waiting limousine, Felicity yawned, unable to suppress her tiredness.

"Have you had any rest?" Roland asked.

"There's too much to do."

"Can you give me an update?"

In her professional voice, Felicity said, "Yes, the government has declared a national emergency and rescue efforts are in progress. There are 14 employees missing. I believe Santos told you 19. We have located five. Authorities have counted 105 dead and 63 survivors have been taken to rescue camps." Felicity looked at Roland, tears in her eyes.

He patted her hand, digesting the unbelievable horror. "Felicity, it's a tragedy. It shouldn't have happened, but it did. We must recover from this as best we can." Felicity crumbled and wept. After a few moments she regained control and wiped her eyes. "Sorry, Sir."

"No need. Can you fill me in on the potential environmental crisis?"

"The tailings have entered Rio Plata and are dispersing downstream. That's all I know."

"Okay. Where is Santos now?"

"He's still at the mine. They're bulldozing a levee in place, but the tailings have all escaped."

Roland sat in silence for a while.

"Sir?"

"Yes."

"The media are demanding blood for this."

Roland smiled sadly. "I expect nothing less. Let me handle the media. I want you to concentrate on helping me find out what happened, helping who we can, and minimizing whatever damage we can."

"Yes, Sir."

After a few minutes, Felicity asked, "Mr Cavendish?"

"Yes."

"I know I'm being selfish, but will we have jobs after this?"

"A good question. I don't know, but I'll look after you. Don't worry."

They arrived at the Carlos City Office for Zagreus Minerals and drove into the secure parking garage. Roland noticed a pack of press outside as they disappeared into the bowels of the garage. Felicity and Roland disembarked from the vehicle and used the elevator. They ascended in silence.

A hive of busyness greeted Roland as he entered the office. Tired faces looked up at him as he surveyed the scene. He sensed he should give words of sympathy and encouragement, but couldn't find any that met the severity of the disaster. A few people gave wan smiles, while others nodded before they returned to their work. His silence made him feel inadequate.

Felicity showed him to his office which would become the base for operations. "I'll be next door if you need me. I'll send a secretary to organize coffee or food."

"Thank you." Roland leaned back in his chair and considered his country manager. *Felicity is caring and quick. She can be hard-nosed when she needs to be too.* Roland chuckled to himself. *I've been on the receiving end of that.* He retrieved his laptop and other items from his briefcase and set himself up for work.

A woman knocked on his door. "Shall I get a coffee for you, Mr Cavendish?"

Roland looked up, seeing another tired person. *These people need to get some rest. Otherwise they won't be any use in the days ahead.* "Yes please, just black."

"I've been informed," she muttered and disappeared.

She returned with coffee and biscuits.

"Thank you..." Roland looked at her nametag, "Viki."

Viki nodded and turned to leave but stopped. "Excuse me for interrupting you. I know you are busy, but the media is overloading the switchboard, wanting a comment. What should I tell them?"

"Tell them we are still assessing the incident. I will give a press conference later today... wait. Come with me." Roland walked into Felicity's office, Viki close behind. "Felicity, I need a helicopter at first light to see the aftermath. We can then fly to the mine to meet Santos and the others. Should we conduct the press conference at the mine or back here?"

Felicity paused to think. "At the mine. It shows you are in the center of the action and not staying apart."

"Good idea, should midday give me plenty of time?"

"It should. I suggest one o'clock just to be sure."

"Okay." Roland turned to Viki. "Tell them I will give a press conference at 1pm at the Vermelho Mine Office.

"Felicity, we need to send these people home. Start two shifts. Otherwise they will collapse from exhaustion and won't be here when we need them."

"That's what I think. I'm outlining a plan before talking to them, although convincing them to go is another matter."

"Okay. When will the helicopter be ready?"

"I have arranged it for five."

Roland looked at his watch. Another three hours. "Thanks." He walked back to his office and sipped his coffee while considering his plan for the day. He logged onto his computer and opened the financial accounts for the business. The balance sheet showed the business had $100 million dollars in available cash. The bottom line will suffer, but Roland thought it the least of the company's problems, given the ongoing ramifications in the months or years ahead. Legal fees may come to that before they settled everything. *Goodness knows what the stock market will do when it opens today.* He wanted to offer the money as good-will for the rescue effort. He needed to call a few board members before the press conference for approval, but he felt confident.

They must find the cause of the collapse. They needed the best civil engineering consultants to review the data and work out what happened. *One of Felicity's people can handle that.*

Roland wanted to meet the families of the missing employees personally. He hoped Santos knew who they were. Then he realized they may not find the families, they might be gone, too.

Roland busied himself for another two hours before he decided he needed to shower and change for his trip to the mine. Refreshed but still in shock, he and Felicity boarded the chopper where his country manager promptly fell asleep. Roland couldn't blame her. Her day had been exhausting. He stayed awake as sunrise dawned on the horizon in the east.

Chapter 7

Vermelho Mine

R oland and Felicity arrived over the Rio Plata two hours later and followed it upstream. He saw a rusty-red stain begin to appear in the river soon afterwards. He shook Felicity awake as the scar advanced. When she looked down she was shocked. "That's terrible," she said.

"Indeed," Roland said solemnly.

They continued up-river, the intensity of the redness increasing as they stared. An hour later, they reached the point of origin. The helicopter veered away from the river and followed the snaking corridor of red mud to the failed tailings dam. The deluge of mud and its destruction confronted them. Stranded vehicles and the tops of buildings jutting up through the mud resembled excavations at an archeological site. The scene left Roland speechless. He couldn't fathom the devastation and suffering inflicted on these people. How could this happen? It showed how destructive large corporations could be, changing people's lives forever.

When they landed at the mine's helipad, reporters were

crowded at the front gate. Roland and Felicity disembarked from the helicopter, and an employee from the mine escorted them to the offices inside the administration complex.

The conference room acted as the command center for Vermelho Mine. Six people carried the weight of hundreds, maybe thousands, as they dealt with the disaster. They all looked up when Roland and Felicity arrived. A worried Santos got up to meet them. "Hi," he said, tired and unenthusiastic, as he shook Roland's hand and then Felicity's.

"Hello Santos," Roland said. He glanced around, nodded his head at the others, "Everyone could do with a five-minute break." The room's atmosphere lighten. He studied Santos. "Let's go outside into the fresh air."

Santos led the way to a courtyard sometimes used for social activities. Santos's shoulders slumped from exhaustion, stress and total devastation. He leaned against a picnic table and looked at Roland in desperation. "This disaster is so big, so terrible, I don't know if I can cope."

Roland didn't have the words to reassure his manager while harbouring similar feelings. So he said, "I don't understand what's happened at the moment, but I know that it's a disaster. Seeing the river and the devastated landscape during the flight here sobers anyone into realizing both the insignificance of the human race and what destruction we can cause." He sighed. "We can't turn back the clock. We can only move forward. Make amends for what we can and take responsibility for our failings. Now, I need you to help the company recover from this and look after our employees. I need you to help me understand what went wrong."

Santos stammered. "It is difficult... looking at these people, knowing they want answers, knowing they have relatives and friends affected by this, seeing their despair."

Roland searched his soul for a moment. "I'm here to give them hope and restore their dignity."

They stood in silence.

Roland asked, "What can you tell me? I'm having a press conference at one."

Santos gathered his thoughts. "The failure of the dyke wall released 43 billion liters of tailings. There are nine employees of the original 19 still missing, presumed dead. We have recovered five and accounted for the other five."

"Any idea of the downstream impact?"

"We don't know what the casualties are, except it may be hundreds. The flood destroyed several villages in the path of the tailings. The river is diluting the tailings, but we don't know its effect on the river's ecology."

"Okay. That gives me something. I'll get more details as I refine my statement. Go have a few minutes."

Santos returned to the conference room. Roland leaned on the table, considering his words for the press conference. He developed an outline in his head and headed back inside where he called the board members to get approval for the expenditure. He expected resistance to his proposal, but the support he received surprised him.

The time to confront the press arrived, and Roland entered the canteen building with the assembled media. Several camera flashes blinded him as he walked to the podium. Felicity and Santos stood on either side. The audience quietened as Roland cleared his throat. He fixed his gaze on the reporters. "Ladies and gentlemen, I will deliver a statement today. I will not be taking questions. An incident occurred yesterday afternoon with the failure of the tailings dam dyke at this Vermelho Mine, resulting in the release of 43 billion liters of slurry. A tragic loss of life, both Vermelho mine employees and civilian, occurred and my heartfelt condolences go out to everyone affected." Roland licked his dry lips. "The reason for the dam's failure is being investigated. Zagreus Minerals is engaging independent consultants to investigate the circumstances behind the failure and make recommendations, ensuring it never happens again."

Several reporters shouting question on how the disaster could have occurred, what effect it would have on the community and the environment and how the consultants can be unbiased. Roland waited patiently for the commotion to abate before continuing.

"In the meantime, we will cooperate with the authorities in our endeavors to find survivors, rejuvenate the landscape, and help people return to their lives as much as possible. In that respect, the board of Zagreus Minerals has approved the immediate release of $100 million for rescue and recovery efforts." Roland paused to gauge the response. "Zagreus Minerals regrets what has happened and again, I offer my heartfelt condolences to the families who have lost loved ones."

Roland prepared to leave.

"How can you stand there and say you regret it when you caused this destruction?" shouted a reporter. "Why are you always putting profit before the welfare of our people? Why won't you answer our questions? Have you something to hide?"

Roland gritted his teeth as he turned to face his accuser, anger in his eyes. The reporter was trying to provoke him so he would lose his temper and say something scandalous. He took several deep breaths and intended to ignore the questions but changed his mind and returned to the microphones. Felicity reached for his arm, warning him to be careful. He glared at the reporter, tears building. "These last 24 hours have been the worst in my entire life. I cannot imagine the suffering and pain these people are going through. But I promise you one thing..." Roland pointed his finger at the reporter, "... I will do everything within my power to help these people in whatever way I can."

Roland rushed back to his office and slammed the door behind him, rattling the frame and venetian blinds. He collapsed into the chair, bowed his head onto his folded arms and cried.

Chapter 8

Evacuation Center

S anchez woke drained after a disrupted and sleepless night. He wandered around the Evacuation Center and noticed various booths with essential items, finding one with toiletries and another with clothing. With a ration from each, he located an amenities block and showered. Refreshed, he walked to the canteen and ate breakfast while he considered what he should do. Catina and Donato must be somewhere. He would ask the authorities if they had any news for him.

A helicopter landed as he mused and Sanchez glanced over, as did other evacuees. Two people covered in red mud disembarked. Lifeless faces. He wondered, *Did I look like that yesterday? Do I still look like that?* He hoped not. The shock of the disaster had worn off, and he sensed an urgency to locate his family. But he didn't know where to start, still finding his own feet.

He wandered over to the processing centre to ask after his family but each person just shook their head and pointed him to another table. Frustrated, he stood in front of the last table with any officials. A man ushered him to a seat.

"How can I help you?"

"I'm trying to find out if you've located my wife and son. You have their details."

"I see," said the man sadly, accustomed to delivering unpleasant news. "What are their names?"

"Catina and Donato Barbosa."

"I will see," he said with a sympathetic smile. He typed the names into the computer database and Catina's name came up first, then Donato's. He frowned. "I'm sorry, but they are still missing. The notes say they are still searching for them, though."

"They were in a tank. It'll be miles away by now if it's still floating."

"It's recorded in the notes. A search for the tank is underway, but they haven't located it yet. I'm sorry. It's early days still. I'm sure they will find them." The official tried to give Sanchez a sense of hope, even though he didn't hold much hope himself. He had dealt with too many reports of dead bodies when families believed them to be missing, leaving him as distraught as the survivors.

"Okay then," Sanchez said, disappointed by the lack of information. "Thanks." He rose and trudged away. *At least he didn't say they are dead*, he thought, comforting himself.

Someone approached him with little purpose, as if needing to talk with someone. Sanchez stopped and let the man advance, watching him as he came closer. Worry lines etched the man's brow.

"Hi," the man said as he stood in front of Sanchez. "I'm Danito."

"Hi. I'm Sanchez."

"Saw you wandering on your own and thought I'd come over and chat."

Sanchez looked around to see if they were alone. "I was just thinking what I should do. My wife and son are still missing."

"Oh," Danito said resentfully. "My wife is dead. I have no family."

"I'm sorry."

Danito shrugged his shoulders. "What are you going to do now?"

"I don't know. We can leave if we want, I suppose, but I don't have anywhere to go. I guess it's destroyed my house, though I should go back and check, try and find my stuff. But my house is on higher ground, so it might still be there."

"I'm stumped what to do. I have no money, no ID, nothing," Danito complained.

"At least I still have my wallet and cards and my phone. It needs charging soon, though."

"At least you have that. Your village near here?" Danito appraised Sanchez.

"Vila Feliz."

"How will you get there?"

"I don't know. Find someone going there."

"A lot to clean up, valuables and other belongings."

Sanchez started feeling uneasy but couldn't pinpoint the exact cause. He wanted to get away from this man. He was asking too many questions. "I don't know. I'll have to find out." He walked away.

"I'll come with you."

"Can't stop you." The suspicion grew stronger as they ventured back to the main pavilion. Sanchez made sure he held his phone and wallet in his pockets. He scoured the Center for people providing transport, or other essentials for independent living, to get his life back together, so he could search for his family. Danito stood next to him, too close, but Sanchez couldn't escape without being obvious. He needed to talk to someone and knew the Center's management by now. He ducked into a bathroom and hoped Danito would get sick of waiting and bug someone else. He was gone 20 minutes later.

Sanchez remembered his boss lived near El Grieta, so he found somewhere quiet and called his number. Enrico answered just before it rang out.

"Hello?"

"Hello Enrico. It's Sanchez."

"Oh, Hi! How are you?"

"I'm alive. Don't know what's happened to Catina and Donato yet. They can't find them."

"Oh, I'm sorry. Hope they find them."

"And you?"

"I'm okay. We're upstream of the disaster."

"Is the business okay?"

"It's still there. I don't know what'll happen now, though. I might open again soon, once everything settles."

Sanchez fidgeted, embarrassed to ask. "Do you have room for me until I get settled back in Vila Feliz?"

"Um... g... I don't know. Our relatives are in the spare rooms."

"It's okay. Just thought I'd ask. Someone around here will have room."

"Sorry."

Televisions in the Center were broadcasting continuous updates of the disaster. Sanchez watched the CEO of the mine company giving a press conference and gritted his teeth, feeling rage towards the man. He'd give him a piece of his mind if he ever saw him, but Sanchez presumed his inferior status too far below the man's importance to be worth noticing. He knew the man's remorse was more about lost profits than people.

Media crews arrived at the Center mid-afternoon and started interviewing people affected by the disaster. Sanchez moved well away from them. He didn't want them poking their noses into his suffering just to make good TV. He disappeared behind the helicopter pad until he realised one was coming in to land. It looked different to a rescue helicopter, bright blue and white, and didn't have any Red Cross markings. *More media.* He rose and found a hiding spot elsewhere.

Roland jumped from the helicopter and surveyed the site with a sober expression. He wanted to visit the Evacuation Center first. He offered a few words to the survivors, hoping he could comfort them. Only a few spoke back. One or two said nothing while others stared at him angrily. Roland could tell they blamed him, each scowl plunging another dagger into his soul. He stepped through a doorway and walked into someone coming the other way.

"You..." Sanchez said, recovering from the collision. "How dare you come here after what you've done?" Sanchez's loathing and spit sprayed Roland's face.

Roland flinched, repulsed, but didn't reach for his handkerchief.

"Hope you've made enough money from us," Sanchez fumed. "What are you going to do now, keep gouging your profits out of us? Send more of us to our deaths. Go back to your mansion. We don't want you here, unless you can tell me where my wife and son are."

Sanchez was drained, all the injustices exhausting him, and he started to sob.

Roland couldn't move. He stood erect as the insults buffeted him, letting the man vent his grief. "I'm sorry," he said when the abuse was over. "I'll find your family."

"You've done enough. I don't want your help." Sanchez walked away.

Roland stood motionless for a few moments until Felicity brought him away from where his mind cowered.

"Maybe we should go," she said.

Chapter 9

Depression

Roland couldn't get Sanchez's condemnation out of his head. He sat in silence in the helicopter as it cruised back to Carlos City. Felicity glanced at him but said nothing. He hoped she understood the pressure he was under, and the responsibility he shouldered.

"I will go straight to the residence," Roland said, as the helicopter approached the office building for landing. "It's been an exhausting day. You should rest."

"I will arrange for the limousine."

"Thanks."

They climbed out of the helicopter when the rotors slowed. Roland's feet felt leaden as he made the journey to the waiting car.

"Good evening, Sir," the chauffeur said.

"Evening," Roland said with the same lifeless tone.

"Shall I take you case, Sir?"

Roland looked at the briefcase in his hand, wondering what it was doing there. "Yes, I won't be using it."

The chauffeur drove to the property owned by Zagreus Minerals, for the use of senior management and guests.

Roland used the residence often. He poured a whisky as they travelled, but it tasted sour. The acidity lingering in his mouth refused to disappear. When they arrived, Roland struggled from the vehicle while the chauffeur collected his bags and placed them inside.

"Will you need my services again, Sir?" the chauffeur asked.

"No, thanks. Pick me up at seven tomorrow."

"I will. Have a pleasant evening."

"Yeah," Roland replied, although he couldn't see how.

A maid waited for him at the entrance foyer and asked if he would be dining tonight.

Roland gazed at her, disorientated. "Er... yes, I will." He looked at his watch and saw it was past seven thirty. "Will half an hour be okay?"

"Yes sir, I will take your case to the study and your bag to the main bedroom." The middle-aged maid stood tall and muscular. She lifted the bag and case with little effort and carried them away.

Roland followed in her wake to the main bedroom and closed the door of the bathroom where he washed his face. It still carried the stain of Sanchez's anger.

Roland couldn't recognize the man in the mirror. The physical features looked the same, although he may have developed an extra wrinkle in the past couple of days, but as he penetrated the eyes, an uncertainty welled up within him. He coasted along when things were in control. Nothing serious had happened in his life for the past decade to challenge his self-esteem. But this catastrophe had challenged him to the core, his confrontation with the man that afternoon in particular. *Do I care for people's safety, or is my conscience creating a facade? Am I putting profit before people's safety? Am I the caring man I consider myself to be?* Roland interrupted his chain of thought, not wanting to dwell on the topic. After a quick shower, he donned fresh clothes, casual jeans and T-shirt with sneakers before going to the dining room for dinner.

He sat and ate his meal alone, sipping wine occasionally. He preferred being alone, but just then he wanted company, someone to distract him from the dark thoughts in his head. He retired to the study to watch television. When every station was showing footage of the dam disaster, he was about to turn it off when he saw himself appear on screen.

"This afternoon Sanchez Barbosa from Vila Feliz ran into Roland Cavendish, CEO of Zagreus Minerals, at the El Grieta Evacuation Center," the reporter said over the images. "As you can see, the meeting became emotional and Mr Barbosa vented his frustrations at the Zagreus executive with a dramatic ending. We caught up with Mr Barbosa afterwards."

The reporter turned to Sanchez. "Mr Barbosa, that was a very heated exchange with the Zagreus executive this afternoon."

"Yes, I was very emotional. I was angry. He needs to know the pain we are going through, having lost loved ones. Not knowing if they are dead or alive, in my case. He needs to understand that the actions of multinational corporations affect the lives of normal people. They need to take responsibility for their actions. They need to be more careful." Sanchez choked back tears.

"I'm sure that if Mr Cavendish is listening, he will take your words to heart. What do you think of the company's promised donation of the hundred million dollars towards the recovery effort?"

Sanchez stared at the camera. "One hundred million

dollars does not bring back these people's loved ones. It does not find my family. We need people to find my family. I need to find my family." He started crying as he fumbled for his wallet. He opened it and held up a photo of Catina and Donato to the camera. "I need to find my beloved wife and son. Please come back to me..."

The reporter was sympathetic. "Well, as you can see, Mr Barbosa is distraught. His wife and son are still missing. Rescue personnel still believe they will find people alive, but hope is dwindling as time elapses..."

Roland turned off the television. The photo of Sanchez's wife and son haunted him. Didn't they realize he was hurting too? He felt their agony. He strode to the wall safe and worked the combination. The lock clicked, the door opened, and he removed his pistol, running his hands over the steel's smoothness. He didn't understand why he removed the gun, but he did. He wondered what his senses would register if he put it to his head and pulled the trigger. Would there be any pain? Would he hear the detonation? What would death be like? Was there any awareness? Would he still sense the pain in his soul afterwards? As he toyed with the gun, he realised his thoughts were cowardly. He would just be transferring the pain to others, his wife most importantly. After cradling the black steel object, he placed it back in the safe and locked it.

Chapter 10

Cave

Donato ventured into the forest, the sounds of strange birds and creatures reverberating in his skull and dampening his courage. The light faded as the canopy thickened, even though the sun glared overhead. His stomach grumbled, and he looked around for something to eat. No food grew where he walked, so he returned to the river. His father had told him you could always find food near a river. He followed the tree line as he walked upstream. A slight inlet stopped his progress, but he spotted an Amora berry bush with ripe fruit. Rushing over, he plucked the berries and stuffed them in his mouth. He picked more and placed one berry in his mouth at a time until he had none left.

A Jaboticaba tree grew further up the creek, and Donato saw fruit still on the trunk. The fruit grew out of reach, so he searched for a stick. He leaped and tapped the lowest berries, flicking a couple to the ground and ran after them before they rolled into the creek. With the fruit safely in his hands, he sat on the bank and bit into the skin, peeling it to reach the juicy flesh and spitting out the seeds.

Watching a pool of water in the creek as he ate, he saw a tortoise swimming. It made him hungry, but he didn't know how to cook the meat, even if he caught it and removed it from its shell. He needed to survive on the fruit at present. He wiped his mouth when he finished eating.

Donato wondered what he should do. He needed to find shelter before nightfall. It was the rainy season, with the guarantee of an evening or nighttime downpour. He remembered the rocky outcrop he saw from the river when he escaped the tank. It appeared to be nearby. He returned to the river, and looked in the forest's direction, locating the tor. After confirming the direction, he headed out on his trek to the elevated plateau of denuded ground. Mosquitoes and other insects started attacking him in the humid conditions. He swatted and slapped at the pests, but welts soon covered him. They itched, but he resisted scratching the spots. He knew from experience that scratching only made it itch more. Still, he couldn't resist the occasional easing of the discomfort. The ground rose as the walk continued and the exercise taxed his stamina, and he often paused for a rest. The trees started thinning out after an hour. He broke through the trees and saw his destination nearby, although the ground turned gravelly and difficult to traverse without slipping and falling. He reached the top and looked around at his panoramic view of the landscape. The river and tank lay to the south, the sun descending to the horizon over his right shoulder. Forest encircled him in every direction beyond the rocky outcrop. Donato imagined it to be a large pimple erupting from the smooth surface of the forest canopy from the air.

The rocks being scaled, Donato was uncertain of his next step. He was thirsty, and he wished he had a container of water, but he didn't. The treeless expanse had much to explore, so he walked around the rocks. A small waterfall cascading from higher up came into view as he cleared a large rock, making him smile in delight. A pool of water congregated around the base of the falls before the water overflowed to continue its journey to the river. He rushed over to the pool and scooped up handfuls of water, drinking the cool transparent liquid with pleasure as it quenched his thirst. *I won't die of thirst while I'm here.* He kept exploring after his drink and climbed to the top of the highest rock on the hill. Donato studied the landscape again and noted no gaps in the canopy to show locations of villages or towns. The revelation and his predicament distressed him and he sat on the rock, distraught. He must be a significant distance from help to find Papa. A frown etched his face as he brought his knees up and hugged his legs and thought of his options.

The sun lowered in the sky as he sat thinking. He needed to find shelter for the night at least, so he crawled off the rock and continued his exploring. A gap between two rocks large enough for him to scamper through appeared. When he crawled through the gap, he saw a small cave to his left. He continued to the cave and explored it. It provided a cozy spot for the night, he thought, but he wondered if any wild animals used it. The thought frightened him. What could he do if they arrived during the night as he slept? He decided he needed a large stick to chase one away if it came. No evidence of animals littered the cavity, so he considered himself safe. He crawled out again and strolled to the forest line in search of a stick to protect himself and gather more food before the sun set. He wished he could light a fire, but he had no implements to light one with, and he didn't know other means of lighting one. A Jaboticaba tree grew nearby, so he knocked more berries to the ground and took them back to the gap between the two rocks.

Donato sat next to the fruit and picked up a stone, rotating the rough fragment in his hands. He got sick of it and threw it to the ground. It hit another rock and sparked, which made Donato jump. Maybe he could light a fire. He rushed to retrieve the rock, and he struck the two together again, with more sparks flying from the contact. Putting the rocks aside, he ran to the forest and collected dry sticks and twigs and dry grass. He placed the larger sticks and wood aside and made a nest of twigs and the grass. With a deep breath, he took the rocks and struck them against each other. A spark flew out, but missed the tinder. He repositioned himself and tried again. Again, the spark flew in the wrong direction. After several attempts, he directed a spark into the tinder, but nothing happened. Donato grunted in frustration. He tried again and again without success. After several more attempts, a slight wisp of smoke rose from the fuel, but extinguished straight away. Encouraged by the prospect, he continued producing spark after spark until a continuous column of smoke started. He recalled how Papa started fires sometimes, so he placed the rocks on the ground and leaned over near the tinder and puffed at the base of the smoke column with pursed lips. Flames burst into meager life after a few blows. Donato jumped back, but tamped the pile closer to the flames to increase the size of the fire. The flames grew over time, so Donato started placing larger twigs and sticks on the fire until it blazed at a respectable size for a fire, he thought. He sat back, proud of himself.

Twilight encroached on the day, and Donato realized he needed more wood, so he dashed to the forest and gathered more while he could. He found two larger branches, parched from the sun, and dragged one at a time to the cave and placed them aside for later. He had enough wood for the night, he thought, so he sat again and fed the fire before grabbing a Jaboticaba berry, opening it to eat the flesh. The fire built in strength and Donato fed more wood, as the material on the fire burned. He dragged one of the large branches over and plonked it on top, producing a large stream of sparks swirling up into the night sky. The night's darkness surrounded him, except for the fire blazing away. Donato had located the fire near the gap in the rocks, hoping to deter animals from venturing inside the cave. He yawned. Before retiring for the night, he relieved himself, and gazed at the sky. The stars twinkled above him. He stared up at them, wondering what they were. Papa said they resembled the sun, but they were so distant they only appeared as small spots of light in the sky. He wished he was with Papa. He felt sad and afraid on his own. Tears escaped from his eyes until he steeled his resolve and brushed them away. He returned to the fire, inspecting it one last time before retiring to the cave and sleep as best he could.

Something woke him, screaming, at one point, grabbing for the stick that lay nearby. He thought an animal sniffed him, but he realized a nightmare woke him. Convinced of his safety, he drifted back to sleep.

Chapter 11

Cave Boy

Donato woke early the next morning, having survived the night without any visits from wild animals, despite the frightful dream. He crawled out of the cave, between the gap in the rocks, and stood, stretching the kinks from his body. The sun warmed the day, and the humidity soaked into Donato's skin. A storm had passed during the night, judging by the moisture on the ground. *Maybe the storm woke me*, he wondered. He relieved himself and went to the pool to quench his thirst and wash his face. He stood and surveyed the vista. *I am an intrepid explorer*, he imagined, as he pushed his chest out with pride. But then his loneliness returned, and he slumped to a scared boy again.

He realized he could catch a small animal or a bird to eat, since he could now start a fire. He made a note to use part of his day hunting, but he would need a weapon or a spear. *The rocks provided for me yesterday, so they might offer a solution again.* He searched the stones and rocks around him and found one with a sharp edge. Once he found a long stick, he tried sharpening one end to a point.

It was hard work, but he pared the wood into a crude spear.

He inspected the remains of the fire. The log had only burned where it sat over the flames. It came apart, and he was left with two smaller logs. Donato collected more wood from the forest for a fire that night, including larger branches and dry grass for tinder, putting the grass and twigs inside the cave in case it rained.

With the evening taken care of, Donato ventured into the forest with his spear-stick to hunt for food. He moved towards the pool where it ran into a small rivulet, hoping other varieties of fruit grew there and might attract animals. He found both. The animals, guinea pig-like animals but larger, the size of a small dog or cat, proved hard to catch, scampering away as soon as they saw him. He needed to be more cunning and stealthy. In the meantime, Donato stuffed his pockets with Brazil nuts until they overflowed, taking them back to the cave for later, and returned to the forest looking for more food, including more Jaboticaba.

Reaching his fill of fruit and nuts for the day, Donato concentrated on developing his hunting skills. He was frightened about having to kill something, even for food, as he had killed nothing before, although he knew that the meat they ate at home came from animals. That felt different. He hadn't seen the animal killed. Papa even gutted the fish he sometimes caught and brought home. Determined to brace himself with a man's courage, he ventured off into the forest searching for prey, not once considering that he too could become prey. He crept through the trees in silence, once or twice stepping on a twig that sounded like thunder when it snapped.

He snuck up on two of the guinea pig-like, creeping as close as he dared, and raised his spear-stick and, taking aim, he threw it. The spear missed, jamming into the ground past the animals and frightening them away. Donato retrieved his spear in disappointment. It required practice and skill to hunt, he realized, so he set out again, determined to catch something.

Two hours later, Donato hit his mark. The rodent squealed and cried when the spear pierced it through the abdomen and tried running away, but it weakened and collapsed with the spear still sticking through it. Donato approached the animal with caution, not knowing what to do next. He wanted it to stop squealing, so he pulled the spear out and jabbed it back in through the chest. Donato cried. He didn't want to kill such a cute-looking animal, but he needed to eat. He scratched his head, knowing that he had to gut the animal, but unsure how without a knife. He picked up the heavy carcass to take it back to the cave where his sharp-edged rock was waiting.

He used the rock to break the skin of the abdominal cavity. It cut open after a few slices, nicking an intestinal tube, and the excrement oozed out, releasing the acrid gaseous contents. Donato recoiled at the stench. He needed to wash it, so he took the carcass over to the creek and put his hand inside, pulling out the intestines and organs and throwing them away into the water. The offal tumbled downstream with the current. He washed the meat and carried the carcass back to the cave where he lit the fire. Once the fire started, and enough coals covered the ground, he tossed his dinner into the flames, not knowing any other way. The fur burned first, sending sparks and Donato wrinkled his nose at the acrid burning-hair smell.

His supply of timber disappeared quicker than expected, so Donato built a stockpile to last the day. He used a stick to turn over the meat and, considering it cooked, pushed it from the fire. When he tried ripping off a leg, he jumped back as the sizzling skin burnt his fingers. He grabbed some fresh leaves off a tree, spread them on the ground and rolled the meat on top to cool off without getting too much dirt on his meal. He munched on a handful of Brazil nuts while he waited, gazing across the horizon. The river appeared bright red like a gigantic angry serpent until it disappeared from sight.

Once cooled enough to eat, Donato discovered the guinea pig meat tasted like chicken and he let juice dribble down his chin. He chuckled, imagining Mama telling him off for using his hands but then he remembered Mama would never scold him again and he missed her dreadfully.

That night, he cried himself to sleep.

Chapter 12

Vila Feliz

After his altercation with Roland Cavendish, Sanchez spent the day asking people for any news of Catina and Donato. He became increasingly frustrated as the day wore on, relying on others to do something. He needed to return to his village. He found out the Maintenance Team was sending a vehicle there the next day, so he made arrangements with the supervisor to go with the group.

He arrived at the departure point by seven. A group of three men stood around waiting next to a twin cab four-wheel drive. A tray on the back held various tools, including shovels, axes and a chainsaw. The men wore khaki-green trousers with rolled-up, long sleeve shirts.

"You coming with us?" one of them asked Sanchez as he walked over to them.

"You going by Vila Feliz?"

"Yeah."

"Then I am."

"Okay, jump in. We're ready to go. I'm Rafael, but call me Raf. These are Pedro and Angelo."

"Left or right?" Angelo asked.

Sanchez shrugged.

"You're left," he said, taking the initiative.

Nearby, the man from the dining hall who had asked too many questions was looking at them.

"Let's go before he wants a lift," Angelo said jerking his head his away.

Sanchez looked over, "Yeah, he talked to me two days ago. I felt uncomfortable, as if he was looking for the best places to loot."

"Not wrong there," Pedro said. "He's come with us a few times. Not done much, but he acted suspiciously.

Raf started the engine and looked at Sanchez in the mirror. "What's your interest in Vila Feliz?" asked Raf.

"I come from there. Want to check what's left of my house."

"Be prepared for a shock. We haven't seen that village yet, but the flood destroyed the others."

"I know. There wasn't much left when they rescued me. How long til we get there?"

"Two to three hours."

"Oh."

They drove south out of town on the main road. The 4WD rocked as it negotiated the winding road.

"You clean up every day?" Sanchez tried to start a conversation.

"Have been," Pedro replied. "We're getting paid to help clean up and start rebuilding where we can. Paid by the government at the start, but Zagreus Minerals are paying now."

"You're the one that spat at the boss guy, aren't you?" Angelo asked.

Sanchez nodded, embarrassed but with no regrets.

"Thought I recognized you. Some nerve."

"Well, he upset me," Sanchez said indignantly.

"You got a wife and son missing, don't you?" Pedro asked.

"Yeah."

"Any news?"

"No, not yet."

They drove on in silence, turning onto a secondary road after an hour and a half. The scenery became familiar to Sanchez as he gazed out the window. When they drove into the remains of Vila Feliz, red mud, now dry and cracked, covered all the low-lying areas of the village. They stopped where the road met the edge of the mud. Electricity poles no longer existed in the village, swept away by the torrent.

"Are you going any further?" Sanchez asked.

"We'll hang around here first. See what cleaning up we can do. We'll move on when we finish, but we have a full day's work ahead of us, by the looks of it."

"Good, let me know when you go. I want to return to the camp tonight."

"Don't worry," Raf said, with a bemused smile. "We won't forget you."

Sanchez walked in line with the edge of the mud, filled with remorse, wondering why he survived and how many had died. He glanced at the park where they had picnicked. No trace of grass or playground remained.

When Sanchez arrived at his house, he was surprised it was still standing. *I should consider myself lucky*, he thought. *At least I have a house left, more or less.* Inside, the floor was covered in red mud and furniture had smashed into walls. Everything was soaked. He sighed. *Where to start?*

In the kitchen, the refrigerator lay on its side in a cake of mud with the door flung open, rotting food spilling out. The main bedroom looked the least damaged, furthest from the torrent of mud. A photo of him with Catina and Donato stood on the bedside table. He wept as he cradled the picture in his arms.

"Bit of a mess," Raf said from behind him.

Startled, Sanchez looked around. "Yeah, I don't know where to begin."

"I'll get some shovels and we can start by digging out the mud. After that, we'll see what needs doing next."

"Thanks."

Raf and Sanchez spent the rest of the day shovelling dirt. The water was still on even though the power was out so they hosed off the rest, realising the carpet was beyond repair. Raf helped him right the fridge but they didn't bother plugging it in.

"It probably won't work anyway," Raf told Sanchez. "They shouldn't be on their sides. The refrigerant leaks out or something. The motor is wet too. It might work once it's dried out."

"We'll see. I don't think the power is coming back on anytime soon."

Raf looked at his watch. "We'd better get going. We should get back before dark."

"Sure. Are you coming back tomorrow?"

"We'll see how the others have fared, but more than likely. There're at least a few properties worth restoring. Needs a dozer to remove the rubbish, though."

"Good, I want to make the house liveable as soon as possible. Not sure what I'll use for transport. Might look for a car."

"You might get a grant to buy one. Ask around when you get back."

"I will."

They returned to the vehicle with the shovels and hose and had a drink.

Raf got out his phone and called Pedro. "You guys ready?"

"Give us five."

"Okay." Raf put the phone back in his pocket. "They'll be five minutes. There's poor reception around here."

"Yeah, I had to make a call from the top of that rise," Sanchez pointed to the hill. "That's what saved me."

"Lucky."

"I suppose." Sanchez didn't consider it lucky.

On the way back to El Grieta, Raf asked his co-workers what they had found.

"Cleaned up one house. Demolished another. Wasn't worth saving." Angelo reported.

"We spent the time cleaning up Sanchez's house. It's not too damaged. Should be liveable once they restore electricity. Enough here to come back tomorrow?"

"Yeah, two or three days."

Sanchez thought the mens' work very noble, despite them being paid to do it. *They have jobs and families to look after, but they're doing this instead, even if they are being paid.* He wondered if he should ask to be part of the team until he got his life back together. "You looking for any new recruits?" he asked hopefully.

Raf looked in the mirror. "Yeah, we're one short but we won't just be going to your village."

"I know. You're doing a good thing, and I want to contribute. Better than hanging around the center."

"Okay. What do you two think?"

"Yeah," Angelo and Pedro replied in unison.

"Four is better than three," Angelo added. "Gives us two fronts."

"Okay then. I'll take you to the supervisor and, if he okays it, they'll sign you up and fill out the paperwork, so you get paid. You can start tomorrow."

"Good," Sanchez said, satisfied. "I'll sure sleep well tonight." He yawned.

The others laughed. "You'll get used to it," Pedro said.

"What happens to the valuables?" Sanchez asked.

"Depends," Raf answered. "We catalogue and photograph what we can save and then advertise to try and find the owner. We place everything else of value in one pile."

"Relies on trust," Sanchez mused.

"It does, but we can't do much else."

Chapter 13

Helicopter

Donato was broadening his hunting skills and tried to spear fish in the pool the next morning but without success.

He made another attempt in the afternoon and this time waded into the pool up to his knees, raising his spear and waiting. After a minute, a fish braved the open water and swam towards Donato. He lined it up and stabbed the water, missing by several centimeters. *Why do I keep missing?* Donato berated himself in frustration. When another fish approached, he aimed closer to himself than the direct line of sight and thrust. He missed again but was closer. Donato thought he had worked out the problem so he waited for the next fish and this time he aimed his spear at where the fish would be rather than where he saw it. Success! He jerked up the spear with the fish flailing, pierced through the belly. Satisfied, Donato waded to the shore where he lowered the fish to the ground and let it flap its life away. Once the fish stopped moving, he grabbed the spear and carried his trophy back to camp.

After cooking and eating the delicious fish, Donato

patted his fat stomach and felt sleepy from all the food. Nightfall started overtaking the day, so he added wood to the fire and retired to his cave.

Donato woke with the sunrise the next morning, stretching his arms and legs. He left the cave and strolled to the pool where he washed himself, then returned to the cave and ate nuts and Jaboticaba. He planned to collect more during the day to restock his dwindling supplies. He grabbed his spear and walked into the forest, keeping track of his direction so he could find his cave again, although the rocky outcrop was always in sight from any clearing.

Late in the morning, Donato thought he heard something. The noise became louder and constant. He stood still, wondering what it was. It sounded like an engine, but thrummed. Donato scanned the sky for a helicopter and realised the sound was coming from the river. The young boy started running back to the cave, crashing through shrubs and bushes and tripping over several times, stopping often to listen for the chopper's thrum. At one point it sounded like it was hovering but then started moving again. Donato's lungs threatened to explode from effort, but he kept running.

The helicopter grew louder. *It's coming my way. Maybe it's seen the camp.* It hovered over the cave site. He kept running, desperate to break free of the forest canopy to attract their attention. The helicopter started moving again and went straight over him. Donato shouted and jumped and waved his hands above his head to attract its attention, but it zoomed past and the sound faded away into the distance. He sat on the ground and cried.

Wiping the tears from his cheeks, Donato knew crying would not make the helicopter return. He tramped back to the cave, his search for food forgotten in his misery. As he sat on a rock near his campfire, he picked up several stones and threw them one at a time at nothing. When he got bored, he wandered to the pool and drank. He needed them to notice him the next time, even if he was foraging in the forest. At the far side of the rocky outcrop facing the river, he started scratching large letters into the ground. He wrote 'ME AJUDA' (help me). *That should get their attention*, he hoped.

It was early afternoon, and he had no inclination to fossick for food, so he wandered over for a swim in the pool. He walked over and stripped. As he waded into the water, he felt the chill on his skin, the water rising with depth. He could swim, being taught by Papa in the swimming hole near the village. His feet left the bottom, and he started stroking and kicking his feet. He headed for the waterfall, approaching its base from the side. A mist of water droplets filled the air as he approached. The bottom of the pool was too deep to stand so he swam to the edge, finding a grip and climbing up next to the cascading water. The rocks were wet and slippery, so Donato stood carefully, making sure he didn't fall. Moisture settled on his skin and a rainbow scintillated as the light diffracted through the mist. It was delightful.

He spied a rock ledge behind the waterfall and inched along the slippery shelf, reaching the other side which was blocked by the cliff face. As Donato turned to walk back, his foot slipped and he fell into the waterfall's force, with the torrent of water pushing him under. In a panic, he tried swimming away but couldn't. He hit the bottom and pushed himself clear, swimming faster while desperately holding his breath. As he burst above the surface, he filled his lungs and paddled on the spot while he calmed down. He waded out and fell onto his back, gazing at the sky as he regained his strength. The exhilaration of the experience made him laugh, despite the danger.

He put his clothes back on and returned to the cave to start a fire as the sun sunk low in the sky. He still had meat left over from his hunting two days ago, so he ate that with fruit once the fire blazed, retiring to bed and sleep afterwards.

The sun came up with a blazing fierceness the next morning. Donato felt the heat as soon as he crept from the cave. After washing himself and satisfying his thirst and hunger, he ventured into the forest for fruit and nuts. He kept near his cave and open ground in case the helicopter came back. He wondered why it had come. It had hovered near the river and then circled past the rocky outcrop of his cave on its way back to wherever it came. It might have seen the tank and investigated. He hoped they did. At least they might get Mama. He had a large stock of fruit and nuts by midday and ate enough food to stop his stomach grumbling.

When he heard the faint noise of the helicopter again, he rushed to the clearing around his cave. He shielded his eyes against the sun as he squinted into the sky in search of the helicopter and saw a speck travelling low over the river, coming his way.

Donato leapt with excitement, but the helicopter pilot was focussed on the tank, landing nearby. They wouldn't see him from where they were, so Donato ran to them. He rushed into the forest and clamoured down the hill, careful not to trip over any debris. He perspired and panted, his lungs bursting from exertion. His legs ached but he kept running. He didn't see the stick in his path and tripped over, hitting the ground hard. He cried out in agony as excruciating pain seared his left ankle, which he twisted when he tripped. He lay still, waiting for the pain to subside, but it didn't. His ankle swelled up quickly and swivelling it shot pain up his leg, but he thought he could bear it. He tested the leg but couldn't put much weight on it. *How am I going to get there now?* Donato thought, dejected.

He looked around for a stick to support him and walked as fast as his sprained ankle would tolerate but he knew it was pointless. The river was too far away. He heard the helicopter engine start as he was climbing back up the hill. The noise intensified before fading away and Donato presumed it had gone back the way it came never to return.

Chapter 14

Catina

S anchez woke up in the rear seat of the four-wheel-drive vehicle returning from the day's clean-up activities. Tired from working, he stretched and yawned, glad to return to a meal and a well-earned sleep.

"Need help with the valuables?" Angelo asked Raf.

"No, Sanchez and I should be able to handle it. There wasn't much today. You and Pedro can go home."

"Okay. Thanks. We'll see you tomorrow then."

Raf and Sanchez picked up the boxes from the vehicle, one with items someone might claim, the other a mishmash of valuables with no identifiable owners. They lugged them to the supervisor's office and handed them over for sorting. A woman sitting by the door rose as they entered. "Is one of you Sanchez Barbosa?"

"I am," Sanchez said.

"Oh. Good, I have news for you."

"I'll just get rid of this lot."

Raf was uneasy. "I'll take care of this. You go talk to her. It might be important."

"Thanks." Sanchez placed the box on the counter,

wiped his hands on his trousers and strolled over to the woman.

"I'm Marie," she said, as she extended a hand.

"Hi Marie," Sanchez said, holding his hands up, showing her how dirty they were. She looked nervous.

"Um... I'm not sure how to tell you this. We've found your wife, we think." Concern and worry etched her face.

Sanchez couldn't tell how he should take the news. "And..."

Marie lowered her head, fidgeting with her hands and sighed, "I'm afraid that the person we found is dead. We believe she's your wife but not 100 percent."

Sanchez stood speechless. He felt light-headed, so he sat in the chair where Marie had been sitting.

"Do you want a drink of water?"

"No." He sat in silence for a moment longer. "What makes you think it's her?"

"They found her in a tank as you described 200 kilometers downstream in the Rio Plata."

"Oh." Fear gripped his stomach. "And Donato? The boy?"

"He wasn't in the tank. They conducted a quick search of the surroundings but couldn't find any trace of him, I'm afraid."

Raf listened to the exchange from the counter as he signed in the salvaged items. He walked over to Sanchez when he finished. "You okay?"

Sanchez looked up, misery in his eyes, and shook his head. "They found Catina. She's dead."

"Oh... I'm sorry." He placed a hand on Sanchez's shoulder and squeezed, offering what comfort he could. "I think you should stay here tomorrow. You'll have things to do," he said with sympathy.

Marie cleared her throat. "Yes. We need you to identify her as soon as possible, if you can. We can then release her for burial."

"What do you mean 'if I can'?"

"I've been told it might be too difficult." Marie bit her lower lip.

Sanchez sat in silence for a few moments. "Can I see her now?"

"If you're up to it. It might not be pleasant."

"I'd prefer to do it now."

"Okay."

"Do you want me to come with you?" Raf asked.

"No, I'll be okay."

"Sure?"

Sanchez nodded. He rose from the chair. "Let's go then."

Sanchez followed Marie to the temporary mortuary set up at the center. She led him to the reception and talked to the man there. He picked up a phone and 10 minutes later, a man wearing olive hospital scrubs with a mask hanging from his neck came through a set of doors.

"Mr Barbosa, I'm sorry to put you through this. Let's hope to do this with minimal distress for you. I will lead you to a room with a window partition. The deceased is on the other side. When you are ready, we will ask you to view the deceased and identify her if you can. Do you understand?"

Sanchez looked bewildered. Events were moving too fast. "I just want to see my Catina."

The man glanced at Marie, knowing what lay ahead. "Okay then. Come with me." He led Sanchez to the viewing window, shielded by venetian blinds. "Stand here," the man said. When Sanchez moved into position, the man asked, "Are you ready?" Sanchez nodded and the man pulled on the cord, rotating the slats.

Sanchez staggered back when he first saw her corpse. This could not be Catina, could it? He felt dizzy as he tried to compose himself. Bile rose in his throat and he heaved. He leaned against the wall and took several deep breaths, steeling himself. As the initial shock eased, he examined the body in greater detail. The face was bloated and somewhat marbled, but his Catina's features still showed. Tears rolled down his cheeks. An unmistakable mole sat by the base of her nose, the mole he often told her he loved. She was wearing her picnic dress which still looked beautiful despite the red stains. Sanchez looked dolefully at the mortuary attendant. "That is Catina," he croaked.

The man was about to close the venetian blind when Sanchez said, "Wait, just a moment longer." Sanchez looked at Catina again, memories of the carefree times they had shared flashing through his mind. "Farewell my love," he said as he placed a kiss on the glass of the window.

Chapter 15

Lights

Donato burst out of the forest with another kill in his hand, another guinea pig creature, despite the slight limp from his sprained ankle. His foot had recovered during the night and was only a minor impediment. He beamed with pride at his latest success, his hunting skills improving daily. This animal was larger and should last him three or four days if he also caught a fish. The day waned as he looked across the expanse of greenery stretching below him. He considered his future and still could not decide on his best course of action. One option was to stay at the cave, hoping someone would find him, but he considered that unlikely, given they had found Mama and not him. They might think he had wandered off and become lost. He could try hiking back upstream, but he saw no signs of civilization and he wasn't sure how he'd survive if he left the sanctuary of his cave. He needed to stay near the river and hopefully he would reach the village. How far had he travelled? How long would it take to return? It was a conundrum.

He kicked stones as he plodded his way to the pool. His

thoughts drifted to Papa. A panic attack seized him. Papa stood on the hill when he jumped into the tank, so he must be alive. The panic subsided, and he arrived at the pool. He drank his fill and returned to the cave and the cooking meat. When the meat had cooked, he rolled it off the fire and let it cool, before tearing it open and devouring the succulent flesh, until he sated himself of food. The sun started setting, so he took the leftover meat into the cave and returned outside again. Not tired yet, he placed more wood on the fire for light and sat, leaning his back against a boulder.

Donato saw the sun lower below the horizon in the west. Turning to the east, he watched the moon, full and shining yellow, rising. It looked so large and close Donato could touch it. The moon rose higher, shrinking in size, and the day's light faded to nothing. Moonlight shimmered on the river as it snaked into the distance, competing with the stars as they battled to have their scintillating light share the night sky. Donato sat, mesmerized by the light on the river as it sparkled, reflecting off the ripples. He didn't notice an anomaly in the light at first, but he emerged from his trance and focussed on an odd patch of light in the distance. It came from near the river and competed with the moon-light's reflection. Donato's heart leapt in his chest and raced with excitement. *It must be a village*, he thought. It looked so far even though he couldn't calibrate distance. *Still*, he thought, *if I walk along the river, I'll reach it in time, and then talk to someone and they will help me find Papa.* He jumped up in glee at the prospect. He rubbed his eyes and looked again, checking he hadn't imagined the light. The glow still shone back at him. Reality started setting in as he realized he had nothing to carry water or food. He didn't want to think of it until tomorrow. Yawning, he retired to the cave and fell asleep.

A disturbance woke him. Yellow, menacing eyes stared at him. He quickly pushed himself against the cave wall, goosebumps rising on his skin. The menacing growl reminded him of an enormous cat, maybe a Puma. The cat growled again but didn't seem interested in Donato. He heard bones crunch as the cat helped itself to his food and wondered if he would be its next course.

The cat licked itself clean and eyed Donato again. It blinked twice and left the cave. He sighed in relief.

He stayed awake long afterwards, frightened the cat might return for its dessert. Finally nodding off, he dreamed he was lost and alone, waking several times with a fright.

Chapter 16

Dreams

oland woke perspiring. He blinked. Moonlight filtered through gaps in the window blind. A nightmare lingered, leaving him with a sense of fear, an animal creeping towards him. He hadn't felt such fear since childhood when, lost in the wilderness, a mountain lion stalked him forcing Roland to climb high up a tree. He wondered why he had dreamed about being hunted. It was unusual.

Sleep escaped him as thoughts of his time as a six-year-old flooded back from long ago.

Roland stumbled over the rocks as he climbed the mountain, looking for his parents. He didn't understand where they had gone. They were there a minute ago, when he had run off chasing a rabbit into the thick forest. The rabbit vanished as it outpaced him. When Roland looked around, he lost his bearings. "Mummy," he yelled, as loud as his six-year-old lungs could manage. "Daddy!" No reply came. He started walking in the direction he thought he had come, but the scenery was unfamiliar. He continued calling out as he lurched around, becoming more lost by the minute. Darkness started engulfing the day, which made Roland scared.

As twilight set in, Roland heard a growl behind him, and a mountain lion crept into view. He froze, entranced, but then scrambled up the nearest tree, climbing higher and higher as the cat hugged the tree trunk and shimmied up behind him. Roland climbed as high as he dared and held his breath as the cat closed the gap. It stopped below him when it ran out of strong branches and swiped its claw at Roland, trying to hook this strange animal. After what seemed a lifetime, the lion grew tired of the hunt, growled again and jumped out of the tree, returning to the jungle. Roland was too frightened to leave his safe haven until morning.

He remembered the terrifying encounter as if it happened yesterday but why was it coming back to him now?

Time was flashing by as he managed the fallout from the disaster, coordinating the rescue and clean-up efforts at the mine and elsewhere. After much discussion with Santos, they closed the mine until further notice, at least until the investigation into the tailings dam collapse had concluded and a new storage dam built. He fronted inter-view after interview with the media, with undeserved accu-sations pummelling him. Government investigators were also circling, looking for regulations the mine had breached or laws it had broken. He sympathized with Santos who, as manager of the mine, endured the government's questions.

Sitting at the breakfast table, Roland munched on muesli as he read the newspaper, scanning political news of the government and opposition bickering at each other. An article about the murder of a prominent member of society shared the front page with the latest attention-grabbing event of the country's celebrities.

His cereal eaten, he grabbed a slice of toast and spread honey on it, turning the page of the newspaper as he started eating. A steaming cup of fresh-ground coffee sat in front of him, which he picked up and sipped. He flicked through the paper and came to a page near the middle, where a photograph caught his eye. The faces of Catina and Donato looked back at him under the headline, 'Wife of Angry Survivor Found'.

'Searchers have located Catina Barbosa, the wife of Sanchez Barbosa, who launched a tirade of verbal abuse at Mr Roland Cavendish, CEO of Zagreus Minerals, when he visited the evacuation center in El Grieta. Searchers discovered Catina Barbosa late on Saturday afternoon, and her body was recovered the next day. She was found in a water tank which had been swept down the river 300km from the mine site. The circumstances of the woman's death are undisclosed. It is understood their son, Donato, was also in the tank when the tailings dam burst but a search for him was unsuccessful. His whereabouts are unknown at this stage. There will be a funeral service for Catina Barbosa on Wednesday in El Grieta.'

. . .

Roland felt sympathy for Sanchez and decided to attend the funeral service discreetly. Any press would make his attendance awkward, risking the solemnity of the occasion. Still, Roland wanted to be there. He made a note on his to-do list and finished his coffee.

Chapter 17

Poachers

The daunting task of hiking to the town forced Donato to consider the provisions he needed for the long trek. He knew it was several days walk, and he wanted to start a fire if he needed to, but the stones he used were too large to carry. Light-weight stones he could carry in his trouser pocket would be better, so he searched for stones of the right size that sparked when he struck them together, settling on two that fit in the palm of his hand. He placed them aside until his departure.

He would need food and decided to use his shirt to carry what he could. He strolled to the pool to catch a fish before he left. With his spear, he ventured to the pool and started stalking, landing a good-sized fish on the second try. He raised the writhing fish from the water and hurried back to the camp to cook it before he left. He would have plenty of water along the river, but Donato wondered how it might taste as he looked at the red stain. Maybe there were tributaries with freshly flowing water further along.

Donato cooked and ate the fish, wiping the juices from his lips afterwards, and prepared to leave the site. He took off his shirt and filled it with fruit and nuts and tied it into a secure bundle. That task completed, he collected the two stones, placed them in his pocket, picked up his spear and the bundle of food and started walking in the river's direction. He looked back towards the cave and his temporary home for the last time, remembering the haven with regret, as he ventured away from it into the forest, beginning his trek to the distant village and uncertainty.

The day's heat and humidity was stifling as he walked through the trees, his path sometimes made difficult with the underbrush and obstacles along the way, reaching the river by mid-afternoon. He walked to the little inlet he had discovered when he first escaped the tank. He strolled upstream to where clean water percolated and, dumping the food bundle, he had a drink, and washed the perspiration from his face. The water looked tempting, but he didn't want to walk in wet clothes afterwards.

His thirst satisfied, he sat to regain his strength for a moment, contemplating his options for the rest of the day. He could set up camp where he sat, knowing that he had a clean water supply, or press on with only the contaminated river water available. He stayed where he was and gathered wood for a fire, thinking he might find an animal to catch for a meal, if he was lucky. His stomach rumbled, so he opened the bundle of food and ate before going off to gather wood. A good pile stood before him after half an hour.

As Donato started preparing the fire, he noticed a tapeti looking at him from the corner of his eye. It sat 10 meters from him and would make a tasty meal if he could catch it, but the thing darted off as soon as Donato moved. With his spear, Donato followed, trying his best to be silent. He saw it 100 meters away, hopping towards the rivulet upstream from where he set up his camp. It stopped and looked behind several times, as if sensing another creature. Donato stood still when it did that, and the tapeti continued on its way. The animal hopped to the water and drank. Donato considered springing out from where he stood to try his luck, but he waited till the animal had sated its thirst and started back in the direction it came. He hoped it would pass near him. Luck being with Donato, the tapeti hopped only meters from him and he threw the spear which landed true, straight through the animal's chest. The tapeti darted a few meters before it collapsed and died. Donato felt proud of his accomplishment, but sad for the creature's death. He picked up the tapeti and returned to the camp, realizing he had no knife to dress the animal. He couldn't find a suitable sharp rock either. Looking for a solution, he walked along the bank of the watercourse and found an old tin can in the water, the sharp-edged lid still intact. Once he washed the tapeti and the tin, he placed the tin next to his food bundle deciding it would come in handy. He lit the fire and cooked the meat, having a hearty meal as dusk settled over the forest.

A cacophony of noise reverberated through the trees as twilight beckoned the night, birds finding trees to roost. Donato found a comfortable spot next to the fire and fell asleep.

He woke early the next morning to the tang of moisture and the sound of a raging thunderstorm. The downpour soaked his clothes and made him uncomfortable. Once the storm passed, the insects came out in force. Donato fought a losing battle trying to keep them from biting him. He ate fruit and nuts, packed his belongings, including his new-gained 'knife,' and started on his way again.

The watercourse blocked his path from continuing upstream, so he ventured away from the river for a time, trying to find a suitable spot to cross. He found a shallow sandy spot 500 meters from his camp and crossed, getting his shoes waterlogged, and squelched his way back to the river. The insects still bugged him, and several bites dotted his face, arms and torso, his legs being protected by the long trousers he wore. He made excellent progress upstream and crossed another three minor tributaries along the way, much easier than the first, and kept a lookout for any fruit trees as he walked.

The sun sank towards the western horizon, so Donato stopped at the next rivulet, tracing his way upstream as he had the prior day. The watercourse had an embankment on his side and when Donato explored it, he saw a small cavity gouged out by the fast-flowing stream after a heavy downpour. There was no sign of rain, so Donato made use of it. He had started collecting wood when he heard voices coming from further upstream. Freezing, instinct told him to hide so he slid into the cavity, hoping the men stayed away from the watercourse.

The intruders crashed through the forest, making enough noise to warn anyone nearby of their approach. Donato lay motionless as they neared the site, and the voices became louder and discernible. Two men travelling together.

"Not having much luck, I haven't seen anything worth taking," one man said.

"Yeah, there should be nests. There're no animals to shoot either," the other said.

"What do you think? Shall we head back?"

"Just a few minutes longer."

Donato felt a sneeze coming on and battled hard to hold it in. A small humph came out.

"What was that?" the first man asked.

"What was what?"

"You can't hear it? You're as deaf as a bat."

They stopped talking and listened, approaching the stream and the embankment. A peephole gap between the edge of the embankment and a tree root allowed Donato to see through, and a leg appeared. He stifled a gasp and flattened himself against the cavity's wall. He closed his eyes in fear and held his breath.

"Look at that," the second man said. Donato thought they had discovered him. "Quick, I'll see if I can shoot it." The sound of a rifle discharging reverberated through the forest.

"Yeah right, you missed by a mile," the first man joked. "We'll get nothing now. We might as well go back."

"Yeah. We might have better luck tomorrow."

Donato heard the men walking away, their presence fading into the distance. He exhaled in relief. They had almost discovered him. Papa had warned him of ruthless poachers, and they disliked being caught in the act. Papa even claimed some people stumbling across poachers had been murdered. When he felt safe again, he crept from the embankment and scanned the forest. He shook with shock at the close encounter. Donato skipped the fire that night.

Chapter 18

Funeral

Sanchez sat in the church dressed in a hired black suit for the occasion, as he waited for the funeral service for Catina to start. Three days had passed since he identified her. He decided to hold the funeral in El Grieta, as Vila Feliz didn't exist anymore. The cemetery was in no condition for burials.

He scanned the church for those who came to pay their last respects. Raf and his family, Angelo and his family, and Pedro were there. Their attendance gave him a lump in his throat, grateful for their support even though he didn't really know them. Enrico and his family came, too. Enrico looked over at Sanchez's solemn face and nodded. Unfamiliar people filled the church pews. The coffin stood in the crossing on a stand adorned with flowers. It embarrassed him he couldn't give Catina more. She deserved more. She loved flowers and loved working in their garden.

The organist started playing a dirge, as the priest entered the church from the vestry and moved to the chancel. The music stopped, and the priest gave the introductory remarks before inviting the congregation to sing a hymn.

Enrico rose and gave the eulogy which Sanchez had written but couldn't bring himself to deliver. Sanchez sobbed as Enrico described Catina's life in a few words, so inadequate for such an angel. Tears flowed by the end. Sanchez heard sniffles behind him, but resisted the urge to turn and see who else grieved. The priest gave a brief sermon, and the congregation joined in singing another hymn. Such a short ceremony to commemorate someone's life. The undertaker's assistants, dressed in white morning suits, carried the coffin. Sanchez thought white inappropriate at first but changed his mind. It provided a freshness that reflected Catina's life. The assistants lifted the coffin and carried it from the church. Sanchez followed, and the rest of the people filed in behind him.

Sanchez remained introspective as he led the funeral procession but spied Roland Cavendish standing out of the way at the back, hands together, his head lowered. Sanchez's initial outrage gave way to respect as he realized it took courage for Roland to attend and he felt honored that the big boss took time from his hectic schedule. He stared at Roland to make sure the man's presence had been noted.

They proceeded to the cemetery behind the church where a plot lay waiting for Catina. The assistants placed the coffin over the hole and lowered it to the supports. People gathered around the open grave with Sanchez at the front with the priest. The priest spoke the traditional words, including 'ashes to ashes and dust to dust' as he threw a handful of dirt onto the coffin. Sanchez placed a white rose on top of the casket and blew one last kiss to his precious Catina. Others threw roses on the coffin. The formalities complete, the coffin lowered to the bottom of the grave.

Sanchez wanted to walk away but the mourners hindered him as they offered their sympathies one at a time.

When Roland Cavendish came forward his uneasiness was plain.

"You have my deepest condolences," Roland said.

Sanchez nodded his thanks. "I almost abused you again when I spotted you, but then I realized you didn't have to come. It must have taken effort to travel here. Thank you."

"I had to come. It's the least I can do."

"Well, thanks."

"You're a symbol of how this tragedy affects people. I'm surprised the media isn't here."

"I'm a nobody in the scheme of things."

They stood in silence for a moment.

"Have you heard news of your son?"

Deeper creases appeared on Sanchez's brow, if that were possible, and he shook his head. "No, he's disappeared. I'm not even sure if anyone's looking anymore."

"I want to help find him."

"Why? What is he to you? What are we to you?"

"If he's out there, I know what he's feeling. I know how scared he must be. Something similar happened to me at his age."

"Oh, well, I don't know what you can do that the others aren't doing, but I would appreciate any help you can give. I would at least have my Donato, if you could find him alive."

"How can I contact you?"

"Do you have a pen?"

Roland handed him one and Sanchez grabbed Catina's Order of Service booklet and wrote down his phone number.

"Thanks. I will contact you if I have any news. Do you have a photo?"

"Only what I gave the reporters and one I still carry with me."

"Oh, I'll get a few copies of that one then. I'll leave you be. Again, you have my deepest sympathies."

Sanchez started walking out of the cemetery again. Raf met him as he left. "What did he want?"

"He wanted to pay his respects and offered to help find Donato."

"Bit of nerve, isn't it?"

"He's not as hard-headed as I thought. He's disturbed by what has happened. I could see it in his eyes."

"If you say so."

"Join me in a Cana?"

Raf peered at him, "Yeah, why not. We'll drink to your wife. I'll see if Angelo and Pedro can join us."

Ten minutes later, they joined Sanchez in the nearby bar and toasted the life of Catina with a bottle of cachaça. The bottle emptied in no time, so Sanchez bought another and soon the men were drunk.

"That's the end of me," said Raf. "I'd better go." Angelo and Pedro agreed and, as they left, Raf turned to Sanchez. "Come back when you're ready."

Sanchez bought another bottle, staggered to a corner table and drank his sorrows away before passing out.

Chapter 19

Decision

Roland left Catina's funeral, disturbed by the news that they may have called off the search for Donato. He made phone calls the next day to clarify. "Hello, are you the person in charge of the search and rescue section?"

"Yes," the supervisor said. "How can I help you?"

"Hello, I'm Roland Cavendish of Zagreus Minerals. I am chasing up any update on the search for Donato Barbosa."

"Oh... Mr Cavendish, please wait while I search through the records."

Roland waited in silence while the person checked the computer.

"I have it. The search was called off two days ago, sir."

"Why?" Roland asked, perplexed.

"Please understand. It's been two weeks and a six-year-old boy is unlikely to survive lost. We haven't found anyone alive for days. The team found a body yesterday, the first one in three days. We are winding back the search and rescue."

"You should still search for him," Roland said, nonplussed.

"I'm sorry, but that is out of my hands. The management team is directing funding towards rehabilitation."

"Can you tell me any information about the boy?"

"There isn't much to say. We presume he climbed into the tank with his mother, but she was found alone."

Roland became frustrated. "Well, can you at least tell me where they found the tank?"

"I can send you a satellite location map."

"That will have to do."

Roland's phone pinged a few minutes later with a satellite image showing the tank's location. Roland was shocked when he realized how far the tank had travelled and it surprised him the search had been extended that far. He probably would have called off the search too, but he still felt it was wrong. It disturbed him. He could still see Sanchez's look of despair. Memories of his own ordeal flashed through his mind, and he feared for the child's predicament... if he was alive.

Roland became exasperated. Sanchez needed closure. He sat in his office in Carlos City, mulling over the dilemma. How much did he need to be involved in managing the disaster for the company? Where should he concentrate his efforts? Keeping shareholders happy or finding a frightened little boy?

He dialled his wife's number. It rang three times before Deborah answered. "Hi, honey. This is a surprise. Are you coming home?"

"Hi sweetie, no, not yet. I need to talk to you."

"Oh... What is it?"

"There's a six-year-old boy still missing. I attended his

mother's funeral yesterday. You remember that news story with the man who abused me and spat at me."

"Yes, it concerned me."

"They buried his wife."

"And you attended her funeral?"

"I had to go, for my sake. He has a son, this man's last hope."

"What do the rescuers say?"

"That's just it, they've called off the search. They say it's unlikely that he's still alive, and resources are needed for rebuilding."

"So..."

"I told you about when I was a child and lost in the wilderness. I just can't think he's dead. Something tells me he's alive and no one's looking for him."

"And..."

"I want to go look for him."

"But what of your responsibilities at Zagreus Minerals?"

"I want to stand aside... only temporarily, so I can search for him. I need to do this."

"Hmm... I'm not talking you out of it. I've seen you in these moods before and you won't budge," Deborah said. "I'll support you, honey, but please, be careful."

Roland sighed. "That was easy." He chuckled. "I think I wanted you to fight me more over it. Maybe I wanted you to talk me out of it."

"You decided before you called. I can understand why. I just want you to return in one piece... and I don't want you devastated, if he is dead. Honey, it's a noble thing that you want to do."

"Thanks. That means so much to me." They fell silent for a moment. "I had better start organizing then."

"Yes, please keep in touch. I want a phone call or text every day. Let me know you're alright."

"I will. Love you, sweetie."

"Love you, honey."

Roland leaned back in his chair in thought. He found the phone number for Charles, the chair of the board, and phoned him.

"Hello Roland. What can I do for you?"

"Hi Charles, I'm going to ask something you won't like."

"Since when has that stopped you? What is it?"

"I want to step aside from my duties and take leave for a few days."

Silence hung in the air.

"Why is that?"

"I want to go find a boy."

"I see. You know the media will see it as running away from your responsibilities."

"I don't give a damn what the media thinks."

"What's so special about the boy?"

"He's the son of the man who abused me the day after the dam burst. I went to his wife's funeral yesterday, and they've called off the search for him. I just need to do this, Charles."

Charles sighed. "The board will grumble. They'll think you're running away too, but that's my problem, I suppose. I can see I won't talk you out of it. Okay, you have my blessing. Just keep me informed. And Roland... please let me know if you need help, you or Deborah."

Roland set to work writing emails, one to the board and the other to his staff, notifying them of his decision to take leave. It made him a free agent. He thought of the things he needed for his trek and called the media outlet to get a copy of Donato's photo. They had asked why, sensing a story, but he fobbed them off, saying he needed a reminder of the human toll of the disaster. It wasn't a complete a lie.

Felicity burst into his office. "What's this about you taking leave?"

"Hello to you, too," Roland replied, a smirk on his face. "You often burst into CEO's offices?"

Felicity's face reddened. "Sorry, sir. It's just such a shock."

"To answer you, yes, I'm taking leave for a special project. I want to find the boy who's missing."

"But what can you achieve that the official search team hasn't?"

Roland turned serious. "I can keep looking until I find him, or at least an answer."

"Oh."

"I'll be back. Besides, I might need help, starting now."

"Sure, what do you need?"

"Where can I lease a good four-wheel drive and buy hiking gear?"

"Umm... I'll get someone to check and send you an email."

"Good."

Felicity stayed where she was.

"Something else?" Roland asked, an eyebrow raised.

"Oh... no... sorry." She left, closing the door behind her.

Roland rose from his seat, a new spring in his step. He peered out the window and stared at the city. It buzzed with busyness, but did it ever stop to consider the human cost?

Felicity returned. "Let's go."

Roland, disturbed from his thoughts, turned. "What do you mean?"

"You won't get a good price. They'll take one look at you and put 100 percent on what they offer us."

Roland chuckled. "Let's go then." He collected his wallet and phone and left with Felicity to go shopping.

Roland drove into the driveway of the company residence in the black four-wheel drive he had just leased, complete with camping equipment, supplies and suitable clothing. He switched off the ignition and sat in his seat for a moment, taking in the afternoon's experience, and grinned. Felicity had such ferocious haggling skills. He shuddered at the thought of being the one trying to negotiate with her. The afternoon's pace tired him, but he felt good. He jumped out and strode into the house.

"Hello, Mr Cavendish," the maid said as he entered the foyer. "Are you driving yourself today?"

"Yes, I'm going to find that missing boy."

The maid's eyes misted over, "That is very noble, sir."

"You're the second woman to tell me that today."

"I will make sure you have a special dinner tonight, sir."

"Meaning you don't make the effort on other occasions?"

"Oh... no, no. We always make it special, sir." The maid's face reddened.

"I know. I'm just joking. The meals are always superb."

The maid blushed. "Thank you, sir."

"I'll freshen up first. I'll see you at dinnertime."

"Yes, sir."

"Oh... before I forget. Can someone bring the clothes and supplies from the car and take them upstairs? Here are the keys."

"Yes sir, I will arrange that."

Roland climbed the stairs, had a shower and changed into casual clothing. The other clothes sat on the bed when he left the bathroom, tags removed. He put a set aside for the next day, including the hiking boots and socks. He placed the others aside to pack later. When ready, he descended the stairs and strolled to the bar, finding himself a chilled beer, and wandered out to the poolside patio to relax before dinner. He knew he had hectic days, or weeks ahead, so he intended to make the evening count. His mind wandered as he speculated on what the next few days might bring.

The maid cleared her throat behind him, bringing Roland out of his rumination. He turned.

"Dinner is ready, sir, or is your preference to eat outside tonight? It is a wonderful evening."

"Yes, it's wonderful, but I'll come inside to eat." Roland finished his beer and rose to follow the maid to the dining room and dinner. He spent the rest of the evening after dinner packing for his departure the next day. He felt tired after he'd completed the tasks, so he had a small nightcap and retired.

Early the next morning, he helped himself to a hearty breakfast. The maid spoiled him. He prepared to leave. The maid and two employees came out to farewell him.

"Have a safe trip, sir," the maid said, with a tear in her eye.

Roland came over and hugged her. "Thank you."

As he drove out the driveway, he realised he needed to make one last stop to run off copies of Donato's photo before leaving the city. It meant winding his way through the peak hour city traffic, but he needed to do it. He completed his task by mid-morning, said goodbye to Felicity and the others, and drove off to find the tank.

Chapter 20

What's The Point?

S anchez rejoined the team two days after Catina's funeral. The monotony at the center was driving him crazy, allowing too many depressing thoughts to invade his mind.

"You sure you're up to it?" Raf asked. "You can take longer."

"Yeah, I'm bored doing nothing."

"Okay then. Hop in and we'll be on our way."

Sanchez climbed into the four-wheel-drive with Raf, Angelo and Pedro.

"How were you after we left the bar?" Angelo asked. "You looked under the weather."

"I was more under the weather after I drank another bottle. I woke up at the center the next day, my head pounding as if a sledgehammer hit it."

"Not the brightest thing to do."

"Yeah, you're right. I just wanted to forget my troubles."

"When are you leaving the center?" Pedro asked.

"I don't know, my place in the village isn't liveable until the power's connected."

"I heard a crew's reinstalling power in the next few days," Raf said.

"Oh, good. They mentioned at the center they're buying cars for people who've lost theirs, although I'm not sure if mine is still there. I didn't check when we went there. My mind was elsewhere. I should have noticed it, if it was. Any chance of detouring past when we return tonight?"

"We can do that," Raf said. "It's not far out of our way. What have you got?"

"A white twin cab tray-top."

"Don't recall seeing it either."

They arrived at their destination and started cleaning, sorting rubbish into piles and finding the odd valuable. The disaster clean-up work was nearing completion and the other crews had disbanded. Raf called it quits early to go look for Sanchez's vehicle and they made a quick circuit of the village.

"I can't see it," Sanchez said, staring out the window.

"Look," Angelo said. "They're bringing power back." He pointed at the new power poles being erected in the main street.

"They might connect the village tomorrow. You'd better get hold of someone to connect your place," Pedro said.

"Suppose so. Well, my tray-top is a lost cause. We may as well go."

"Let's go downstream," Raf said. "It may have washed that way. We didn't go there last time." He detoured to a track beside the stain of red in the valley. They rounded a bend and drove over a slight rise in the landscape where they spotted three vehicles. Two were submerged in mud to their roofs but the third had escaped the drowning, with the wheels bogged and a mud-line 30 centimeters up the chassis.

"That's it!" Sanchez said, pointing to his utility.

Raf drove closer and stopped. They climbed out and walked over to the bogged tray-top. Sanchez looked inside, and to his relief, mud hadn't got inside.

"Pop the bonnet and we'll see how the engine looks," Pedro said.

Sanchez complied.

"A bit of dirt on the sump, but everything else looks good. You got the keys, Sanchez? See if it starts. What's it been, two weeks? The battery should still be okay if nothing's shorted."

The starter motor clicked and started cranking with a slow undulating burr but didn't catch.

"Sounds promising," Angelo said.

"I'll bring the four-wheel-drive over and see if we can jumpstart it. We've got the leads in the back," Raf said.

Angelo collected the jumper leads and connected the two batteries. He gave thumbs up to Raf and Sanchez when he was ready. Raf revved his engine while Sanchez turned the key again. After a few seconds, it started and Sanchez kept it running at higher revs for a while, then idled it to recharge the battery.

"Good to go," Raf said.

"If I can drive out of this bog," Sanchez replied.

"Give it a go, I'll pull you out if you can't."

"Okay." Sanchez engaged the reverse gear. He increased the revs and engaged the clutch. The motor labored as the clutch gripped and the vehicle lurched backwards. Sanchez willed it to move, but the wheels started spinning. "I'll need that pull now."

"Okay, let's get hooked up," Raf said, walking back to the four-wheel drive to position it.

They had a tow rope connected between the vehicles five minutes later, ready to move Sanchez's utility.

Raf moved his vehicle forward and made the rope taut. "Ready?"

"Ready."

Raf hit the accelerator and the four-wheel drive started pulling the vehicle out, the rope as tense as a piano wire. Sanchez put his vehicle in gear and powered it, mud flying. The bog, reluctant to give up its prize, relinquished its hold on the vehicle, and it inched backwards to freedom.

"That worked well." Sanchez smiled.

"Yeah, you can drive it back to the center and give it a good wash," Raf said. "You got enough fuel to get back? Is it petrol or diesel?"

"Diesel," Sanchez said.

"Good, I've got a Gerry Can. We won't need it. We'll fill you up and drive behind you in case there're any problems."

"You don't have to do that. You've done enough."

"Not an argument, we don't want you stranded."

Angelo got the Gerry Can and filled up Sanchez's vehicle with diesel.

"Okay then. Let's go. It looks roadworthy," Raf said.

"Want company?" Angelo asked Sanchez.

"Sure."

Raf and Pedro climbed into the four-wheel drive while Angelo climbed into the tray-top with Sanchez. They drove off, Sanchez staying 100 meters ahead. The two vehicles rolled into the center at 7:30 in the evening.

They jumped out. Sanchez helped the others take the valuables into the office and park the four-wheel drive.

"I might give tomorrow a miss," Sanchez said. "I want to

connect the electricity and clean up my house to make it liveable again."

"Fine," Raf said. "Call us if you need help. We can return the same as today."

"Thanks. I will. I'll let you know what's happening."

The others said their goodnights and left, leaving Sanchez standing next to his vehicle, considering whether he had time to wash off the mud. Tired, he left it until the morning. He walked back to the center for dinner and sleep. Because he found his vehicle, the day ended brighter than he expected.

He rose early the next morning, had breakfast and washed his utility. *It looks new again.* He then found out electricians were scheduled to work at his village that day so he could ask them to connect his house back into the grid. He filled up with diesel before leaving El Grieta and travelled there.

The electricity crew were busy installing poles and threading up wires in the main street of the village as he arrived. He drove up to them and jumped out. He strolled up to the supervisor and said, "Hi, how's things?"

"Good, making excellent progress, although there's little going on here."

The comment was a bitter pill for Sanchez. "Most died, and the village isn't in the best of conditions."

"Yeah, what can we do for you?"

"My house is over there." Sanchez pointed. "Any chance you can re-connect the power?"

The supervisor looked at their progress and the distance to Sanchez's house. "We don't have time today. Should be able to manage it tomorrow though."

"I'd appreciate that. I'll leave you to it then." Sanchez left them and drove to his house. They had washed out the mud, but it needed a thorough clean to make the house live-able. He started moving things around, cleaning furniture and other items, and inspected the electrical appliances. He threw out things that looked water-damaged.

Donato's teddy bear lay on the floor of his bedroom, covered in red mud. He picked it up and sat on the bed, holding it close. Tears started flowing as memories returned. *Where are you, Donato? Are you still alive?* With a groan, he stood and trudged to the sink and rinsed mud from the bear. He walked into his bedroom and looked around. A photo-graph of their wedding day hung on the wall, joyful smiles as he and Catina stood cheek to cheek with him behind her, arms around her waist. He removed the photo from the wall and sat on the bed, his eyes transfixed on the image, and started crying in despair. *Why did you leave Catina? What's the point for me now?* He sat with the picture frame in his lap, hugging it in his arms, unable to move for ages. He eventually recovered from his sadness and placed the photo back on the wall and continued working.

In the afternoon, Sanchez's supervisor, Enrico called to see how he was going.

"Oh, I'm okay, I guess. Still coming to terms with every-thing. I'm at my house to salvage what I can and maybe try to live in it again. I need the electricity connected first, though."

"Good that you're moving on again. Look, I called to check if you want to come back to work. The business is picking up again and we need you to handle the orders."

"Um... yeah, I suppose I can. The clean-up work is coming to an end."

"Can you start Monday?"

"Okay."

"Good, I'll see you then."

Sanchez sat in thought. He'd find it difficult meeting his workmates again after two weeks, with everything that had happened. He wondered how many had similar stories.

"Hello... anybody there?" the power company supervisor called from the open doorway into the kitchen.

"In here," Sanchez said from the bedroom, the unexpected interruption bringing him back to the present.

"We're making better progress than expected. We should have the power connected in the next hour or two."

"Oh, good."

Sanchez didn't know if he could live in this house, alone in a deserted village. Other houses might be liveable after repairs, but the flood destroyed the rest of the place. He saw no-one from the village in the evacuation center and he wondered where they were. Were they still alive? He gazed out the window at what used to be his life. No shops, no park, no school, no church. Why would anyone live here? *What's the point?*

Chapter 21

Vila Rio Dobrar

Donato left the site early the next morning. He kept walking throughout the day, stopping to have a drink when he found clean water, and ate fruit and nuts as he rested. His supplies started running low and he was worried about finding food. He stopped as the sun became low in the sky and set up camp, checking for signs of other visitors. He collected wood for the fire, wishing he had something to cook. The fruit and nuts were nutritious, but his diet was getting boring and his body needed more variety.

The next day started overcast, threatening to storm. He gulped his food, drank a draft of water, and set off again. It started raining an hour later. The downpour saturated Donato's clothes, making him miserable and chilled, and the rain continued for most of the day. The ground became muddy and slippery as Donato trudged along the river. He continued walking until the sky started darkening still overcast. He stopped at a creek running with a small but steady stream of water, taking the downpour to the main river.

With luck, he found a large hollow for sleeping. The

overhang kept him dry from the rain. As everything was wet, there was no point in starting a fire. He sat half inside the hollow, leaning up against the side while he opened his tied-up bundle of food. Little remained, but he had seen nothing to replenish his supply during the day. The nature of the forest had changed. The fruit-bearing trees plentiful before were non-existent where he was now. He ate the food as daylight dwindled and folded the shirt back up, settling back in the hollow to sleep.

Donato woke in darkness, unable to stop shivering. His clothes had dried with the warm night air, but his body was frigid. As he peered up, he noted that the clouds had cleared, with an occasional one fleeing across the sky. He wrapped his arms around himself to try warming up, but with no success. Sleep deserted him as he lay in his chill. Sometime later, he warmed up, but he started perspiring. *I've caught a flu, or something worse.*

The sky started brightening soon after, with birds chirping, welcoming another day, the orange of the sun clawing its way above the horizon. Donato couldn't appreciate the splendor of the sunrise in his condition. He had a headache and started shivering again. To stand caused pain in his joints and he was miserable, so he sat again. He wasn't hungry, despite having eaten little for two days. His shoulders slumped in self-pity, and he wanted to sleep again, but he needed to continue his journey. The sun, above the horizon, started warming him and the day. He rose again and staggered to the creek. As he kneeled, he tried drinking the water. He became nauseous and vomited, although only bile and water came out. The attack subsided, and he wiped his mouth clean of the slimy remains of vomit, gulping a mouthful of water and swirling it in his mouth to rinse out the foul taste. Once he rested, he tried having another drink, which he kept down. He sat leaning against a tree for ages after another drink, trying to gather his strength to start the day.

With a determined effort, Donato gathered his spear and meager bundle of food and looked for a suitable spot to cross. One came into view, so he started across, groaning as he labored through the water. He crossed at a narrow section of the creek, but the pain in his joints made the task tiresome. Halfway across, he lost hold of one corner of his shirt and what little remained of his food supply fell into the water. He quickened his pace and reached the other side, falling onto the bank from the exertion, and crying over his loss when he got there. He rose again a while later and continued walking.

Donato's eyes hurt with the sun's glare and he felt hot, as if he were in an oven, but he continued staggering to the unknown destination as the day passed. Lips parched, he drank water wherever he could find it, not caring for its cleanliness. He couldn't see any food anywhere and his stomach was protesting. To Donato's relief, the day ended, and the sky started paling in the east, any sign of a town or village still a distant dream. He found somewhere he thought looked comfortable enough to sleep and sat, closing his eyes from exhaustion.

Thinking he heard a noise, Donato became alert. He realized he had been sleeping as darkness encompassed the landscape. As he sat motionless, he heard the noise again and followed its direction. A rat scurried past him, stopping not far away to sniff the air. It looked at Donato, inquisitive, before continuing to run from its hunter. Nighttime life filled the air as he sat in the darkness. The forest cleared in the west, so Donato could see further. Light appeared to contaminate the darkness in that direction, but the moonlight masked any other illumination. His illness subsided during his sleep, to his relief, so he tried closing his eyes again, still exhausted from his efforts.

Donato woke to daylight and the eyes of an intruding creature, inspecting the strange animal before it. It darted away when Donato's eyes fluttered open, stopping a few meters away, bravely observing. Its courage disappeared when Donato sat up and it ran out of sight. His stomach lurched from hunger and nausea, heaving into a dry retch before subsiding. He swayed with dizziness when he stood. Looking for water, he saw none, so he started plodding to the west, dragging his feet from weariness and lack of food. A small pool came to view soon after, and he quenched his thirst. He felt exhausted, but drew on his last reserves of energy to continue his trek.

He walked and stumbled for several hours, being unprepared when the forest opened to the view of civilization. A tiny village stood in front of him. He collapsed on the ground and cried with relief.

Chapter 22

Back To Work

S anchez spent the weekend buying supplies for the house and tidying up the place. The electricity was connected late Friday afternoon, as promised. He stayed in the center on Friday but moved back to his house the next day with a tray-top load of food and other essentials. He advised Raf of his return to normal employment on Monday. Raf told him to keep in touch.

A vehicle drove into the village late on Sunday morning. As he peered out the window, he saw it stop 300 meters away next to the remains of a house, its foundations projecting out of the ground like the skeletal bleached timber of a long-lost pier. A family of four emerged from the vehicle, bewildered by the destruction, staring numbly. The woman cried, and the man hugged her, supporting her. Sanchez saw that it was the Rodriguez family. He walked over to them, considering himself fortunate to still have a house.

The man looked towards Sanchez when he heard him approach. "Hi, Sanchez."

"Hi, not much left."

"No, at least I still have my family."

Sanchez became distressed. The woman looked at him. "We are so sorry for you about Catina."

"Thanks," Sanchez said with a husky voice.

"Any news of Donato?" the woman asked.

Sanchez shook his head. "No, he wasn't with Catina and no one knows where he is. The CEO from Zagreus Minerals has offered to help find him, but I don't hold much hope, even with their money. If he's..." Sanchez broke down.

The woman came over and consoled him, placing her hand on his shoulder. "They will find him."

Sanchez nodded, and they stood in silence. "What will you do with your house?" he said, pointing to the remains.

"Not sure. We returned to find our belongings."

"Have you checked at the evacuation center in El Grieta? The valuables are handed to them. There might be something there."

"No, we haven't, we'll do that. We've been staying with Maria's sister since this happened."

They stood in silence again.

"I'll leave you to it," Sanchez said, sensing they wanted to be by themselves.

"Yeah, okay. Good to see you."

Sanchez walked back to his house, leaving the others to lament the loss of their possessions. He felt jealous that they had their family, and he had no one: his parents deceased and no siblings. The loneliness was overwhelming. He spent the rest of the day moping, not noticing when the Rodriguez family left.

He rose early the next morning and drove the 40-minute drive to his workplace. Returning was strange, and he approached the entrance nervous. His fellow workers behaved with consideration when he arrived. Sanchez sensed they didn't know how to behave in his presence, but he understood. The circumstances would make him uncomfortable also if he was in their shoes.

Chapter 23

Grandma

Donato stumbled into the village just before noon. Now that he had arrived, he couldn't decide what to do. He needed food and rest to recover from whatever illness he had, but walking into the village of strangers made him nervous. So he retreated to the forest for cover, sat and waited until nightfall.

He fell asleep and light started fading when he opened his eyes again. His mouth was dry, and he needed water. His stomach grumbled. Twilight turned to darkness, so Donato crept into the village. A small stream ran through the center like his own village. He wished he had known that before, he could have quenched his thirst sooner. To stay hidden, he angled to the edge of the village and slinked to the stream. When he crawled to the water, he cupped his hands and drank until he couldn't drink any more. After scurrying up the bank again, he sat at the top scanning the landscape. The village had 30 or 40 houses, a shop and a bar. A truck stop with a service station and cafe stood at the edge, next to the highway. Donato sat upstream of the village and noticed a bridge where the road crossed the stream. He realized the village was on a major road between two cities.

Donato's stomach grumbled so loud he thought the entire village must have heard. He decided to sneak up to the truck stop and look through the bin. There might be fresh food there he could eat. He walked along the outskirts of the village until he reached the truck stop, then sidled around the back of the cafe. A large bin stood by the rear entrance, illuminated by the light above. As he looked for anyone watching, he crept to the bin. The top towered above his head and he couldn't reach it. A box high enough to stand on rested against the building. He dragged it across with as little noise as he could and climbed up. He grabbed the edge of the lid and opened it. His eyes lit up when he saw chips and a half-eaten hot dog in a plastic bag, near to the edge. Reaching in, he grabbed it.

The back door of the cafe opened, frightening Donato, making him teeter on the box. He lost hold of the lid and it slammed shut. He jumped from the box and dashed into the darkness.

The café worker cursed an animal, but seeing the box, she shouted into the darkness, "Get away from the bin. We have enough theft without you stealing from our bin. Come and buy something." She opened the lid and threw more rubbish in, searching the darkness for the culprit. She couldn't see anyone, so she returned inside and closed the door.

Donato found a tree to sit by and delved into his stash. The chips were heavenly. He grabbed the hot dog and bit into the bun and sausage, letting out a sigh of contentment. Food had never tasted so good. He savored the rest of the hot dog and ate the chips one at a time. Not wanting to chance his luck at the cafe again, he wandered to the stream's bank, had a drink and sat, hidden from the village and cafe. Night wore on and his eyes became heavy until they closed, and he slept.

The noise of several cocks crowing woke him the next morning. A cloudless sky greeted him, and the sun started rising above the horizon. Donato scampered to the water, had a drink, and ran to the cafe for food before anyone stirred. The box was still there. He climbed up and opened the lid, in search of edible scraps for breakfast.

Two arms wrapped around his waist. "There you are, you thief," the familiar female voice said.

Donato screamed, "Let me go!" Losing his grip on the lid in his struggle to get free, it fell on his head. "Ow!"

The woman pulled him from the bin, with Donato kicking and struggling to break free.

"Let me go... Let me go!"

"Calm yourself, you little brat. I won't hurt you. And stop kicking. It hurts."

Donato turned and looked at the woman who was old and obese. Her thick arms held him in a bear hug, so he stopped his struggle, knowing he couldn't get free. She had grey, oily hair and few teeth from what he could tell. A lit cigarette hung from her mouth.

"You going to run away if I let you go?"

Donato shook his head as his body became limp.

The woman put him on the ground and released him. "You should scout better, if you're going to steal. I was standing 10 meters away when you ran up to that bin. Not much of a thief."

Donato stood still with his head hung low. "Not stealing if it's in the bin. You're throwing it away," he mumbled.

"Maybe right. What's your name?"

"Donato."

"Donato, hey, you can call me grandma." She puffed the last of the cigarette and threw the butt into the dirt, tendrils of smoke wafting away. "Come inside, then. No point staying out here."

"Don't want to go with you. Don't know you."

"Hee-hee-hee. Good lad, but I don't bite. Come in or stay here, I don't care. I have to get back in though. I'll leave the door open for you, if you change your mind. Might even give you food you don't have to scrounge." She returned inside, the screen door slamming behind her. She left the wooden door open.

Donato stood staring at the entrance, wondering what to do. He felt afraid. Papa had always told him to be careful around strangers, but she was nice once she released him... and she promised him food. He glanced towards the forest and back again. Maybe he could find out where he was and how far away his home still lay. His legs started moving towards the door, as if of their own volition. He resolved to trust her for the time being as he opened the screen door and ventured inside into a kitchen, the aroma of eggs and bacon seducing him.

Grandma looked up when she heard the door. "Decided to come in then. Hop on that stool," she said, pointing to the corner and returning to her work. Donato obeyed, hefting himself up by the leg rung to the seat. He watched Grandma toil away, moving between cooking in the frying pan, toasting bread and preparing drinks, checking the order as she went. This continued for another 15 minutes at which stage there was a lull after the morning rush. She waddled out the kitchen door, leaving Donato alone for 10 minutes, before she returned. "You hungry?"

"Yes!" Donato exclaimed.

"Like eggs, sausage, bacon?"

"Yes, please."

Grandma stared at him, about to make a comment, but reconsidered. She waddled to the cooking bench and prepared a meal for them both, poured juice for Donato and a coffee for herself and placed the lot on the counter dividing the kitchen from the dining room. "Come with me."

Donato hopped from the stool and followed her through to the dining room. He stood behind her as she retrieved the food and drinks from the counter.

"Here, grab this," she said as she handed him a plate full of food.

Donato's eyes bulged when he saw the quantity. He hadn't seen so much food for ages.

Grandma grabbed the other plate and the drinks and found a table nearby. "Dig in," she said, as she hacked off a piece of bacon.

Donato wanted to grab the food in his hands and stuff it in his mouth but his parents' instructions on dining etiquette restrained him, and he cut off small portions with his knife and fork.

"Where did you learn to eat that way?" Grandma asked.

"My parents."

She grunted. "It'll take you all day. Where you from, then?"

"Vila Feliz."

"Never heard of it. Where's your parents?"

"Papa is still there. Mama died. The red mud swept us downriver, and she died. I'm trying to get back to Papa."

"That dam collapse, then. Put that red shit in the water, killing the fish. Someone should shoot the bastards responsible." She took a gulp of coffee, eyes fixed on Donato, considering her words. "Got nowhere to stay then."

Donato shook his head.

"You can stay with me, but you gotta do your chores, or I'll give you a whipping," Grandma said, as she wagged her fork at Donato.

Donato broke into a smile. "Thank you."

"Don't thank me yet. Your first chore is to get outta those clothes and clean yourself. You stink to high heaven. Where were you?"

"In the forest."

"Think I got clothes at home should fit you." She went back to her breakfast, ending the conversation. They finished their meals in silence.

"Put this stuff in the kitchen sink," Grandma ordered. She went out the front door where Donato watched her through the window. She lit a cigarette, pulled a large draw of smoke and exhaled, coughing and spluttering. Donato turned away and did what he had been told.

When Grandma came back inside, she was with a strange man who looked like a waiter.

"Who's that?" the waiter asked.

"Thief kid picking through our bin. Says the river swept him downstream with that mud collapse."

"Not stealing if we threw it out."

Grandma stared at the man. "That's what the kid said."

"What you gunna do with him?"

"Don't know. I'll shack him up for a time."

"I want to find Papa," Donato said.

Grandma and the man looked at him. "We'll see," she said, looking doubtful. She turned her attention to the waiter, "You okay here, while I take this brat home and wash that stench off him?"

"Sure, it's quiet at the moment. Make sure you're back by eleven."

"Always am, aren't I." She entered the kitchen and returned a few moments later with a bag. "Come on then," she said to Donato.

He followed her to a nearby street. At the fourth house on the right, Grandma opened the rusted gate and invited him into her home. "Close the door behind you," she said.

Donato hesitated at the threshold for a moment before deciding to commit himself. The house was compact, smaller than his house, with a joint lounge room and kitchen. To the left was Grandma's bedroom, and another that appeared empty. A bathroom, laundry and toilet were at the back.

Grandma plopped her bag on the kitchen counter and waddled to the bathroom. Donato heard an explosive fart moments later with an accompanying, "Ahh, that's better." She came out again a few minutes later, the water running in the bath. "Strip off and take a bath. Ought to burn those clothes. Turn the water off when it's deep enough. Don't let it get too hot. I'll see if I can find clean clothes for you."

Donato approached the bathroom with caution. The odor overpowered him and he stifled a dry retch. He tested the bath's temperature and found it was too hot, so turned on the cold till it reached the right height. Feeling shy and vulnerable, he closed the door and undressed. He lay in the bath, letting the warm water clean and refresh him.

Grandma barged in, clothes in hand. Donato tried to cover his nakedness. "Nothing to hide around here, boy. You're years away from having something worth seeing. Here're clean clothes for you. Should fit." She walked out again.

Donato scrubbed his skin and soaped his face and hair, dunking again and again. A black ring ran around the high-water mark of the tub when he got out. He dried himself and put on the clothes. They were too large, but fit. He let the water out. Guilt nudged his conscience for leaving it dirty, so he found a brush, put soap on it and scrubbed the bath. Grandma came in while he was working, impressed with his initiative. "Useful, after all," she said.

Grandma pointed Donato towards the second bedroom. "You can sleep in there. You feeling alright? You look pale."

"I've been sick for two days. I'm much better today."

"Now you tell me. I'll get it now. Guess you need some sleep. Go have a nap. Come over to the cafe when you're ready. Don't go pinching anything. I'll know if something's missing. I have to go now." She turned, picked up her bag and left.

Donato felt tired, so he took up Grandma's suggestion of a nap. The bedroom had a fold-up bed next to a window with a blue and white checkered blanket on top. It also contained a wardrobe and a compact table and chair. Donato yawned. He took his shoes off and crawled under the blanket, feeling the softness as he slid into place. He put his head on the pillow and fell asleep.

Chapter 24

Donato's Cave

Roland spent two days travelling from Carlos City to the tank. He booked into a motel the first night, but he preferred to find a suitable site to set up a camp and sleep under the stars. He couldn't remember the last time he had slept under the stars, lacking the courage after his experience — lost when six years old. The nights were balmy with an occasional storm. After arriving near the location, he searched for a road or track. A narrow gap between the trees emerged. He veered the four-wheel-drive off the highway and drove onto the dirt road but keeping to a low speed with uneven surfaces and tight bends along the way.

An hour and a half later, he arrived at the riverbank. He didn't see any tank, though. When he checked his GPS, he discovered he had gone too far downriver, so he drove back along the sandy bank. The river's redness troubled him. He knew it was caused by the dam collapse. Many dead and rotting fish littered the shoreline. The tank appeared in the distance as he rounded a bend, and Roland drove at a steady pace towards it. He stopped the vehicle next to the tank 20 minutes later.

He jumped out and studied the beach. Many footmarks littered the sand, making it impossible to know Donato's from the rest. He waded into the water to the tank. There wasn't a ladder on the outside, so Roland jumped, grabbing the top lip and pulling his body up, so he could look inside. A broken ladder lay half on the floor and half on the side. There was no sign of Donato having ever occupied the tank. He lowered himself and waded back to shore.

Roland scanned the landscape, wondering where Donato might have gone. A rocky outcrop rose from the forest inland, piquing his interest. *I'd run there if I was a frightened and lonely child. I'd want a view of the area.* As he searched the tree line, Roland couldn't see any driving tracks, so he got his backpack out of the car, checked that he had everything he needed, and set off on foot.

He marked the location of the outcrop on his phone and used its navigation system to guide him there. It took him an hour to reach the clearing. Wiping the perspiration from his forehead and gulping a mouthful of water, he scanned the surrounds. Letters had been scratched into the ground near him. As he read the words, Roland mouthed 'ME AJUDA'. Not knowing what it meant, he pulled out his phone and typed the words into the translation app. 'HELP ME' it read. Someone had been lost here but was it Donato? Roland searched the ground more. He found evidence of a fire near an opening in the rocks. A cave entrance? And bones in the fire. *Someone has been here recently,* Roland concluded. Several sets of child-sized footprints heading off to the north. Roland's excitement grew, as he realised Donato had used the location as a camp. Was he still here?

He followed the prints and came to a waterfall and pool. *A source of water*, Roland thought. It looked clean, so he filled his container up while he inspected the shoreline for footprints. He returned to the firepit and looked into the opening in the rocks, wondering if a cat or other creature used it for its home. Not knowing what lay beyond, he crouched and clambered into the cavity. He shone his torch around the cave, finding evidence of nut shells, fruit seeds, and bones on the floor. Roland marvelled at the resourcefulness of the boy.

He crawled back out again and fished his binoculars out of his backpack. He scanned all around the outcrop but didn't see anything.

The sun started sinking and Roland wanted to camp overnight by his vehicle, so he took photographs of the campsite and inside the cave and trekked back to the river. The spot where the tank stood had an expanse of sandy beach before the tree line, so Roland drove the vehicle closer to the forest and set up camp, starting with his tent and a table and chair. He lit the cooker and boiled water, making coffee. As he sipped the coffee, he prepared food to cook for his supper; baked beans, compressed meat and bread. While the beans and meat heated on one burner, he toasted two slices of bread on the other. He had a meal fit for a king 10 minutes later. Maybe not, but it tasted good. After eating his food, washing and packing up the utensils, he took a bottle of whisky from the vehicle and poured a shot in a metal cup, sipping on it as the sky darkened, his hurricane lantern providing the only light. When he finished his whisky, he packed what he didn't need away, locked the vehicle, strolled to a tree, urinated and settled into his tent, falling asleep not long later.

Birds squawked as the sun rose the next morning, waking Roland from a deep and refreshing sleep. As he lay, he pondered how much stress had evaporated from his life since relinquishing his high-powered job just days ago. The birds jolted him back to the present, so he rose and prepared for the day's activities. As he sat in his chair sipping coffee, Roland considered what he knew and what his next moves should be. Someone had been living near the rocky outcrop, and in recent times, someone who had small feet, child's feet, and wanted help. Although no direct evidence signified it was Donato, Roland thought it probable that it was, but Donato had vanished. The outcrop was deserted, and Roland had no idea of the direction he might have taken.

Roland returned to the outcrop and scouted for tracks. Several wove in and out of the forest, so he followed them but soon lost them in the undergrowth. He returned to the clearing and sat by the cave entrance gazing above the tree line. *Where would I go if I were a lost six-year-old?* Roland recalled his own predicament and tried to remember his thoughts. He remembered that he felt scared and lonely. He just wanted his parents. *Unless he waited here for someone to find him. When the people who retrieved his mother didn't spot him, he decided they weren't coming back to look for him.* Roland looked at the distance between where he sat and the tank. He thought it arduous for a six-year-old to run to the tank, if he saw someone land there. *They may have left before he could attract their attention. So, if I knew I was on my own, I'd return upstream following that route.* But he couldn't conceive that Donato just left, hoping someone would find him.

He selected the map app on his phone and searched for settlements upstream. The village of Vila Rio Dobrar was

60 kilometers away, which Roland thought far for a young boy to travel on foot but considered it achievable. The boy's resourcefulness was plain by how he managed his food supply. Roland wanted to return to the tank first and scout along the river, trying to find any potential routes.

The sun started lowering in the sky by the time Roland returned to his vehicle, so he stopped searching to start fresh in the morning. He walked along the riverbank for a distance, taking in the damage the disaster had caused to the river as he walked. An inlet barred his way, so he walked along that to the tree line and then started back to his vehicle. He stopped after a hundred meters. Small footprints were etched into the soil. The boy had come along here. Feeling excited by the discovery, Roland returned to his vehicle. In the morning, he intended returning to the stream to follow it into the forest. He may find evidence of the boy. When he returned to his camp, he cooked and ate a meal and turned in, wanting to start at first light in the morning.

The day began with a brilliant sunrise. Roland rose and devoured breakfast, then prepared for the scouting afterwards. Entering the forest, he found the ashes of a campfire and animal bones scattered on the ground. As he searched further upstream, he discovered more footprints and followed them. They continued for 500 meters before disappearing in water. He crossed the stream and picked up the footprints on the other side, followed them back to the river and upstream. Roland thought the tracks showed purpose and intent. This person intended going somewhere, somewhere upstream. Roland knew he needed to get to Vila Rio Dobrar. He returned to the four-wheel-drive, looking for a way through the bush. The stream was too deep where it joined the river and he saw no other vehicle tracks into the forest. After trekking downstream for a while, he realized his only route out was the same one he had come in on. The return to the highway was a two-hour drive, and he feared travelling at night through the forest in case his vehicle broke down, so he stayed for another night, intending to pack and move out at first light.

Chapter 25

Alcoholic Comfort

S anchez stopped at the liquor store on his way home from work for beer and Cachaça, and picked up food from a grocery store, before returning home as dusk advanced. He prepared his meal and ate it, swilling beer as he did so. After cleaning up, he went outside to a silence he had never experienced, not even birds chirping, the creatures having huddled in their nests. Only the lights of his house illuminated the village. Clouds scurried across the sky in the moonlight. They too were silent. He felt so alone.

He returned inside and tried watching the television, but he hadn't replaced the antenna yet, so the screen was all snow. Instead, he snatched a bottle of Cachaça and a glass from the cupboard, returning to the outside air. After pouring a glass, he sat and drank in self-pity. As the last drops dripped from the bottle, he staggered inside for another one.

Sanchez woke still outside, a furry tongue in his mouth and slight queasiness in his stomach, the glass in his hand

and the half empty bottle next to the chair. He finished the glass and considered filling it again, but retired to bed instead. It was three in the morning.

Sunlight blazed through the bedroom window. Sanchez woke with a start, glancing at the clock on the bedside table. He groaned as he saw he had overslept. He never overslept. Now late for work, he jumped from bed, but went straight back. A thumping headache pounded in his head and his stomach contents disagreed with being moved. An overwhelming need to vomit overcame him. He rushed to the bathroom. A stream of putrid brown liquid issued from his mouth and onto the floor of the bathroom, just short of the toilet. With two further steps, the rest of the eruption entered the bowl. Sanchez hung his head over the toilet as the last of his stomach's contents dripped from his mouth, dizziness and pain circling his head. The attack subsided after five minutes. Afterwards, he stood up straight and breathed and teetered to the basin to rinse his mouth. He cursed his stupidity as he peered in the mirror and saw an ashen and gaunt face. He brushed his teeth.

Not wanting breakfast, Sanchez donned his work clothes and hopped in his vehicle for the trip to work, buying mints at a service station along the way. He arrived an hour and a half late for work and rushed to his desk.

"Have trouble getting to work today?" Enrico asked as he approached Sanchez's desk.

"Overslept."

"Whoa... what's that smell?"

"Nothing," Sanchez said, turning red.

Enrico placed one hand on Sanchez's chair and the other on his desk as he leaned over him. "You should use the sick room until you're sober. I don't want to catch you drunk at work again. You know it's not allowed. I know what you've been through, but drinking isn't the answer." He left.

Sanchez stared after him, gulping as he realized his stupidity. He rose from his chair and returned to his vehicle, got in the back seat and wept himself sober.

Chapter 26

Sold

Donato started feeling safe, even comfortable. The old woman continued being nice to him, but gruff in her mannerisms. He rose the same time as she did the next morning and accompanied her to the cafe, helping her with the cooking and joining her for breakfast after business became quiet. He enjoyed helping her, despite the cigarette smoke that irritated his nose and throat when he stood downwind.

Grandma looked at him as they finished breakfast, "You comfy here?"

Donato nodded.

"You want to stay?"

He shook his head, "I want to find Papa."

"Well, he's dead."

"He is not," Donato said, as small wells of tears formed in his eyes.

"I read an article on that disaster in the paper last night. Your village is a mess - what was it, Vila Feliz - so he more than likely died with the others."

"Did not. I saw him on the hill," Donato said, obstinate.

Grandma sighed, tired of the conversation, and rose to take her plate and cup to the kitchen. She waddled off, leaving Donato teary. The screen door slammed shut moments later.

The waiter came over. "Don't mind her, she means well," he said, trying to give him encouragement. He picked up Donato's plate and returned it to the kitchen, retiring out the front afterwards.

Donato worked in the cafe, helping in the dining room and kitchen. Truck drivers were the main customers, coming in for a meal to break up their journeys. They looked mean and gruff, and Donato avoided them when he could. A few gave him a friendly greeting, but most ignored him. Others were regulars. They stayed and chatted to the waiter or Grandma long after they completed their meals, catching up on news from other drivers and gathering snippets of information about what to expect on the roads.

Grandma was friendly with one driver in particular, who arrived after dusk. He was tall, large and obese but younger than her. She sat at the table with him. Donato stood by the counter watching them.

"Haven't seen you for a while, Jose," Grandma said.

"Been busy around Carlos City."

"Busy shagging your city girl?"

"Naw, you're the only one for me. You know that." They both laughed, making their bellies convulse.

Jose looked over to Donato. "Who's the kid?"

"Dunno. Caught him stealing from the bin yesterday."

"Not stealing if it's in the bin."

"Why does everyone keep saying that?"

"He got a name?"

"Donato."

"Hey, Donato. Come over here."

Donato stayed where he stood, not sure what to do.

"Come on over," Grandma said. "He won't bite."

Donato walked hesitantly to the table, still wary of the man as he looked untrustworthy. He stood at the table and waited.

"Where you from, kid?"

"Vila Feliz."

"Vila Feliz? You're a long way from home."

"I got washed downriver."

"What a journey and a half!" Jose turned to Grandma. "People say it's a gigantic mess up there. They're calling for a supply of stuff for the recovery work. I tried getting some action but couldn't get a bite. Others are making big bucks, inflating their prices, saying it's out of the way. Guess they aren't that desperate yet." He guffawed. "Well, nice meeting you, kid. You can go."

Donato returned to the counter.

"What you going to do with him?"

"Dunno."

Jose moved closer to Grandma and nuzzled into her breast. "Want to play?"

Grandma knocked his hand away, chuckling. "Not in front of the kid." She looked at Jose, enjoying the attention. "Come on then." Jose and Grandma strolled through the kitchen, the outside door slamming behind them.

Donato followed them to the back door, wondering what they were doing. Soon afterwards he heard grunts and groans, as his Mama and Papa sometimes did at night in their bedroom. The groans climaxed, and Jose came back in moments later, zipping up his trousers. Grandma came in later still, adjusting the top of her dress.

Jose sat at a table again.

Grandma wandered over to him. "Want to stay the night?"

"Can't. Got a delivery due first thing tomorrow morning in Porta Plata."

"Pity," Grandma said with a twinkle in her eyes.

Jose laughed. Grandma gave him a coffee. He got up afterwards and left, Grandma watching his truck leave from the window. The lights caught Jose's wave as he turned onto the highway, the truck's rear lights fading in the distance.

Grandma turned and sighed. She glanced at Donato. "Been a busy day. Why don't you go home to bed? Wait a minute, I got you something." She went into the kitchen and returned moments later with a teddy bear. "Here, you can have that for your troubles today."

Donato took the bear. "Thank you."

"You're welcome. Now scat."

Donato wandered through the kitchen, going outside, caressing the softness of the bear as he walked. With battered fur, and one eye hanging loose, it comforted him despite its disrepair. It reminded him of his bear at home. He walked the distance to Grandma's house and went straight to bed.

The next day was the same drudgery with the clatter of pots and pans ringing through the kitchen as orders were placed and filled. Grandma wiped perspiration from her forehead as the day warmed, and the heat of the cooking soaked into her.

A man walked into the cafe towards the end of the morning rush period. He didn't have a trucker's look. He stood and was quite trim. He wore a charcoal-grey pinstriped suit over a light blue shirt and red tie. His polished black shoes glistened. Reflective sunglasses sat on his tanned face, a thin moustache stretching the length of his mouth converged just under the bottom of his nose. Sitting in a booth by the window where he had a view outside and around the cafe, he grabbed the menu and read through it, tossing it back on the table afterwards.

The waitress ambled over to him. "Ready to order?"

"Bacon and eggs and a black coffee."

"Something else?"

The man stared at her emotionless and mute.

The waitress shuffled on her feet. "Just asking." She placed his order on the counter and went to serve another customer.

The man removed his sunglasses, his pupil's black orbs sucking in information around the cafe. They weaved around the dining room, until Donato appeared from the kitchen, locking onto him with the hunger of a ravenous wolf. Donato saw him staring and stopped. He was spell-bound, but the man scared him. Donato broke the spell and found a table that needed cleaning. Tense, he picked up the dirty dishes and rushed to the kitchen.

When Grandma and Donato emerged from the kitchen half an hour later to eat their breakfast, the man was still in the booth drinking coffee and smoking a cigarillo. Grandma had her back to him, which meant that Donato faced him. The man kept looking at Donato while he ate his breakfast, making him nervous. The man reminded Donato of the strangers his parents warned him to avoid, but something compelled Donato to keep looking at him. He finished his breakfast and rushed into the kitchen to get away from the man, leaving Grandma still eating.

The man swaggered across to Grandma. She looked at him with indifference, as she wiped her plate clean with a piece of toast and popped the morsel in her mouth. They were alone in the cafe.

"That your boy?" the man asked.

"What?"

"That your boy?"

Grandma chuckled, "I'm a mite over the hill for that."

"Maybe you're looking after him."

Donato overheard them talking and crept to the doorway, wondering why Grandma was speaking to the creepy man.

"Naw, caught him thieving from the bin. Says he's from Vila Feliz."

The man's eyes twinkled at the news Donato was alone. "Why are you looking after him then?"

"Dunno, he's cute, and he helps."

The man considered his options, weighing up whether Grandma was someone who might consider a proposition. "You want me to take him off your hands?"

"Why?"

"You going to keep him forever then?"

"Haven't thought about it. He says he's got a father back in Vila Feliz, but I reckon he's dead. Says he wants to go back there."

"A-ha. I can pay you."

Grandma stopped chewing, unsure if she heard right. "What do you mean, pay?"

"I'm offering to pay you to take him."

"What, sell him?"

"You could say that."

Grandma grabbed another scrap of toast and wiped more grease from the plate onto it while she thought. "How much is he worth then?" She put the toast in her mouth.

The man eyed her for a moment, considering what he should offer. "Nice boy his age, I can offer $5000 US for him."

Grandma stopped chewing. She had never seen 5000 American dollars at once. "That much?"

"Yes."

"And what will you be doing with him?"

"That's my business," the man said with a sinister smile.

The look on his face gave Grandma the shivers, but the money tempted her. She had no ties to the boy. He might give Donato a better chance in life than she could. She felt guilty, as if she would be betraying him. But her greed outweighed her conscience so, not being one to accept an offer without haggling, she said, "Six thousand."

The man's smile grew more menacing, "Sold."

Grandma gulped, realizing she couldn't renege now. "Money first."

"You'll get your money. Have him ready here at eight tonight." The man walked out.

Chapter 27

Escape

Donato felt helpless. After he rushed from the cafe, he hid inside a wooden enclosure, next to the gas cylinder. He had discovered it while exploring, wandering around between chores. He squeezed in among the hoses and other gardening implements with the gaps between the boards giving him a limited view. How could she sell him? He had trusted her. She treated him with kindness. She had even given him the teddy bear. Tears streaked Donato's face as he confronted Grandma's betrayal. Who was the man in the suit why did he want to buy Donato? He gave Donato the creeps.

Grandma came outside after half an hour, "Donato, where are you, you little brat? Get your butt in here and do your chores." She went back inside, muttering to herself.

Donato needed a plan to escape the village, but how? The next place along the river, Porta Plata, was 100 kilometers away, according to the map in the cafe, too far for him to survive in the forest. Hiding wasn't an option; they would find and sell him. Maybe stowing away in a truck, hiding under the tarpaulin, would get him away from danger.

Donato decided to wait until it was dark to make his escape. He wanted to take his teddy bear, though, but he had left it back at the house, tucked away in his bed. He settled on the plan to hide until nightfall, rush to the house and grab his bear while Grandma worked, and find a truck to hide in.

The wooden enclosure warmed up as the day wore on, making Donato thirsty. He spied Grandma come out the back door several times to light up a cigarette, muttering to herself as she smoked. She called him a few times, but he didn't answer. The sun poked through a gap at one stage and lit up his hideaway, where cobwebs covered the roof and Daddy Longlegs vibrated their way along guitar string taut webs in search of food. Donato saw a more menacing spider, large and black, sitting in a corner. He wondered if the spider sensed his presence, or just stayed in the corner, waiting for prey. Cockroaches scurried along the dirt floor, eager to put distance between themselves and him.

Daylight faded, and twilight advanced. Donato crept out of his hiding spot when he thought it dark enough to avoid Grandma's notice. He sped to the house and grabbed his bear. As he was about to leave, he saw money on the kitchen counter, which he stole to buy food. *Now I'm a thief.* He left, sneaking back towards the cafe, on the lookout for signs of Grandma. He turned a corner and bumped into her.

"There you are, you little tramp. Where have you been?" she said, as she grabbed Donato's arm, squeezing it tight. He struggled to get free, but she held him too tight.

"Let me go. You're hurting me."

"Well, you shouldn't run off and neglect your chores, you little brat."

"I had to run. You sold me."

Grandma's grip loosened in surprise. Donato squirmed loose and raced off, Grandma waddling after him.

"Come back, you little rascal. It's for the best. He'll look after you better than I can."

Donato ran around the corner and towards the river. He slid down the embankment and hid.

Grandma soon tired and stopped chasing him, coughing and spluttering from the exertion. "You ungrateful little shit," she said when she recovered her breath, and trudged back to the cafe, mumbling, "How will I explain this to the guy when he comes?"

Donato waited until he was sure Grandma had gone into the cafe and given up on him, then sneaked along the bank towards the building, slipping several times on the loose soil. He poked his head above the embankment and searched for signs of Grandma, then for a suitable truck. One stood next to the cafe, out of the glare of the floodlights illuminating the parking lot. It had tarpaulin coverings on its sides, and it was pointed in the right direction for Porta Plata.

He crept to the truck, careful to stay in the shadows. He made it to the side of the cafe unnoticed, stopping to calm his breathing. He darted to the far side of the truck. Donato realized the flaw in his plan when he tried reaching up to the truck's tray, the bottom of the tarpaulin. He only just reached when he stood on tiptoes. He slumped down, dejected. As he took another look at the truck, he noticed the front tarpaulin flapping. The gap was wide enough to squeeze through if he could reach.

His teddy bear tucked in his pants, he clambered up onto the step by the cabin door. If he could manage a foothold on the tie rail, he could swing across onto the tray. He succeeded on the first go and hung from the rail, holding the edge of the cargo frame. He pulled the tarpaulin aside and pushed himself through to the tray, pulling the cover back over as he inspected his transport. More space was down the back so he edged towards it and slumped onto the tray top. "We made it," he said to his bear as he waited for the truck to leave.

After what seemed like forever later, Donato heard someone near the truck and then the tray swayed as a man climbed into the cabin. The engine started, and the truck moved.

Donato hazarded a peak out the back. They were heading towards Porta Plata, as he hoped. A four-wheel-drive turned off the highway into the truck stop just before he closed the flap and settled back for the drive.

Chapter 28

Fight

S anchez woke from an alcoholic haze. The pressure of moving forward in his life felt unbearable as he stumbled out of bed, scratching the stubble on his chin as he plodded to the bathroom. He couldn't move on with his life. He didn't want to forget his Catina. When he looked in the mirror, red-veined eyes stared back at him, desperation forming in the wrinkles of his forehead. He had vowed to stop drinking to excess again after Enrico caught him, but the allure of numbing the pain was stronger than the determination to stay sober, although he had moderated his consumption over the past few days.

He drove to work and started his shift. Enrico strolled past his desk soon after his arrival and greeted him with a smile, as he did each day. Sanchez presumed he checked for the whiff of alcohol on him. Work held no pleasure for him anymore. It had no purpose and he had no one to enjoy the fruits of his labour with, no one to buy that special treat for with the extra cash. The day dragged on, but the shift neared its end, releasing him from his now pointless work.

"Can I have a word with you in my office?" Enrico asked, as he came to Sanchez's desk.

"Sure," Sanchez said, uncertain of the reason for the mysterious invitation. He rose and followed Enrico back to his office.

Enrico sat behind the desk, neat piles of orders and other work-in-progress documentation stacked on his desktop, a computer terminal to one side and an empty coffee cup sitting in the corner. He looked at Sanchez, uncertain how to broach the topic.

Sanchez kept glancing around, with the occasional peek at Enrico, waiting for him to start the conversation.

"You have always been a hard worker, Sanchez. Your performance has been exceptional, and you have been reliable, but this past week has been below what we expect."

"I've been trying my best."

"But you're making too many mistakes on orders that need re-doing because you've made errors in the original processing. I understand you're going through tough times."

"I can't concentrate at the moment. My mind's elsewhere, with Catina and..."

"Maybe I called you back into work too early. You still need to come to terms with your grief."

"I'm okay. I might still have issues, but I can improve."

"You sure? You're still drinking, Sanchez. I've said nothing, because I couldn't smell it on you, but the bloodshot eyes tell me."

Sanchez reddened at the accusation. "But I'm still doing my job."

"But that's it Sanchez, you're not, not to the standard we need."

Sanchez remained quiet in disgruntled silence.

Enrico sighed. "You should concentrate on finding Donato."

"Donato is dead. The rescue people said so."

"Have they found the body?"

"No, and they never will."

"Well, there's always a chance."

"You sound the same as that CEO guy. He's dead," Sanchez said with finality.

Enrico looked at Sanchez as he rubbed the back of his neck and shook his head. "You don't leave me any choice, Sanchez. We can't allow these mistakes to continue. I have to let you go, at least until you sort out your problems."

"You're firing me?"

"I'm giving you time off without pay. Let's see how you are in a month."

"You're firing me!" Sanchez said, anger rising.

"I'm giving you time to get yourself together. I'm sorry."

Sanchez knew the conversation was over and it was pointless to argue any further. He glared at Enrico and walked out. He gathered his personal items from his desk and left, as the others in the office looked on in confusion. He revved the engine and sped out of the carpark, scattering his belongings over the front seat and onto the floor. With tears trickling down his face, he drove in desperation to El Grieta and his favorite bar. As he entered, he cased the room. Few people patronized the place this early. It got busy later. He trudged to the bar.

"Sanchez," the barman said as he strolled over to him. "What will you have?"

"A beer for starters, Dimos."

Dimos moved off and returned moments later with a full glass of beer, froth threatening to overflow from the rim of the glass. He placed it on the towel that covered the full length of the bar.

Sanchez grabbed the glass and took a large gulp. He wiped his froth-covered lips and emptied the glass. "I'll have another one."

"Aggressive," Dimos commented, stoking up a conversation to break his boredom.

"The boss just told me to 'go sort out my issues'."

"I see."

Sanchez looked at Dimos for a moment. "It's not fair. Yes, I've been making mistakes, but who can blame me with what's happened. How can I concentrate?"

"You've been through a rough patch. Can't argue with that."

"Thought I'd have a drink."

Dimos noticed another patron beckoning him. "I'll be back."

"Can I have some Cassava chips when you're ready?"

"Sure."

Sanchez sat alone, stewing over the treatment he had received. Enrico had no choice, but it didn't help him get his life back together. Dimos refilled his glass and brought the chips over, leaving Sanchez alone with his thoughts. He changed to Cachaça after a couple more beers and, as the night wore on, Sanchez became more inebriated.

A woman approached and sat next to him. "Hi, got a light?"

"I don't smoke," Sanchez said, knowing she was flirting with him. He resented the presumption at first, but he was no longer married, so he was unconstrained, although he never had the urge to stray.

"Oh, could you buy me a drink then?"

Sanchez looked from his drink to the woman. He found

it hard to focus. She looked his age, mid-30s, curly black hair and slim. A cute nose, Sanchez thought. Her dress revealed her cleavage and most of her legs. He wondered whether she was in the bar with friends or was the local prostitute. No harm in buying her a drink. He signalled to Dimos. "A drink for the lady."

Dimos glanced at Sanchez to make sure he heard right. He shrugged. "What will you have?"

"A margarita."

Sanchez resumed staring at his drink.

The woman's drink came, and she settled herself on the stool next to him as she sipped. "You got a name? I'm Rosita."

Sanchez looked up. "Sanchez."

"Come here often?"

"No."

"Talkative guy, aren't you?"

Sanchez, warming up, moved his stool to face her. "Sorry, I'm not in a very good mood. Things've been rough."

"Fight with the wife?"

"No, not that. I don't have a wife."

"What's that ring for then?"

Sanchez looked at his finger and saw he still wore his wedding ring. He hadn't noticed, putting it on was just automatic, but after thinking it over, he wasn't ready to take it off yet. "Married, but she's dead now." Sorrow etched his face.

"I'm sorry," Rosita said, as she touched Sanchez's forearm.

Sanchez had not been touched by a woman other than his wife for so long, the gesture felt like a violation.

Rosita jerked back. She stayed quiet, wondering if she had crossed the line.

He realized the concern was innocent. "She died in the dam disaster." He kept his eyes on his drink, not wanting to look at her.

"Oh, that's horrible." She reached out for his arm again, by reflex, but pulled back.

Sanchez turned to her, tears threatening. "And my son is dead, too. Or he's out there somewhere, lost."

An overwhelming sadness flowed from Rosita to Sanchez and back again. Her hand reached for his arm again and she left it there. Sanchez did not mind anymore. "That is so sad," she said.

Sanchez emptied his glass and ordered another. He fell silent, and Rosita didn't disturb his reflections. As he wiped the moisture from his eyes, he asked, "And you? Why are you here?"

"Me?" Rosita giggled. "I came with friends. They're over there," she said, pointing in their direction. Two women waved. "I said you looked cute, and they dared me to come over and talk to you. It scared me. Today's the first time."

"You should be careful."

"I am, but I took an exception with you."

Sanchez smiled, the first smile he could remember for a long time.

"That's a nice smile."

Sanchez's grin widened at the compliment. "Thank you."

They studied each other for a moment.

"Don't you have a guy? Someone like you?"

Rosita blushed. "No. I'm not too good with men."

"Bet you think you bombed out again."

"No. You're the nicest man I've met for a long time."

"Well, I'm poor company at present." Sanchez noticed that Rosita had finished her drink. "Another one?"

"Oh... yes, please."

Sanchez ordered one for her.

"It's not my place and I shouldn't mention it, but you're guzzling down drinks."

Sanchez restrained himself from saying something nasty, knowing she commented out of concern. "Things haven't been going too good. Work's put me on leave to sort out my issues, with everything that's been happening. Fired me."

"I'm sorry. I can't imagine it. It must take time to heal, though. It must be awful."

Sanchez changed the topic and his mood. "What's your story?"

They continued chatting, becoming more intimate the more they talked and drank.

"There you are," bellowed a gruff male voice behind them. "What are you doing with him, you slut?"

Rosita jumped in surprise and froze, recognizing the voice. They turned to face the man, Sanchez's height, but wiry.

Rosita reddened. "You don't own me. We broke up months ago," she said in an angry but timid voice.

"We break up when I say we do." He went to grab Rosita by the arm.

Sanchez seized his arm as he hopped off the stool. "You don't treat a lady that way. You heard her. Go away."

The man grunted. "She's no lady."

Scared, Rosita said, "Don't Sanchez, please. He'll hurt you."

Dimos intervened, "No fighting in the bar or I'll call the police."

The man glared at Dimos and spat on the floor. He pushed Sanchez, who fell back.

Sanchez picked himself up, anger rising, both from the effects of alcohol and the man's contempt. "Looks to me she made an excellent decision to get away from you."

The man, fury in his eyes, stepped forward and swung at Sanchez, hitting him on the cheek, drawing blood and sending him crashing over a table. Sanchez exploded and retaliated. They traded punch for punch and were both bloodied. Dimos and another patron tried to separate them without success, so Dimos called the police who arrested them both.

Sanchez held his head low in shame as he searched out Rosita, who was with her friends, crying. She dared a glance as the police escorted him from the bar.

Chapter 29

Breakdown

The truck jumped and bumped as it travelled along the highway. Donato hit a crate several times as the jostling threw him around. It was fortunate the tray had sideboards, as he may have slid off otherwise. He felt tired, but the ride drove sleep away with every jolt and bump. The smell of fruit filled the space under the tarpaulin, and it made his mouth water. He tried finding a gap between the crates to snatch some fruit but couldn't find any in the darkness, resigning himself to sitting and waiting.

A vibration and loud noise blasted from under him and the left side of the truck fell to the road, screeching metal on bitumen, tossing Donato around until the truck slowed and stopped. The cabin door opened and slammed shut, and the tray swayed. A torch light filtered through the tarpaulin as the driver inspected the remains of his predicament.

"Fuck, what do I do now?" the driver cried. "Where the hell's the back wheel?" The axle had sheered and the wheel, separated from the truck, travelled its own journey, once it received its freedom.

The light disappeared and Donato heard muttering fading away. The driver returned a few minutes later with the missing wheel, tipped it over and rotated it to a standstill. "I won't get this fixed tonight. I might as well have a sleep and wait for morning," the truck driver said to himself.

Left alone and marooned, Donato tried to sleep but he had to pee. He snuck out and found a spot in the bushes nearby. He crawled back in and fell asleep.

"Who the hell are you?" said a loud voice, as sunlight streamed onto Donato.

He sat up with a jolt. The truck driver stood in front of him with the tarpaulin pulled aside. Donato slid back into the crates, covering his face with his arms for protection.

"Don't worry, I'm not gunna hurt you."

Donato lowered his arms and sat blinking as his eyes adjusted to the sunlight. He looked at the plump driver. He had a round face and a two-day-old beard with a moustache, one black front tooth prominent against his normal white ones. Despite the rugged appearance, Donato saw a kindness in the man. "Donato," he mumbled.

"Well, Donato. What are you doing in my truck?"

"I had to escape from Grandma at the cafe. She wanted to sell me. So, I crawled onto your truck last night, hoping to get to Porta Plata."

"That woman from the cafe sell you? Nah, not her."

"She did. Some man came yesterday and offered her $6000 to buy me. He was supposed to pick me up last night."

The driver scratched his head. "Well, I'll be. You got on the wrong truck, though. I'm going to Carlos City. I was until this happened," the driver said, pointing to the broken axle. He stood looking at Donato for a few moments more, "You hungry?"

Donato nodded.

The driver pulled the tarpaulin back further and picked up two papayas from the top tray of the crates. "Here, have one of these. You would've stayed hidden, if I wasn't getting one myself."

Donato took one. "Thank you." He peeled the skin away with his fingers and started eating it, juice dribbling down his chin, the aroma and texture of the fresh fruit filling his mouth.

The truck driver sat on the sideboard and ate his, throwing away the seeds as he ate. "Want another one?"

Donato didn't answer, as he didn't want to appear greedy, even though he wanted one.

"Of course, you do. I'm having another one. You may as well have one, too. You probably haven't eaten since yesterday."

It was true and Donato was grateful the driver offered so he didn't have to ask.

"I called a mechanic earlier. He'll be another couple of hours before he gets here. He's coming from Porta Plata, so he might take you back with him. Why Porta Plata? Where's your parents?"

"My Mama is dead. She died in the tank. Papa is back in my village, Vila Feliz. I'm trying to get back to him."

"Sorry your ma's dead. What's this tank you're talking about?"

"The flood swept Mama and me away and Mama died. I walked to the village where Grandma lives. I thought Grandma was kind, but she wasn't."

"Well, there're different people everywhere. I see enough of them in my travels. You're taking a risk by yourself, though."

"What else can I do? I can go to the police in Porta Plata."

"Don't do that. They're as corrupt as the crime gangs there."

"I'll just have to take my chances then."

"Maybe."

The mechanic came late in the morning and took several hours to repair the truck.

"Hey, Donato, where are you?" the driver called, raising his voice.

Donato appeared from around the truck, where he had been playing with smooth round pebbles. "Here."

"I'm off now. The mechanic will take you to Porta Plata. Look after yourself."

"Thank you." Donato looked at the mechanic. He didn't have kind eyes, but he looked harmless.

"Come along then," the mechanic said. Grease streaked his clothes and face. He wiped his hands with a rag and rubbed his face, before tossing it back in the tool rack of his van.

Donato hopped into the van and waved goodbye to the truck driver as they passed.

"Are you going to Porta Plata?" Donato asked.

"Hope so, or I'm lost."

They drove in silence for an hour, when the mechanic pulled over and stopped at a service station. He filled the vehicle, bought food and then parked away from the service station lights. The mechanic grabbed Donato by the arm. "Now, kid. If you want something to eat, you gotta earn it."

Donato froze as he tried to work out what the man meant. "What do you mean? You're hurting me." He struggled to get loose.

The mechanic hit him across the cheek. "Behave yourself."

Donato bit down on the man's arm, quickly opened the door and jumped out.

The mechanic grabbed at him. "You little shit, you'll pay for that!"

Donato raced into the surrounding bush and hid behind a tree, shaking with fear.

"You had better come back before I leave," the mechanic shouted.

Donato didn't move.

"One last chance before I go."

Donato stayed put. Walking to Porta Plata was better than returning to the van.

A few minutes later, the vehicle drove away. Donato sighed with relief. He should never have trusted him. *Why are people so mean?* At least he was heading in the right direction. He didn't think he was too far from the city.

Chapter 30

Clothes

Roland pulled into the truck stop at Vila Rio Dobrar after dark. The taillights of a truck glared back at him as it pulled out to continue its journey. The trip onto the highway proved long and tiring, and he looked forward to a bed. He parked and walked into the cafe.

The doorbell rang as he entered. A few truck drivers glanced up but soon lost interest. He found a table by the window and sat.

A waitress waltzed over to him. "Coffee?"

"Yes, please. And nachos."

Roland gazed around the dining room. An old fat woman worked in the kitchen, a cigarette in her mouth, unlit to Roland's relief. *She looked ready to go outside before I turned up* . The cafe was typical of a highway truck stop. It looked clean, at least. He considered asking if anyone had seen the boy but was too tired.

Roland's meal arrived, and he ate it with his fingers, only picking up a fork now and then as he stared out of the window, thinking of the boy's alternatives if he made it that far. The journey from the tank was a vast distance for a boy. Roland believed he could have managed it if he kept to the river. But Roland didn't know how long it was since Donato left the cave.

Roland walked over to the counter and paid his bill. "Is there a hotel in town?" he asked the waitress.

Surprised, the waitress told him about a guest house in the main street. "You can't miss it. It's got fancy woodwork on the front. They put people up sometimes."

"Thanks."

Roland found the place easily. He parked and walked the short distance up the footpath to the front door and knocked. He didn't hear any movement from behind the door, so he knocked again, louder. There were footsteps moments later.

The door opened and an elderly man peered at him. "Can I help you?"

"Yes, I was wondering if you had a room for the night? The waitress at the cafe said that you run a guest house."

The man looked worried. "It's late."

"Who is it?" an aged woman bellowed from inside the house.

"Someone wants a room," the man shouted back.

"Well, don't leave him standing there. Let him in," said the woman as she hobbled up the hallway.

The man opened the door. He raised his eyebrows. "You heard the woman."

Roland chuckled at the couple's antics as he walked into their house.

"You looking to rent a room?" the elderly woman enquired.

"Yes, if I could."

"Just one night?"

"I'm not sure yet."

"Well, it doesn't matter if you stay longer. We don't do meals, though. Go to the cafe for them."

"That's okay."

"Come with me. I'll show you your room." The woman limped back up the hallway. She passed two doors and stopped at the third one, opening it and turning on the light. "My legs don't work too good anymore."

Roland smiled. A typical elderly couple, complaining about everything but content with life. He looked into the room. "This will be fine. How much?"

"Eighty a night."

"Good."

The woman glanced at him, as if considering whether she should have charged more.

Roland laughed. "Don't worry. I know it's high, but it's okay." He got his wallet out and paid her. "I'll give you more tomorrow if I stay longer."

The woman fumbled in her apron pocket, pulling out a key. "That opens the front and back doors. There's a sliding lock on your door. Park your car out the back, driveway's on the side, bathroom's there." She pointed to a door.

"Thanks." Roland took the key.

"Have a pleasant stay, young man." She wandered off.

Roland walked out the front and drove his vehicle around the back. He got his bag and entered via the rear door. He lugged his bag to his room and on the bed, grabbed his toiletry bag and strolled to the bathroom with a towel to prepare for bed. Back in his room, he looked at his watch. Still early, he called Deborah.

"Hi, honey, how you doing?" Deborah answered.

"Tired. It's been an exhausting day. Thought I'd call you."

"Where are you?"

"A place called Vila Rio Dobrar. It's a tiny village, but I got a bed for the night."

"How's the boy hunting going?"

"I think I've found a trace of him. I found a cave near where the tank settled. There's evidence of someone living there and small footprints, a boy's shoe size. That's why I'm here. I believe he came here, but I haven't asked around yet. I only just got here."

"Well, that's something. Hope you find him. You can come home to your lonely wife then."

"You missing me?"

"Of course I am. Don't tease me."

"I'm sorry. Any excitement happening your end?"

"Oh, just the usual…"

They talked for a few minutes longer.

"I'd better get to bed," Roland said.

"Okay. Thanks for calling. Love you, honey."

"Love you too, sweetie, goodnight."

Roland sighed. He missed Deborah. He got into bed and turned off the light, falling asleep soon afterwards.

A rooster greeted Roland as he woke the next morning. It sounded nearby. He peered at the time and groaned when he saw it was 5:30. With a flop backward, he closed his eyes, hoping to doze again. He smiled as he thought how his lifestyle had changed since relinquishing his corporate duties, where he'd have jumped up and out of bed in the past, ready to tackle the coming day's problems. He enjoyed the soft bed, a sheet and light blanket covering him in the mild subtropical conditions. When he opened his eyes again, he saw 6:20 on the clock. He must have gone back to sleep. Resolving to start the day, he sat up and stretched his arms. He grabbed the towel and toiletry bag and showered in the bathroom.

Refreshed, he strolled outside and surveyed the surroundings. The air, still cool from the night, washed over him in a gentle breeze as the sun rose higher above the horizon.

"Pleasant day, isn't it?" the old woman said from behind.

Roland jumped and turned. "I didn't hear you come up. Yes, it's wonderful. Makes life worth living, don't you think?"

"Yes, it does. But at my age, the days blur together. Still, I woke up this morning. That's something to be thankful for, I guess."

Roland laughed.

"Not very often we get Westerners staying. What's your business?"

Roland smiled, impressed with the woman's directness. "I'm looking for a boy." He pulled out his wallet and extracted the small picture of Donato. "Have you seen him?"

"You police then?" the old woman quizzed, looking nervous.

"No, I'm not. I'm trying to find him so I can take him back to his father."

"Well, I ain't seen him around here."

Roland put the picture back. "I'll leave my things here. I might stay another night, so here's another eighty."

"Sixty will do. You're a nice enough man."

Roland smiled again. "Sixty then." He pulled twenty out of the wad and gave the rest to her.

"Have a nice day."

"I hope so. Is the cafe open yet?"

"Been open for hours."

"Oh, good."

The woman wandered back inside, leaving Roland to his own devices. He walked to the cafe. Houses on both sides of the road looked rundown, with rusted iron roofs. Several had gates hanging open and fences spotted with neglect. The sun, rising higher in the sky, warmed Roland's neck. The main street connected to the highway, so he turned left, arriving at the cafe five minutes later.

A bustle of noise blasted him as he entered, the boisterous conversations of the truck drivers reverberating throughout. Roland found a spare table, sat and looked through the menu. A waiter came over five minutes later, and Roland gave his order of coffee and bacon and eggs. He realized he had come at the busiest time of the morning, but he had plenty of time to ask questions later.

Roland gazed out the window. Large rigs with long trailers sat in the parking bays, but the most common trucks were smaller two or three axle rigid chassis design, a few in desperate need of maintenance. Roland's meal came, and he consumed it while pondering the day ahead. The cafe started emptying by the time he finished. He drank his coffee and asked for another one. The last driver departed, and the cook rushed out the back door. She came back five minutes later. Later on, she waddled into the dining room with a plate of food and sat eating. The waiter sat at an adjacent table sipping on a cup of coffee.

Roland called the waiter over, signalling for a refill. The man rose, grabbed the pot and wandered over. Roland showed him Donato's photo. "Have you seen this boy?" he asked.

The waiter glanced towards the cook and then back

again. He stared at the image of the boy. "No... haven't seen him around here." He filled the cup and left.

Roland thought he was lying but couldn't think of a reason he should. He let it go, drinking his coffee. Later on, he strolled over to the cook who lit a cigarette. She looked at him suspiciously. Roland sat at the table opposite her. "Excuse me for interrupting, but have you seen this boy?" Roland showed her the picture.

She stared at him, unblinking, while she drew on the cigarette and let the smoke drift out of her mouth, before she replied. "You a cop or something?"

"No, I'm not. I'm looking for this boy so I can return him to his father."

"Snooping can be dangerous."

Roland didn't understand why the woman was avoiding a simple question. Her obstructive behavior annoyed him. "I just want to know if you've seen him."

She took another puff of her cigarette. "No."

"Thank you," Roland said as he rose from the table. "That wasn't so hard, was it," he muttered when out of earshot. He walked over to the waiter. "What do I owe?"

The waiter rose and strolled to the counter. He tallied the bill and gave it to Roland, who paid in cash. "Is there a bathroom here?" Roland asked.

"Out back," the waiter replied.

"Thanks." Roland felt the woman's eyes burn into him as he exited, making him feel uncomfortable. He knew they had lied, he just had to work out why.

After using the bathroom, he took in the surroundings in the open air. Dry stubble covered most of the ground, although several patches of grass added greenery. A few trees followed the line of the riverbank as it snaked past. Roland was unsure what to do. He glanced around and spotted a large bin. He strolled over and took a peek, feeling guilty for trespassing. It was mainly discarded leftovers, but Roland caught sight of something else. He reached in and grabbed a shirt out of the layers of garbage and, when he pulled it out and shook it, he saw that it was a boy's shirt, the same color that Sanchez said Donato had been wearing. On the inside of the collar, a sewn-on label read 'Donato'. He looked up and at the café. "You lying bastards," he said to himself.

The door opened and the cook appeared. She saw Roland and stopped. With a hostile glare at him and the shirt, she blushed with guilt. "What you doing snooping in other people's bins, you thief," she said, as she seesawed the two steps to the ground.

Roland shoved the accusing evidence at her. "Thought you said you hadn't seen the boy."

She pulled a cigarette out of a packet in her apron pocket and lit it. "Didn't want any trouble. He may have been here."

"When?"

"Last few days."

"Where is he now?"

"Dunno."

"When did you last see him?"

"Last night. The thief ran off with my money from the kitchen bench at home."

"What, he broke into your house?"

"No, I let him stay for a few days."

"Why did he leave?"

The woman looked guilty. "Dunno."

Roland felt frustrated. "I don't understand why you didn't tell me this when I asked."

"Didn't want trouble."

156

Roland walked away in disgust, keeping hold of the shirt as evidence. He trooped back to the guest house, pulled a plastic bag from his four-wheel drive and stored the shirt in it. He sat out of the sun on a bench seat by the back door. *Why did Donato leave and where did he go? Did he walk or did he get a lift?*

Chapter 31

Released

S anchez sat on the bench in the jail cell at the local police station feeling miserable, both from the hangover and his predicament. He had never been aggressive or violent his entire life, even after drinking too much, and couldn't understand why his behavior had changed so much. The police had charged him and put him in the cell to cool off. Rosita came to mind. He liked her, and she didn't deserve the embarrassment he had caused. The thought disturbed him, but he couldn't understand why, since they'd never meet again.

The jailhouse door opened, and a police officer entered carrying two bags. He came over to Sanchez's cell. "Here's breakfast," he said, as he handed the bag to him through the bars. He did the same at the next cell, occupied no doubt by Sanchez's foe.

"What happens now?" Sanchez asked as the police officer returned.

He stopped and looked at Sanchez. "This your first time?"

Sanchez nodded.

"Sometime this morning you'll face a magistrate, and we'll see what happens then."

The police officer left the jailhouse, locking the door behind him.

The two meters by three-meter cell had little circulation so it felt stuffy and reeked from frequent use and insufficient cleaning. Sanchez opened the bag and pulled out a bacon and egg roll and a bottle of water. After a sip of water, he ate the roll, sipping the rest of the water to wash the bland taste away. He needed a toilet, and a bowl sat in the rear corner of the cell. He used it, uncomfortable with the lack of privacy, and washed his hands in the basin afterwards, wetting his face and hair at the same time.

Two police officers returned three hours later. One of them opened a flap in the cell's door. "Hold your hands out," he ordered. Sanchez obeyed, and the officer put handcuffs on his wrists.

The second police officer did likewise with the person in the other cell. They opened the cell doors and led them both out, keeping one hand gripped around the prisoner's arm, and the other on the handle of their baton ready for use.

"Why didn't you mind your own business?" Sanchez heard from behind him.

"No talking," the police officer said.

Leaving the jailhouse, the police officers led them next door to the court, and into separate rooms. A door on the opposite side opened 10 minutes later. "Come with me," a different police officer said.

Sanchez followed him into the main courtroom.

"Stand over there."

Sanchez obeyed.

"If the judge asks you a question, say 'Your Honor'."

Sanchez nodded.

A few minutes later, the judge entered and leafed through the papers in front of him, grunting a few times, then peered at Sanchez. "It says here that they arrested you for brawling in Griego's Bar last night. Is that correct?"

Sanchez looked at the police officer who gestured for him to answer, annoyed with the delay.

"Yes, Your Honor."

"Says you were fighting over a woman. Is that correct?"

"No, Your Honor. I was defending her dignity, but it got out of control," Sanchez said, lowering his head, embarrassed.

"I see."

"Do you have convictions for prior felonies?"

"No, Your Honor."

The judge looked at Sanchez, deciding his course of action. He consulted his notes again. "You lost your wife and son?"

"Yes, Your Honor, my wife died in the dam disaster. My son is still missing, but I know he's dead." Tears clouded his eyes.

The judge looked at the police officer and back at Sanchez. "I'm sorry," he said. "Since you haven't committed a crime before and because of your circumstances, I will give you a fine of 1000 Real plus court costs without a conviction."

"Thank you... Your Honor," Sanchez said, breathing a sigh of relief.

The police officer led Sanchez back to the holding room. He removed the handcuffs. "You caught the judge in a pleasant mood this morning. Appreciate your good fortune."

"I do," Sanchez said, rubbing the soreness from his wrists.

"Go back next door. Once the paperwork comes through, they will hand you your belongings and present you with the fine notice. You'll have 30 days to pay."

"Okay." Sanchez left the courthouse.

He retrieved his vehicle from the Bar's carpark two blocks away and returned to his house where he gazed at a photograph of Catina and Donato, tears trickling down his face. That night, he drank himself to sleep.

With no reason to rise from bed the next day, he slept until noon. He then moped around doing nothing. He went for a walk outside, meandering through the red mud-caked streets of his non-existent village. The Rodriguez family hadn't returned. He didn't blame them. They had no reason to come back. He drank himself into oblivion again that night.

He woke late again the next day to the sound of a vehicle pulling up outside the house, but his hangover kept him in bed. The visitor knocked on the door. "Come in," Sanchez shouted, before he realized how much pain the noise induced in his head.

The outside door to the kitchen opened. "Phew, smells like a brothel in here," Raf said. He poked his head through the open bedroom door. "You okay?" he asked with concern.

"Why wouldn't I be?" Sanchez said, with too much resentment.

"Things've been tough for you."

"Shit happens."

Raf looked at Sanchez, considering what to say next. "There was a ruckus at Griego's Bar on Thursday night."

"That was stupid. I shouldn't have let the guy goad me over a woman."

"They said it was Rosita you were defending. She's not just 'a woman'. She's something special, but has a knack for falling for the wrong men."

"Well, she'll just add me to the list then, won't she?"

Raf looked around again. "Being here on your own isn't healthy."

"Got nowhere else to go."

"Why don't you stay with us for a while? We've got a spare bedroom you can use. Just until you get on your feet again. You've been through a tragedy. Company will be better for you."

Tears flowed from Sanchez's eyes. "I'm not worth it."

Raf approached him and sat on the bed. "Hey, I know we haven't known each other for long, but to me we developed a reasonable friendship when we were together. I consider you a friend. Friends do this, they help each other. Now, what do you think?"

Sanchez wiped the tears away. "Okay."

Raf stood. "Let's get you cleaned up and pack a few things."

Sanchez got out of bed. He showered and shaved, dressing in clean clothes. Raf helped him pack other clothes and toiletries into his suitcase, placing dirty clothes in a bag as well to take and wash. They placed the items in Sanchez's vehicle. "Follow me," Raf said as he jumped into his own.

Chapter 32

Porta Plata

onato woke early the next morning, hungry and thirsty. Grandma had fed him well, so he could tolerate hunger for a while. He started walking, returning to the highway and following it, careful to hide from any passing vehicle. He didn't trust anyone anymore. He wouldn't be tricked again.

The highway crossed a stream not long after he started, a bridge spanning the width. Donato ducked under the bridge and quenched his thirst before submerging himself in the water, soaking away dirt and exhaustion. As he waded from the stream, dripping wet, he looked around for something to eat but the area was bare. He crossed the bridge, continuing his journey to Porta Plata.

The vegetation soon changed, and he entered a dense jungle with the scar of the highway plowing through it. Strange noises filtered through to him from high in the trees. Midday came, so Donato stopped and searched for food in the surrounding forest. He found a fruiting Cajá tree, so he climbed the buttressed trunk and reached for a limb with fruit dangling down. He grabbed two bunches, tore their stems loose and let them fall to the ground. After scampering back down, he peeled the skin from the fruit and ate the mango-tasting pulp around the seed. With the hole in his stomach filled, he rested, falling asleep. A slithering thing on his shoulder woke him, and he jumped up, seeing the tail of a snake slithering up the tree. He shivered, shaken by the fright. The sun was well past overhead, so Donato started walking again, drinking water as he passed watercourses along the way.

Daylight faded as he approached another bridge over a stream, so Donato stopped for the night. He had carried fruit with him, so he ate the rest before light deserted him. Clouds came over the sky after dark and a glow of light reflected off them, giving him confidence that Porta Plata lay nearby. He settled to sleep, only waking to the sound of a large downpour. He was glad he chose to sleep under the bridge to protect him from getting wet.

The clouds dissipated before dawn, and Donato woke to a cloudless sky. He started walking again, eager to reach Porta Plata that day. The vegetation started thinning out mid-afternoon, with tracks regularly forking from the highway. Donato was crossing one track when a revving vehicle appeared from around a bend. He hid behind a tree as he heard the shouts and hoots of drunken men. The car swerved and skidded to a stop next to where Donato hid.

"See that?" someone said.

"See what?" another asked.

"Something darting through the trees."

"I saw nothing, but let's check." Three quick rounds echoed from a rifle as the person fired randomly in the air.

"You idiot!" the other person said, laughing. "Nothing's hanging around after that."

"Well, I need a piss."

A door opened and slammed. Donato froze as footsteps came closer to where he hid. They stopped behind the tree. The tree's trunk was large and wide so Donato remained hidden and crouched in silence. The sound of flowing water reached his ears, and the smell of urine irritated his nostrils. He stifled a gag as the formaldehyde reek of urine wafted past him.

"Ahh..." the man said as he completed his business. Footsteps receded back to the vehicle. "Another beer?" he asked as he rustled in a container.

"Nah, I've had enough for now."

"Suit yourself." A can opened, followed by a door opening and closing. The engine fired up, and the men drove away, dust and gravel flying as the driver spun the wheels. The sound of the vehicle faded into the distance, but Donato stayed where he crouched, his heart pounding.

When he felt safe again, Donato emerged from his hiding place and continued his journey, coming to the outskirts of the city as the sun started sinking in the west. A few shambolic huts stood before him, announcing the city's edge. Donato wasn't ready to see people, so he skirted the perimeter and ended up back at the river. He thought he might follow the riverbank without being too conspicuous. A gouged-out bank allowed him to walk along the river without detection from above. The other side was thick with housing and industry. He walked under a large bridge as the last of the sunset turned the sparkling red water to murk. Donato kept walking until wharves blocked his path.

Chapter 33

The Truck Driver

A nightmare woke Roland. He was nestled high in a tree, keeping away from predators as he tried to sleep. No matter where he slept, a predator found him, trying to devour him. 'Keep away,' his dreaming self said. 'Don't touch me.' He was covered in sweat when he woke. He felt somewhere else and in danger but didn't understand why. What did the dream mean? The implications disturbed him. Calming himself, he lay back and drifted off to sleep again.

Roland searched around Vila Rio Dobrar the next day for clues of Donato's presence but found nothing. It frustrated him he came so close, only to lose track of him again. What happened to the boy? He asked the village people, but they hadn't seen him. Despite the bristly reception, Roland continued eating at the cafe. Grandma resisted sabotaging his food.

He consulted a map, considering Donato's potential destination and how long he might have taken to walk there on foot. That Donato walked to the village showed the boy's wish to return upriver. Porta Plata was the next place with any population, but it was 100 kilometers away, much further than he had walked to Vila Rio Dobrar.

Sipping on his coffee, Roland watched as three truck drivers walked in and greeted the staff with familiarity before taking a table.

"Something weird happened to me a few days back," one driver said.

"What's that?" another asked.

"I left here on my way to Carlos City and my rear axle broke. It was night, so I slept and called a mechanic the next morning. When I lifted the tarp for a bite of fruit, a kid popped out."

Roland immediately homed in on the men's conversation.

"No kidding?"

"Truth."

Roland's walked over to the group. "Do you mind me interrupting you for a moment?" he asked.

The drivers shrugged.

Roland sat down. "Did I hear you say you found a boy in your truck?" he asked the man.

The driver stared at Roland, suspicious. "Well... yes."

Roland pulled the picture of Donato from his wallet. "Is this him?"

The driver's brows rose. "Yeah, that's the kid."

The other drivers leaned over to see.

"What's he to you?"

"I'm trying to find him, to take him back to his father. The mining disaster swept him downriver."

"That's what he said. But he was going the wrong way. He wanted to go to Porta Plata. I was going to Carlos City."

"What happened? Where is he now?"

"The axle on my truck snapped, so I called a mechanic

from Porta Plata, the closest place for major repairs. He left with the mechanic, headed for Porta Plata."

"Okay. Well, thanks for that. That's a great help. At least I know where he's going. Do you know the mechanic's name?"

"No but he came from Porta Plata Mechanical Repairs & Service. It's a small business. Should be easy to locate the guy."

Roland wrote the name on a scrap of napkin. "Thanks."

The driver leaned over to Roland. He whispered, "The kid said he ran because the cook wanted to sell him. Don't believe it myself."

No wonder she didn't want anyone to find out, Roland thought. The information decided his next move — travel to Porta Plata the next day and search for Donato there. The trip would take the whole day. He needed to find the mechanic.

Chapter 34

Prostitutes

Darkness fell over the port as Donato sat next to the wharf, thinking. He had the money he stole from Grandma in his pocket and he felt hungry, so he decided to buy food and then find a safe place to sleep. He retraced his steps to find a place he could scramble up the riverbank, finding a spot nearby that looked easy to scale. A rising track appeared, as if someone used the path often.

Donato found himself in a dead-end street, darkness concealing his presence. The other end of the street connected to a wide thoroughfare with streetlights and shops. A shiver crept over him as he looked back along the darkened alley and he noted his position in case he needed to escape back that way later.

He stepped into the light and was met by a sea of strangers as couples and families strolled along the footpath in the early evening. People stared at him on the street alone. He heard someone say, "Where are his parents?" in disgust. Many of the shops were closed for the day — Clothes shops, and other specialty establishments that kept regular business hours. Many eateries were still open: fast-food places, cafes, bars and restaurants, the sound of people enjoying themselves filtering out into the street. He walked past many children holding on to their parents' hands as they pointed out various things with excited squeals. They were confused to see Donato on his own, sometimes noticing the teddy bear hanging out of the top of his pants, one eye dangling, as if looking at the ground. Donato couldn't decide which shop to choose. He settled on a fast-food shop that sold Picanhas.

He walked inside and waited at the counter where the attendant snapped at him. "What do you want?" he said.

"Can I have two beef Picanha skewers, please?"

"Can you pay?" the man asked, suspicious, searching for an accomplice.

"Yes." Donato was careful to only pull out one note from his pocket. "See."

"Okay then. That it?"

"A drink. I'll go get one." Donato walked to the refriger-ator and grabbed a bottle of water.

The attendant came back five minutes later with two steaming skewers in a paper bag, the grease soaking the paper. He placed it on the counter. "Five-sixty."

Donato pulled out the 10 Real note and the man gave Donato change, which he counted before putting it in his pocket. The man was smiling. "Making sure I didn't short-change you, huh?"

"My parents taught me never to trust strangers," Donato said, as he recalled all the strangers who had proven the wisdom of his parents' warning lately.

Donato left the shop and found a suitable spot to sit and eat his food. He finished the meal, licking his fingers and drank some water.

Afterwards, as dusk turned to night, Donato wandered down the street and found himself in a seedier area. He thought he should go back but curiosity tempted him to look further. He came to an intersection and turned into that, the lack of lighting creating a menacing gloom.

At a corner, he found two women, glittery split dresses exposing their legs and not leaving much to the imagination elsewhere either.

"Oh, look at the cute little boy," one of them said.

"Yeah, what's he doing hanging around here?" the other asked.

The first woman bent down to Donato's level. "Are you lost?" she asked with concern.

Donato shook his head. "I'm trying to get back to my Papa."

The woman glanced at the other. "Isn't he cute? I could take him home."

"If you say so." The woman pulled a cigarette from her clutch bag, lit it and inhaled a long drag.

"Where is your Papa?"

"In Vila Feliz."

"Where's that?" she asked, glancing up at her associate.

The woman took another puff. "Dunno."

"Hey, hey, hey..." a male voice shouted from up the street. "This ain't a child-care center. How you gunna get customers with a kid hanging off your ankles?"

The woman stood up. "Oh, shut up Silvio. The kid's cute."

"I'll give you cute if you don't stop talking to me that way," Silvio said, offering the back of his hand.

The woman stepped back, frightened. "He just appeared."

"Well, you got work to do." He looked at Donato,

"Scram kid. You're bad for business... or maybe we can find extra with a boy."

"Don't you dare," the woman warned, defying him despite the prior threat. "He's just a boy."

"Yeah, yeah, yeah. Just trying to scare him."

The woman leaned down again. "You'd better go before he hurts you."

Donato couldn't believe how many adults couldn't be trusted. He returned to the safety of the riverbank and found a slight hollow, large enough to hide him and protect him from the elements. Donato felt alone and miserable as he lay on his side trying to sleep. Why did this keep happening to him? Why are nasty people everywhere? Where are you, Papa? His misery gave way to sleep.

The noise of a blaring horn woke Donato with a start. The sun had risen. A barge chugged up the river past him, coming closer to his bank, as if to dock at the wharf. It blasted its horn again. The deck, piled with bales, bobbed with the gentle undulations of the river. Other boats moved along the waterway, the red silt staining the sides with a residue of rust.

Donato stood and stretched. He wondered if he could sneak on board a boat and hitch a ride home. He wouldn't know which was going where, though. He decided to go for breakfast and found a fruit store where he chose a banana and mango.

"Hey, what're you doing?" the shopkeeper shouted as he ran out to stop Donato.

"I can pay," Donato said hurriedly, as he handed over the fruit.

"Oh. Well, let's see. Forty centavos will do."

Donato fished through his pocket to find his loose coins.

"Where are your parents?" the shopkeeper asked.

Donato shrugged and walked off, tired of explaining things to everyone he met. He peeled the banana and ate it as he strolled. A bench seat stood nearby, so he sat on it as he ate the mango.

Morning turned to afternoon, and he found himself in a fenced off warehouse section near the wharf. One warehouse looked vandalised, windows smashed, and wall panelling pulled off. He crawled through a gap in the fence and squeezed through the warehouse wall where he was met with a vast expanse in the dim interior. Various boxes and rusting bits and pieces littered the floor, long forgotten. An office lined the far wall, so Donato strolled over and looked inside. Two desks covered with dust and wonky chairs stood crippled nearby. Cobwebs hung from the ceiling. He tried the door and the hinges squealed in protest as Donato pushed. After brushing away the cobwebs, he discovered the space under the desks would make a comfortable and safe spot to sleep. And the finger-sized hole in the office wall under the desk was the perfect spy hole.

Chapter 35

Rosita

Sanchez settled into the spare bedroom at Raf's house. He appreciated Raf's kindness and didn't want to abuse his generosity. As he had no job and little else to do, he volunteered for odd jobs around the house.

He sat on a bench seat on the back verandah in the early evening reading the newspaper. A knock on the front door disturbed his concentration but he didn't get up as he knew Raf and his wife were both home.

Raf came out a few moments later. "You have a visitor."

"Who?" Sanchez asked, as he didn't realise anyone knew he was living at Raf's house.

"Come see," Raf said with a hint of mischief.

Intrigued, Sanchez went inside with Raf. They passed through the kitchen and into the family room. He froze.

"Hello Sanchez," Rosita whispered, afraid to look at him as she sat on the sofa.

His mouth half opened, but no words came out. He looked at Raf, who had a cheeky grin on his face.

"I'll leave you two alone," Raf said.

Sanchez's eyes followed Raf, pleading for him to stay, but he still couldn't talk.

Left alone in the room with Rosita, he was uncomfortable. "I didn't think I'd meet you again after my behavior," he mumbled with effort.

"It wasn't your fault Manuel's such an idiot."

"I shouldn't have let him bait me as he did."

"Well, that's in the past now. Come. Sit," Rosita said, patting the sofa.

He walked over and sat down. He found his nerve again. "Why did you come?" he asked, gazing at her.

Rosita was wearing a tight white top with a frilly neckline and blue jeans with casual black sandals. She giggled. "Raf asked if I could. He's my cousin."

Sanchez was annoyed at Raf for going behind his back. "He didn't tell me that. No wonder he knew about the fight."

Rosita laughed. Her smile was contagious. He remembered she made him smile the first time they met, too.

"You've impressed Raf. He wants to care for you."

"You haven't answered my question."

Puzzled, Rosita asked, "What question?"

"Why did you come?"

Rosita lowered her eyes, a slight reddening colored her cheeks. "I found you interesting, despite how the evening ended. I wanted to find out what you're like when you're sober."

Sanchez reddened. "I don't drink that much as a habit. It's just that..."

"You don't have to explain. Raf told me what happened. It must be so hard for you."

"Still doesn't excuse my behavior."

"No, it doesn't."

Sanchez chuckled.

"What's so funny?" Rosita asked, confused.

"Raf told me you had a habit of picking the wrong men and I said you can add me to the list. I hope I'm off that list now."

"I think you are," Rosita whispered, but then she frowned, "Raf should keep his opinions to himself."

Sanchez laughed.

"What's so funny now?"

Sanchez stopped laughing and became self-conscious, blushing, "You're so gorgeous when you're angry." He looked away, not wanting to become any more intimate.

Rosita blushed. "It's getting hot in here. Only when I'm angry?"

"You're more gorgeous when you smile."

Rosita's face turned beetroot red, and she looked away.

Sanchez, seeing her discomfort, said, "Maybe we should stick to more general topics for now."

She looked back at him, relieved. "Yes, we should."

Raf poked his head through the doorway. "You two want a drink?"

"Coffee," Rosita said.

"Me too," Sanchez said. "Let's go out back."

The sun, half set, played soft golden and mottled sunlight on them as the last of its rays shone through the leaves of a nearby tree. A cooling breeze drifted over them, and Sanchez smelled Rosita's perfume. They sat in silence, neither wanting to be the first to speak. Raf came out with coffees, bringing over a small table for the cups. Sanchez watched Rosita glance at Raf, a sparkling glint of approval in her eyes. Raf gave a brotherly smile and left.

"You two appear close," Sanchez said.

"Me and Raf? We lived a few houses apart. We played

together as children. Got up to too much mischief sometimes. I can still feel the beltings my father gave me, well deserved too."

Sanchez chuckled.

"Raf's always cared for me. I've ignored his advice sometimes and suffered the consequences, with men in particular. He's an excellent judge of character."

"And what did he say of me?"

"I don't tell secrets," Rosita said with a teasing smile.

"That's not fair."

"You'll just have to live with it."

They sipped their coffees.

"Do you have a photo?"

"A photo of what?"

"Your family."

Pain crossed Sanchez's face.

"I'm sorry. I shouldn't have asked."

"It's okay. I suppose everything's still raw." Sanchez pulled out his wallet and slid out the photo. "Here."

A smiling Catina stood next to Donato, waving. "She's stunning," Rosita said.

"Yes, she was."

"Still no word of your son?"

"No." Tears started welling in Sanchez's eyes. He stared at the photo for a while longer before putting it back in his wallet.

"I should go."

"No, please stay longer."

They sat and talked for another half an hour.

"I must go now," Rosita said.

"Okay. Can we do this again soon?"

"If you want to, and it's not too soon. Things must still be hard for you. We can be friends if nothing else."

"Yes... friends," Sanchez said, a smile radiating from him.

Rosita rose to leave.

"Where do you live?"

"Two kilometers away."

"How did you get here?"

"I walked."

"You can't walk back. It's getting dark. I'll drive you."

"Okay," Rosita said, blushing.

They walked inside the house.

"Just taking Rosita home."

"Oh?" Raf asked, his eyebrows raised.

"I'm coming straight back," Sanchez said, annoyed.

He led Rosita to his pickup, and they drove off, Rosita directing him to an apartment block three storeys high. He idled the vehicle when they arrived.

"I'm glad you came, and we talked," Sanchez said. "It's what I needed."

"I'm glad, too. We'll get together again soon."

Their eyes locked before they both became nervous and broke contact.

"Bye," Rosita said as she opened the door.

"See you soon."

Sanchez watched Rosita walk into the building and drove home.

"That went well," Raf said, as Sanchez entered.

"Bloody matchmaker," he replied, a sheepish smile on his face as he headed for his room.

Chapter 36

Mechanic

Roland woke just before seven the next morning. He packed his belongings and put them in his four-wheel drive and searched for the owners.

"Are you off?" the old woman asked, wiping her wet fingers on her apron and waddling across to him, smiling.

"Yes, I am. Thank you so much for having me."

"You were no trouble."

"And thanks for doing the laundry."

"My pleasure."

"Here's the key, then." Roland handed the key to the woman.

"Hope you have luck finding that boy. Can't believe he was under our very noses."

"So do I." Roland walked to his vehicle and drove to the cafe where he had a quick breakfast and set off for Porta Plata.

The drive to the city took longer than Roland expected, being delayed several times by slow-moving trucks over-laden with cargo, and the condition of the road, which meant his progress was slow, even when he had empty highway ahead. Time vanished as he turned the radio up, listening to the music. He hit the outskirts of Porta Plata mid-afternoon, and pulled over to find the mechanic's business in his Maps app, finding the workshop in the port district. He pulled up in front of the workshop 45 minutes later.

Roland walked into reception where several mechanical parts lay on the front counter and the floor. Mechanics worked on two trucks in the workshop, with one half inside the engine cavity. Roland tapped the bell on the counter and waited.

A middle-aged man with little hair came in from the workshop, using a rag to wipe grease from his hands, his overalls smeared with grime and dirt. "How can I help you?" he asked.

"I'm Roland Cavendish. I'm looking for the mechanic who repaired a truck."

The man looked at Roland suspiciously. "You a federal agent?"

"No, I'm not. I just want to talk to him."

"When was this?"

"Last Friday. He was out on the highway."

"Let's check the log." The man produced a book from underneath the counter and flicked through the pages, checking the jobs list. "It was Fernando," he said, looking back at Roland. "But he's not here. He's out at a breakdown. He should be back by five."

"Okay. I'll wait."

"Can I help you?"

"I don't think so. He gave a boy a lift into Porta Plata. I just want to talk to him."

The man's eyes widened in alarm at mention of a boy.

"You'll just have to wait," he blurted, and rushed back to the workshop.

That was strange, Roland thought.

He spent the time looking at the nearby businesses and ships in the port. Five o'clock arrived and a service vehicle drove into the workshop, avoiding the other mechanics busy packing up for the day. Roland walked back into the reception again.

Another man walked in moments later, looking at Roland warily. "Heard you're looking for a kid."

"Yes, I talked to the truck driver who's truck you repaired on Friday. He mentioned that he had a boy with him, and you took him, because you were going to Porta Plata. Is that right?"

"Yes."

"I'm trying to find him so I can take him back to his father. Where did you drop him?"

"I didn't."

"What do you mean?"

"I pulled into a service station to fill up not far from town. When I got back from paying, he'd bolted, left. Bought food for him too, the ungrateful scamp."

Donato's disappearance disturbed Roland. It sounded similar to fleeing from the cook at the cafe. "Can you think of a reason why he would run?"

"What are you suggesting, hey? You think I did something to the lad?" Fernando started getting angry.

"It's just unusual he should run." Roland wondered why the driver was being so defensive.

"Well, he just did. That's all I know."

"Where was the service station?"

"Fifteen kilometers out on the Carlos City road. You passed it."

Roland remembered the spot. "Yes, I did. Well, if you have nothing else, I thank you for your time."

"Not a problem."

Roland left, feeling Fernando's eyes drilling into his back as he walked away. He hopped into his vehicle and drove off, heading for the center of the city, looking for a suitable hotel, settling on Plata Continental. It stood near the river in the tourist part of the metropolis. On check-in, the receptionist gave him a room on the fifth floor over-looking the river. He parked his vehicle and unpacked his suitcase before gazing out the window. A red snake wove its stain through the landscape, making Roland cringe. The mistakes of the company he led had produced that red snake. He hoped the company was doing its best to return the river to its pristine state, reminding Roland to call the Carlos City office tomorrow to get an update on progress.

Darkness encroached on the city, so Roland descended to the hotel bar, waiting for dinner. The bar had a casual atmosphere and various sports telecasts screened on the televisions scattered throughout. It served meals too, so he stayed. A notice on the wall advertised a live band playing later that night.

He ordered a meal in the bar after his second beer. After he finished his meal, he saw a pool table near the far side. Since no one was playing, he walked over and played a few games solo. The monotony bored him, so he played left-handed instead of his usual right. Roland felt it might give him a slight edge over an opponent, if he mastered it.

"Want to play a real opponent?" Roland heard over his shoulder as he finished potting the black ball. A young woman stood nearby, red T-shirt top and blue jeans. She looked appealing.

"Sure," Roland replied, thinking her no challenge.

The woman helped Roland collect the balls and Roland racked them, ready for the break. A waiter passed, so he ordered a beer and bought the woman a drink.

"I'm Roland," he said.

"Maria."

"You can break."

Maria looked at Roland with challenging eyes and accepted his invitation. She completed the break and continued as she potted five balls from the break demonstrating her skill. The bar started filling with women, and he realised it was a bar local women patronized, hopeful for a man for the night, or a longer relationship, with luck. His attention returning to the game, Maria gestured it was his turn to play. He ruined the shot and potted no balls. He shrugged as Maria moved into position. Roland's game improved as it progressed, but he had given Maria the edge and lost.

"Another?" Maria asked.

"I don't enjoy getting beaten, but why not?"

Maria set up the balls and allowed Roland to take the break. He played much better and won the game. They played another in the best of three, which Roland won with impressive, if lucky, shots.

"You win," Maria said.

"You're an excellent player."

"That was impressive," a man said, as he approached them. He spoke English with a heavy Germanic accent. "Maybe you play me?"

Roland looked at Maria, not wanting to exclude her, but she indicated it was fine. She stayed. Roland noticed she kept close. "Okay. I always enjoy playing."

Maria set up the balls for them. The German signalled for Roland to break the pack. He did, potting a ball and potted three more balls, much to the German's annoyance. The German started using distraction tactics after Roland had potted the third ball and lined up for his fourth. He started talking just before Roland played to put him off his shot. Roland potted the fourth. On the fifth, the German stood in Roland's line-of-sight and coughed just as he moved to hit the ball, causing Roland to miss. The German continued with the tactics, reducing the margin so the game hung in the balance. Roland became frustrated but said nothing. He wanted to smash the guy with his cue at one stage but won the game by one ball. The German wanted a rematch, which Roland accepted. Roland cleared his mind to relax more and ignore the man's distractions. He wanted to enjoy the game and accept whatever result eventuated. The German broke, and the game seesawed as each had their period of excellent play, despite the German's distractions. Two of Roland's balls sat packed together by one corner pocket with one of the German's and Roland had another ball by the other corner pocket. He attempted an advanced shot to pot both balls in the same pocket for the hell of it. He lined up and hit the white ball which struck the first ball in a perfect spot. It hit the next ball, dropping it into the pocket. With the spin, the first ball followed the second into the pocket. Meanwhile, the white ball ricocheted off the first ball over to the third ball and hit it into that pocket, leaving just the black ball for Roland to down. The German stood open mouthed. He couldn't believe his eyes. Roland couldn't believe it either, but accepted the good fortune, and the humiliation it produced in the German. Roland then potted the black ball with a straightforward shot and won the game.

"That was lucky," Roland confessed.

"Yes, luck," the German agreed. He refrained from challenging for a third game.

As Roland had satisfied his hunger for pool for the night, he put his cue away.

The band set up while Roland was playing, so he settled in a spot at the bar where he could watch the band perform. Maria followed and sat on a stool next to him. Roland knew Maria's intentions, but felt happy with her companionship for the night. They talked in between listening to the band. Maria moved closer to Roland as it got later.

Midnight approached, so Roland bid farewell to Maria, as he wanted to get up early the next morning. He understood where Maria wanted the night to end. She looked disappointed but smiled when Roland mentioned he was staying at the hotel several nights and would be in the bar again.

Chapter 37

Extortion

Donato's teddy bear stared back at him as he opened his eyes the next morning. His back felt sore as he moved to a sitting position. He crawled out from under the desk and arched his back to stretch. Subdued light from the overcast sky outside filtered through the smashed windows of the warehouse. Once he retrieved the half-full bottle of water, he took a drink to quench his thirst. He needed to urinate, but he hadn't seen a toilet in the place. He went out into a corner of the warehouse and relieved himself. His bladder empty, he returned to the office and picked up his bear, as he didn't want to leave it there in case he didn't return and tucked it into his pants again.

After squeezing through the gap in the wall, Donato walked back to the shops. It hadn't rained overnight, but the sky appeared threatening. He didn't spot anyone else until he came to the shops. Most stores still had their doors closed, too early for business. Food vendors displayed their wares and were busy preparing meals for the rush of people soon to descend on them. The smell of the cooking made

Donato salivate. After buying food and a drink from a nearby vendor, he walked off looking for somewhere to sit and eat. He passed two intersections before he noticed a small park with a lawn, flower beds and bench seats. With a dash across the road, he sat on a seat away from the curious and well-intentioned. He devoured his food, licked his fingers and looked around at his surroundings. Small birds hopped back and forth on the grass towards him, searching for crumbs to scavenge. He sat and watched them for a time. People started walking through the park, on their way to somewhere else — jobs and other destinations — ignoring the waif boy sitting on the bench, the sight a common occurrence.

"What are you doing here, son?" a male voice asked Donato from behind.

Donato froze from the unexpected presence sneaking up on him. An aged man in his sixties stood by the seat, stooped and weary. Kind and tired eyes looked at him, a grey-bearded face matching the grey hair and worn-out rags for clothes and hat, advertising a homeless man. The man smiled and shuffled towards the bench seat. "I didn't want to scare you. You see, that's my seat, where I sit watching the world most days. I suppose it's not really my seat, I don't own it, but I sit here. I don't mind sharing, though. It's good to share."

"I'm sorry. I didn't know it was your seat," Donato apologized. He made to move.

The man waved him back. "It's okay, son. As I said, it's good to share. I never meet anyone who wants to share my seat with me. You can share my seat, if you can spare the time."

Donato smiled at the kind but lonely old man. "I have time."

"Good, good." The man sat next to Donato and leaned on the backrest. "Ahh... that's better. Now, what are you doing here all alone? Little boys shouldn't be running around all alone. They shouldn't be talking to strangers like me either. But I'm harmless. Some are not. You need to be wise to pick the harmless ones, otherwise you can get yourself into trouble."

Donato felt unsure if he should answer. The man talked so much he couldn't get a word in anyway. Uncertain, he sat in silence.

After a pause, the man turned to glance at Donato. "Cat got your tongue? I know I talk too much, but you can interrupt."

"It's not polite to interrupt."

"Your parents taught you something, then. Speaking of parents, where are they?"

"Mama is dead, and Papa is far away in Vila Feliz."

"Sorry to hear that, son. Not good, not having a mother. A boy needs his mother. Needs his father, too. What's he doing in what you called?"

"That's where I live. The red flood swept me away."

"Oh. I read that story in an old paper. It was the story of the day. Nasty business that, making the river red and everything. Hope they clean up the mess. Made a terrible mess. All the fish died. Don't know if they all died, but a lot died. They washed up along the riverbank and stunk to high heaven, they did, until they came along and cleaned them up. You get washed down here, then?"

"No, I floated further downriver in a tank. That's where Mama died, in the tank. I've been walking back upriver, back to my home. I got here yesterday."

Compassionate eyes looked at Donato. "Sad to hear that. A boy shouldn't see death that way, especially when it's your mother. Very sad. Too young to experience things like that. Such is life, I suppose. You got a name?"

"Donato."

"Well, Donato, looks like you've had something to eat. Hope you didn't steal it."

"Oh, no sir, I paid for it."

"That's good. Too much stealing around here, stealing this, stealing that. Police have their day cut out trying to catch everyone. They're the thieves half the time. And you shouldn't tell strangers you have money. They might steal it from you." The man winked as he gave a whimsical laugh.

Several teeth were missing from the man's mouth, the others stained and black with signs of decay. As if catching the old man's mood, he said, "I didn't say I had money now."

The man laughed again, jovial. "Good boy."

"What's your name?"

The man gazed at Donato before answering. "You can call me Vovo."

"Okay, Vovo. Have you eaten?"

"I had a few nibbles before this. Thanks for asking. Good to be polite to people. Solve the world's problems if everyone was polite, but everyone's too busy, rushing every-where, trying to get on in the world, it's moving too fast. People should learn to slow down and enjoy life. But here I am complaining to a boy who doesn't know what I'm talking about. Please tell me when I talk too much. I talk too much, you know."

Donato smiled at the confession. "What do you do then?"

"Oh, a bit of this and a bit of that. I look in bins for discarded things to sell. It's amazing the things people throw away sometimes. People are so wasteful,.Things that haven't even been used sometimes. I found a full packet of biscuits once, still wrapped and everything. They lasted me a week, they did."

"I'm glad you came along today. I was feeling lonely."

"Yes, well, you were on my seat, you see. You'll never be lonely if you sit on my seat. I'll come along, in time. It's not really my seat. I don't own it, but I like to think it's my seat."

"You already said that."

"Did I? Good thing someone's listening, otherwise I'd just keep repeating myself."

Donato laughed. "That's funny."

Vovo chuckled.

"Where is your family?" Donato asked.

"Oh, that's a sad story, I suppose. Wife died long ago, and kids have long gone. They're not interested in a foolish old man." The man looked sad from remembering a deep hurt that had left scars. He sat in melancholic silence.

"Don't you work?"

"Work's for people who're useful. I'm past my use-by date. Nobody needs an old man."

"Why not? You can talk to people. You're a good talker."

Vovo chuckled. "I may be a good talker, but am I a good listener?"

"You listened to me."

"I'm glad."

"What are you going to do now?"

"Oh, I don't know. I think I'll just sit here with you for a while. There's no hurry. The world won't end if I sit with you for a while. It's been a while since anyone has sat with me. I think I'll just sit here for now."

Silence spread between them. Donato said nothing further, and the old man sat, content and watchful. The sky still threatened rain. Birds chirped in the trees and bright red and yellow flowers bloomed in the beds nearby, their scent wafting past with the breeze now and then. The old man's presence comforted Donato in a way he couldn't understand. It made him happy to have the old man sit with him.

"You hungry?" Vovo asked.

Donato realized that he was. "Yes, I am."

"Here," Vovo said, reaching into his trouser pocket and extracting money with his arthritic fingers. "Go find something for both of us. There's a shop two blocks away, a grocery store." He pointed to the street fronting the park. "Biscuits and chips and stuff. And fruit if they've got any." He held out the money.

"Shouldn't show people you've got money," Donato said.

Vovo sniggered. "You're learning. I think I can trust you though."

Donato hopped off the bench. "You'll be here when I get back?"

"You've got my money and food, I hope. I'll be here."

After two blocks, Donato saw the grocery store the old man described. A man leaned on the counter, dark rings around his eyes. His head jerked up when Donato entered, fear turning to indifference when he saw it was only a young boy. The shopkeeper returned to reading the paper.

Donato grabbed a basket and navigated the aisles of groceries. He guessed Vovo would like chips and found a packet of cassava chips. He heard the door to the store open and close. A chill followed.

"It's that time of the month," a deep menacing voice said.

"I don't have your money yet," the storekeeper said, obvious fear in his tone. "It's been a quiet month. I'm sure I'll have enough tomorrow."

"Well, that'll upset the boss. You know it takes money to keep your store safe. Ain't that right, Bruno?"

"Sure does," Bruno said. "The boss gets upset when he doesn't get paid. Gets him mad, and you don't want the boss mad at you. He got mad at the shop owner further along the street... oh, that's right, it ain't there anymore." He chuckled a sinister laugh. "I might take a walk."

Donato crept to the far end of the store, trying to keep quiet. He huddled behind the shelving and peeked at the counter through a gap in the shelves. He spied one of the stand-over men headed towards him.

A turnstile rack with packets of candy hanging from it stood in front of the row of shelves. Bruno hooked it with his finger and pulled it over, the packets crashing to the floor. "Oops, how clumsy. Accidents will happen." He continued strutting through the aisle. Donato slid into the next aisle and waited, hoping he remained hidden. The man's shape loomed over Donato as he cleared the aisle and stood in front of a freezer door. Bruno made a quick movement with his arm, and one door smashed. "Oh dear, things are breaking real easy."

"Please," the shopkeeper pleaded. "I will have the money tomorrow, I promise."

"Hear that Bruno, he'll have the money tomorrow."

"Yeah, can we wait that long?"

"Well, you know, the boss was in a good mood today, and he said to me before we left, 'the stores' been doing it tough since that dam thing. I'm feeling generous today. If our patrons can't pay today, I'll let them have a couple more days.' That was generous of him, don't you think?"

"Yeah, he must be in a good mood. Must have had an excellent lay," Bruno said, laughing as he grabbed a packet of ice creams, ripped it open and took one.

"Maybe. So, we'll do this. We'll let you off today, and we'll come back tomorrow. That's fair. You think that's fair, Bruno?"

"Fair to me," Bruno said in between slurps of ice cream. He turned into the aisle where Donato hid. "Well, well, well. What have we here?" He snatched for Donato and grabbed him by the arm, squeezing tight as he lifted Donato off the floor.

"Let me go!" Donato yelled as he struggled to escape the firm grip.

"What's that?" the other man said.

"A mouse hiding behind the shelves," Bruno said, teasing Donato with his other hand.

"He's just a kid. Let him go."

"He heard us." Bruno reached the counter again.

"He won't tell anyone, will you?"

Donato shook his head vigorously.

"See. He's a good kid. Let him go."

Bruno eased his grip and dropped Donato to the floor. Donato scrambled away, keeping his eyes on the men. He reached the back of the shop and hid in a corner. The men laughed.

"Anyone'd think you got laid too, the mood you're in," Bruno said.

"Gotta be kind sometimes, Bruno. Let's go."

The owner gazed at the smashed freezer door, his shoulders stooped in despair. He picked up the turnstile and found Donato. "Sorry, kid. Did he hurt you?"

Donato shook his head and took time to calm himself. He went back to his basket and chose more biscuits, two packets of candy and fruit. After spying a packet of muesli bars, he grabbed that too before going to the counter. The shopkeeper added up the bill, and Donato paid. The shopkeeper put the items in a paper bag for Donato and he left. He ran back to the park.

Vovo sat in the seat where Donato had left him. "Thought you shot through for a minute."

Donato struggled to regain his breath. "Two mean men came into the store and wanted money from the shopkeeper and then they saw me and one of them grabbed me."

Alarmed, the old man scanned the street. "Hope they didn't hurt you, lad."

"No, I'm okay."

"Good." The man's look changed from alarm to resolution. "Did you get their names?"

"One was Bruno. I don't know the other person's name."

"That's fine, lad." Vovo sat staring into the distance, calculating his next move.

Chapter 38

Police

Roland's plan for the day was to speak to the local police, so he drove to the station and approached the counter. A uniformed police officer sat looking at his phone, not paying any attention to Roland. He waited for the officer to notice him.

"Yeah," the police officer said, not taking his eyes from his phone.

"I'm trying to locate a lost boy."

The officer raised his head. "What makes you think we got him?"

"I'm not saying that you have him, I wondered if anyone had reported seeing him in the last few days?"

"Boys go missing every day. They either show up or they don't. Sometimes we catch them in a felony, or they turn up dead somewhere. Why's this one special?" The police officer placed his phone on the counter, looking at Roland with more interest.

"The Vermelho mine disaster swept him away from Vila Feliz, and I've traced him coming to Porta Plata yesterday. He may have come to the police for help."

The officer eyed Roland again and looked back to his phone before sighing. "Let me check." He disappeared into the station.

Roland stood by the counter waiting for his return. On peaking at the person's phone, he saw that he had been surfing through one of the social media sites. *A useful pursuit for a police officer*, Roland scoffed. Several minutes elapsed, and Roland wondered if they had forgotten him when the officer returned.

"Nothing in the reports. Not any at the other stations either."

"Oh, okay." Roland pondered his next move. "Could I report a missing child?"

"You could. Not sure what good that will do. We're overworked around here."

"I'm sure you are," Roland said, flicking his eyes to the man's phone.

"What's he to you?"

"I'm trying to return him to his father."

"So, you're not a relative?"

"No."

"Well, only a relative can report a missing person."

"What if none are alive?"

"Thought you said the father was alive."

"It was a rhetorical question."

"That's an exception."

Roland realized the officer was becoming increasingly annoyed with him, so he retreated.

"What's your name then?"

"Roland Cavendish."

The police officer studied him. "You're that head guy from the company, aren't you?"

"Yes, I am."

"I wouldn't mention that too loudly around here."

"I'm not afraid of facing up to the consequences."

"Really? I'm not sure you realize what retribution people around here could demand."

Roland shivered at the warning. Or was it a threat? "Anyway, the boy's name is Donato Barbosa. Can you please call me if he surfaces?" Roland wrote his phone number and other details on a piece of paper and gave it to the man.

The police officer gaped and frowned at Roland with a 'you're joking' expression but said, "Yeah, okay."

"Thank you for your time." Roland turned to leave, as a suspicious and calculating guise appeared on the police officer's face. He walked to his vehicle again, hopping in. *What now?* He picked up the map sitting on the passenger side seat and unfolded it. He saw the Carlos City Road and the roadhouse where the mechanic lost Donato. *Where would he go?* Donato had been travelling along the river, so Roland presumed he would continue to do so. The Carlos City Road neared the river as it entered the city. If Donato didn't want to walk along the road (he already had two nasty experiences; Roland felt sure the mechanic hadn't been honest with him), he would have gone back to the river and followed it into the city. Roland traced the river until he reached the port precinct and tapped his finger. Donato would have gone to the port. He had money from the woman at Vila Rio Dobrar, and Roland considered he might try boarding a boat upriver. Roland headed to the port.

Chapter 39

Bullies

"I'd better go," Donato said to Vovo late in the day.

"Okay. I've got things to do, too. There's always something to do. Never a dull moment."

Donato hopped off the bench, reluctant to leave. "Will you be here tomorrow?"

"Oh, I'm here most days. Always like sitting on my seat. I told you it's my seat, didn't I? It's not really my seat, but I like to think it's mine."

Donato smiled, but said nothing. "I might see you tomorrow then."

"Always welcome to sit on my seat, little boy."

Donato set off under Vovo's watchful eye until he disappeared around the corner. Needing food, he first returned to the grocery store, buying more for the night. The shopkeeper had cleaned up the glass and taped the broken freezer door with plastic . He strolled back to his hiding spot with a bag of supplies.

As he turned a corner, Donato ran into a group of older boys who looked between 10 and 15.

"Who have we here?" one boy taunted. He pranced in front of the others as if preening himself.

"Someone got us some snacks," another boy said.

They came closer and surrounded Donato, trapping him.

"Give me the bag," the older boy said.

"It's mine," Donato replied, cowering with fear.

"Ohh... it's mine," the leader said, mimicking Donato. "It's mine now." He made to grab the bag, but Donato jerked away from his reach.

"That was a big mistake." He nodded to a boy behind Donato, who moved forward and grabbed him, pinning his arms behind his back.

"Let me go," Donato screamed as he struggled to escape.

The leader punched him in the stomach. "You need to obey orders. Didn't your parents tell you not to talk back to your elders?"

Donato buckled over, dropping the bag of groceries. Tears trickled from his eyes as the pain engulfed him.

"What a sook," another boy said.

The leader picked up the bag and looked inside. He pulled out a packet of chips and ate them in front of Donato's face. Enlightenment dawned. "How did you buy these? You got money?"

Donato was now even more afraid. He couldn't buy any more food if they took his money. He shook his head.

"Let's look in his pockets!"

"What are you boys doing?" Vovo called, as he came around the corner leaning on his walking stick.

"Mind your business, old man."

"That boy is my business. Leave him alone."

"How you going to make us?"

The gang gathered around their leader, who strutted

towards Vovo, even though he only came up to Vovo's chin, despite the man's stoop.

"Don't be foolish. Now leave him be. Donato, come over here."

Frozen with fear and unable to move, Donato stood where he was.

"Donato," Vovo said again, bringing him from his stasis.

He scurried over to Vovo and hid behind him. The leader stood facing the old man and shoved him hard, but could only sway him where he stood. Vovo stared the leader down. "Just leave," he said.

Vovo watched the teenager slide his hand into his pocket and pull out a flick knife. With lightning-fast action, Vovo had the boy pinned to the ground before he could open the knife. The leader stared up at the man, stupefied by Vovo's speed. Vovo glared at the boy. "Leave now before you get hurt."

The leader nodded. Vovo grabbed the knife before releasing his hold. The other members of the gang, waiting for instructions, stood motionless. Vovo stepped back two paces.

The leader stood up, massaging his wrist and arm where the old man had grabbed him. He was humiliated and burning with rage at being bested by an elderly man. "Get him!" he yelled to his gang. They moved forward, confident their numbers outweighed any skill.

Donato stood to the side, unable to help. He didn't need to worry. Boy after boy flew from the old man as each tried to gain a hold or a punch, Vovo reacting like a ballet dancer with lethal force. In less than a minute, the confrontation was over with one boy groaning on the ground, others nursing their injuries.

"Go, before I get warmed up," Vovo threatened, approaching the group menacingly.

The gang backed off. "We'll get you one day," the leader warned as he walked away with his gang.

The old man brushed off his tattered coat and walked over to Donato's grocery bag lying where it spilled. He gave it back to Donato. "Here. You should be more careful walking around these parts. If nothing else, they'll force you to join them. I'd get you to stay with me, but that's not possible. I have things to do, many things. Things only an old man must do."

Donato grabbed the bag and nodded. "Thank you."

Vovo patted Donato on the shoulder, looking at him with fatherly love. "Go."

Chapter 40

The Port

Roland drove around the port, hoping to spot Donato. He stopped people to ask if they had seen him, but no-one had. He returned to the hotel, depressed by his lack of progress. In his room, he called Felicity at the Carlos City office to get an update of events.

"Hi Roland, how's things?" Felicity asked.

"Slow. I've picked up a trail of the boy, but he's disappeared in Porta Plata somewhere."

"Be careful where you go there. Porta Plata can be a dangerous place."

"What do you mean?"

"It's popular with drug traffickers, amongst other things."

"I'll take note. The police aren't interested."

"I'm not surprised."

"So, how are things going?"

"A political hot potato, as you can imagine. The various government departments are getting heavy-handed with us. I think they're being pressured. Several executives from head office have flown in to manage the fallout. There's significant public anger over the entire incident. Social media is on fire, the flames being fed by environmental activist groups. The main hostilities are coming from people far removed from the incident. Those affected just want to get their lives back together. Feedback suggests they're very appreciative of the counselling services we're providing. With the angst, I just want to resign and curl up sometimes. It's depressing."

"I can imagine. Isn't providing funds for the clean-up helping soothe things?"

"Yeah, somewhat. That's getting its share of flack, too. People are saying it's blood money."

"What's happening with the clean-up?"

"That's progressing well. The mess is cleaned up and rebuilding teams are helping people return to their homes as soon as possible. That will take time."

"What's happening at the mine?"

"It's still shut down. I don't know when it will start up again. They have to get tailings storage organized and approved before the authorities will allow it to start. The investigation is progressing. We've brought two leading experts in to find out what happened. It will take several months before they can issue a report, though."

"You don't need me then."

"I'm missing your support. There's negative talk that you're shirking your responsibilities. They want you to front up."

"I realized that might happen. Let's hope I find the boy soon."

"Yeah."

"I'll let you go then."

"Okay. Be careful."

"I will."

Roland hung up and sighed, feeling helpless. He doubted his decision to search for the boy, but he couldn't forget his own experience. He needed to find the boy to bury his demons. Depression crept up on him again, but he had no way to stop the downward spiral. Loneliness engulfed him and he wished he could reach out and hold Deborah. After freshening up, he went down to the bar for a drink and watched basketball on television. He dined in the restaurant before returning to the bar but had no interest in playing pool. He watched more sport while sipping his drink. Thinking of retiring for the night, he looked at his watch — nine-thirty. He had one more drink.

"Hi," a familiar female voice said from behind him.

Roland turned to see Maria, dressed elegantly. "Oh, Hi," he said with little cheer.

A little put out, Maria asked, "What's eating you tonight?"

"Oh, nothing. Just a depressing day."

"Want to talk?"

"Maybe. Want a drink?"

"Thought you'd never ask." Maria sat next to Roland and ordered a drink from the bartender. The drink came a minute later, and Maria took a sip. "So, what's up?"

Roland shook his head, unsure if he wanted to divulge his problems. He didn't know Maria. He took a chance. "I'm trying to find a lost boy from the mine disaster the other week. It's been difficult. I tracked him here, but I've lost him again."

"What's the boy to you?"

"I'm trying to find him, to return him to his father."

"That dam collapse was terrible with so many people

killed. I'd give that company's boss a piece of my mind, if I saw him."

Roland's face turned white. "I'm the boss," he whispered to Maria, hanging his head in shame.

"You're what?" Maria stared at Roland in disbelief and shock, and then a mien of disgust overcame her. "You disgusting, filthy, money-grabbing pig. I don't know how you can show your face around here, you slime." Maria worked herself into a frenzy, as her face darkened, and her voice rose. Other patrons started turning around. As she noticed interest from the others, Maria announced, "Here's the person responsible for that mining disaster."

Other people in the bar became agitated, and Roland shifted in his seat. They started contributing their own abuse and a few looked like they were going to get physical. "I'm sorry," Roland said to Maria and ran out of the bar. He dashed to the elevator and jumped in, breathing a sigh of relief when the doors closed. He arrived on the fifth floor and sped to his room, locked the door and collapsed onto the bed, shivering with fear. He imagined the crowd might lynch him if he stayed any longer.

Roland headed to the mini-bar and opened a small bottle of whisky, drinking it straight down. He opened another and poured it into a glass, adding an ice cube. Stumbling over to a chair next to the small table, he slumped into it, placed the glass down and stared at it. He wondered if he should have pulled the trigger when he had the chance. How he needed to be in Deborah's arms at that moment, just for the comfort it would give him. He lifted the glass and drank half the contents. The self-pity threatened to drown him, so he tried to think of something constructive, but he couldn't. He felt fenced in and cornered. With nothing else to do that night, he drank the whisky and flopped onto the bed, tossing and turning, hoping to fall asleep.

Roland ran as fast as his little legs could go as he tried to out-run the predator behind him. His heart pounded in his chest, pumping oxygen through his arteries to fuel his muscles. He stumbled several times as he crashed through the undergrowth, his position obvious to anything on alert. Sweat threatened to blind him, as the salty water dribbled into his eyes, returning as soon as he wiped it away. His progress, hampered by the dim moonlight, was too slow to escape his pursuer, whatever it was. His pace slowed, as fatigue set in, and his will to continue waned with each step.

The ground turned rocky, making running even more hazardous, an abyss of nothingness fast approaching up ahead, as he neared a cliff. He veered right but realized the futility of his efforts as the cliff edge faded in the distance. He stopped running. Bent with exhaustion, he struggled to get air into his lungs to recover. He couldn't hear anything chasing him, so he searched around for his hunter. Everything was still, except for the swaying trees 20 meters away, the breeze rustling the leaves.

A black form slinked towards him, the reflected moonlight shining in its eyes, as it edged to within 10 meters of him. Roland noticed it was feline but couldn't recognize the species in the dim light. It stopped and sniffed the air, a quiet growl reverberating from its throat. Roland edged towards the cliff, as close as he dared to keep his distance, but he could only retreat so far. Fear emanated from Roland's body, adding to the cat's heightened hunting instinct. He whimpered and wet himself. The cat kept low to the ground and continued its slow slinking walk, swaying, as if considering the most entertaining method of the kill. It decided and pounced...

Roland woke, perspiration pouring from his body as he screamed. He breathed in spasms as he woke, his sensation of being trapped and helpless returning to him after so many years. That dream had not replayed itself since his childhood. He gasped for air to calm himself and got out of the bed for a drink of water. Returning to bed, he lay on top willing sleep to return.

Dawn bled through the curtains as Roland tossed and turned, hoping for more sleep. Tiredness still weighed on him. Sensing the futility of continuing his attempts to sleep, he rose and had a shower. Dressed, he descended to the restaurant for breakfast before preparing for his day's activities. He returned to the port, showing Donato's photo to shopkeepers and others to see if anyone recognized him.

He pulled up at the port just after 10 in the morning and showed Donato's photo at shop after shop. Ready to give up, Roland tried the grocery store where the shopkeeper, stocking a shelf, returned to the counter when he saw a potential customer.

"Can I help you, sir?" the shopkeeper asked.

"I was wondering if you've seen this boy?" Roland asked, as he showed the man the photo.

The shopkeeper peered at the image. "Yes, he was in here yesterday."

Roland's eyes lit up at the positive news. "Do you know where he is?"

After shaking his head, the shopkeeper said, "No, I haven't seen him before, and he hasn't come in today. I thought he was just another waif roaming the streets. They end up here, homeless with nowhere to go. Although he had money, which was surprising. They often come in to steal food."

"Can you tell me which direction he came from?"

"No, why are you looking for him? Is he in trouble?"

"No, he's from upriver and I'm trying to return him to his father."

"He won't last too long if he stays around here. It's a rough neighborhood at night."

"Can you tell me where he might go?" Roland asked as he scratched his head.

"No, you might try further in the port. There are plenty of vacant buildings there where a child could hide."

"Thanks."

Roland left the store and walked along the footpath with more purpose, now with Donato's presence confirmed. He passed an electrical goods store with televisions in the window. The images of two men on screen distracted him. The reporter announced they had been found dead that morning, murdered execution style. The reporter said the names, but Roland only caught 'Bruno' as a loud truck motored past the shop. Noon approached, so Roland bought food and, seeing a park nearby, strode over. As he sat on a bench seat eating, his mood improved.

A group of men entered the park, but they looked innocuous, so Roland ignored them, taking in the scenery while he considered his next moves. He didn't notice the men approaching him until he was surrounded.

"You're that boss guy from the mine, aren't you?" one man asked, menace in his stance. "I saw you on the TV."

Roland blinked as fear swelled up from his stomach, his face blanching.

"Hey, guys. This guy killed those villagers. What's say we teach him a lesson?"

Mob mentality gripped the group and Roland cowered as one of them reached out and grabbed him, pulling him from the bench and punching him in the stomach, felling Roland to the ground, winded. The others joined in the melee as one and then another kicked him, blood spurting from his nose and mouth. Roland curled in on himself for protection, but they lifted him up and punched him, before dropping him to the ground again. Distant sirens stopped their vigilante justice, and they ran off, leaving Roland unconscious in the park.

Chapter 41

Crash

The day after Rosita's visit lasted forever. Sanchez found it impossible to think of enough activities to keep busy. Inaction ate away at him until his depression started to return. Having one's family ripped from you was a significant shock for even the most robust constitution, and Sanchez could sense his mental health slipping. If only his life held a promising future. He had no job. His home, although suffering only minor damage, was like being in isolation in prison. No one else was living in the village and there were no signs of anyone returning. His life in Vila Feliz had ended with the death of his family. Sanchez realized his best way forward was to sell his property and move closer to El Grieta. He had savings for a deposit, he thought, although he hadn't researched the property market in the city. Still, the casual, free existence of Vila Feliz, far away from the buzz of any metropolis, had attracted them there. Sanchez sighed in indecision. He could investigate the property market in El Grieta at least and rent a unit or house until he made a final decision.

As night approached, the evening meal with Raf and his

family began, always a festive occasion, even with the meager, but adequate, provision on the table. Raf gave Sanchez a beer as they both retired to the bench seat in the backyard.

"I've been thinking of moving to El Grieta, selling up and buying something here. What do you think?" Sanchez asked as he took a sip of beer.

Raf gazed out towards the dwindling sunset in considered thought before answering. "I can see advantages for you in the short term. It's not healthy for you living alone out at Vila Feliz."

"That's what I'm realizing."

"Why make a permanent move?"

Sanchez took another sip from his beer. "That life's finished. I can't explain it, but it's as if it's a shrine to what I had with my family, and I don't want to disturb it."

"You don't know that Donato is dead."

"I know he is. It won't be the same living there, without Catina."

"Hmm... you have a point. It won't be easy selling, although I hear they're setting up a special building fund for those who want to move to higher ground. You could tap into that, instead of finding a buyer for your house, if they'll agree to do it."

"That's something I can ask. Do you know the property market here?"

"No, I know someone who can help, though."

"That'd be good. In the meantime, I'll find a place to rent. Get out of your way."

"You know you're always welcome here, but it's a good first step in rebuilding your life."

"I might drive out to Vila Feliz tomorrow and pick up a load of stuff."

"Fine."

Sanchez rose early the next morning. He wanted time to sort through the belongings he intended bringing back with him. After breakfast, he jumped in his vehicle and drove to Vila Feliz. He parked near his house and got out, the sounds of nature the only thing greeting him. As he expected, the surroundings had not changed since he left. The loneliness returned, and he knew his intended plan to move to be the right one. He grabbed bags and boxes he brought with him and started sorting through the items he wanted to take back. Lunch came, and he ate the food he packed after breakfast. He considered walking to the park, but the pain became too severe when he glanced that way. He started packing up by mid-afternoon, deciding the rest could wait until he found a place to rent.

Driving back, he tuned the radio to a station he and Catina liked. As he fiddled with the dial, a car appeared over the rise and veered onto Sanchez's side of the road before correcting. Just before they passed each other, the car swerved and headed straight towards Sanchez, who pulled the steering wheel tight and skidded onto the gravel shoulder, spinning the car which dropped off the edge and rolled to the bottom of a steep incline, throwing Sanchez around like a rag doll. When the vehicle finally came to a stop, Sanchez was unconscious. It was several hours before someone noticed and called emergency personnel.

The light brightened, and a door appeared. He pulled on the handle, it opened, and he walked through it. A glorious meadow welcomed him, the kind Catina had always described. The sun shone, and the breeze ruffled his hair. Bright yellow flowers bloomed, and a lone tree stood at the top of the rise, its foliage spreading out, providing shade. Sanchez walked toward it, taking his time as he enjoyed the serenity. He saw someone sitting under the tree as he approached, someone familiar, someone who shouldn't be here. As the person's features became clearer, Sanchez increased his pace until he ran. His pulse quickened.

"Catina!" he shouted as he neared the tree.

She looked around and smiled, the smile Sanchez loved so much. "What are you doing here, my love?" she asked when he stopped before her.

"I came through the door."

"You're not meant to be here. It's too soon for you. You need to care for Donato."

"But I'm here now," Sanchez said, with tears of joy.

"It is not your time," Catina said, standing and approaching Sanchez. She lifted her hand and stroked his cheek. He closed his eyes in ecstasy at the touch.

Her gaze of loving adoration turned sad. "You cannot stay. You must go back."

"No, I won't."

"But you need to care for Donato."

"He is dead."

"No, he's not dead. He is alive. He needs you. Someone will find him, and he needs you to be there for him."

Sanchez sobbed.

"Shh," she whispered. "Do not be sad. Rejoice in the time we had together. We'll meet again when it's time."

"I don't want to go back. There is so much happiness here."

"Please you must, my love."

An irrefutable force pulled Sanchez away from her

towards the door. He tried to grab her, to hold on to her, but he lost his grip, "No, I don't want to go. Please let me stay!"

"You will return one day. I promise my love. Until then, live life and remember me with joy."

He fell back through the door. The light faded to a pinpoint and disappeared.

"He's waking up," someone said, as Sanchez regained consciousness.

Something was wrong, but Sanchez couldn't decide what. He remembered his pleasant dream, and he wanted to be with his wife again. As his consciousness increased, pain seeped into his body, intense pain.

"Increase the morphine," the person said.

The pain subsided moments later, but it lingered, threatening to return with a vengeance.

"Leave him rest and check him every hour."

Sanchez went back to sleep and woke again, time indeterminate. Energy had drained from him and a throbbing reverberated through his body.

"You're back with us," a familiar voice said to him.

Sanchez opened his bruised eyes as far as slits. He couldn't focus for a few moments before the blurriness cleared. He moved his head to the side and saw Raf sitting beside him. "Where am I?"

"You're in hospital. You had a car crash."

Sanchez creased his brow, trying to recall. "I remember. I swerved to avoid a car. It veered to the wrong side of the road. But I saw Catina, and she was so happy. She sent me back. She said Donato is alive."

"So that's what happened. The police suspected as much, but the other vehicle didn't stop."

"How bad am I?"

"The doctor said you almost died, but you'll live and make a full recovery. Broken bones to mend. Physiotherapy to undergo and you'll be right again. You need rest though, so I'll leave you now. The doctor said I can't stay too long. You're still very weak. I'll see you again soon."

Sanchez nodded as he closed his eyes, feeling exhausted.

Chapter 42

Drug Deal

After the old man's heroics, Donato returned to his hiding spot. He ate what was left of his food. The memory of the mean boy eating his chips came to mind, and he grew angry. He had looked forward to them and they now lay scattered on the road where they fell. After having a drink, he packed the rest away at the back of his cubby. His teddy bear sat by the side of the desk, waiting for its owner's sleep, so it could take part in any mischief teddy bears get up to beyond people's gaze.

Donato yawned as light faded inside the warehouse. He swung his legs over the desk as he considered the day ahead. The old man was nice but strange. He could fight, though. Donato wondered where Vovo learned to fight, and why he sat around the entire day. Despite that, Donato decided Vovo was a good person, unlike grandma, the mechanic, those men and the boys. They were bad people. Donato frowned. Why do more bad people exist than good ones? *Papa is a good person and the truck driver, too. That evens it up*, Donato thought, brightening. He wondered if Papa was looking for him. A lot of time had passed since the flood. *Maybe Papa has given up*, Donato thought. *Don't give up yet. I'm coming home.* He yawned again, so he jumped off the desk and curled up underneath.

With a start, Donato woke, confused by his surroundings. He didn't realize he had fallen asleep. Something woke him. He heard a noise coming from the warehouse. A vehicle being driven inside. Fear prevented Donato from leaving his cubby to look. Headlights flashed against the wall. He remembered the small peephole in the office wall, so he inched over and looked through. A large black car sat in the middle of the warehouse, two men leaning against it, waiting. They had guns in their hands, making Donato shiver with fear. He had seen guns on television, but not actual guns, except on police, but they needed guns. These people weren't police. One man held a cigarette, the red glow of the tip intensifying as he inhaled.

Donato heard another vehicle as it came closer. Headlights appeared in the opening and it parked in front of the first. The smoker dropped the cigarette and squashed it with his shoe, as both men readied themselves, coming to attention with their guns raised. The rear passenger door opened, and an obese man in a white pinstripe suite stepped out. Donato couldn't see a gun.

"Why the guns?" the man asked. "Haven't we conducted business long enough to merit a small amount of trust?"

The men exchanged glances. One of them said, "Standard procedure, nothing personal."

"Have it your way." The man walked away from his car and into the warehouse, peering into the darkness, his footsteps on the concrete floor echoing against the steel walls. After his inspection, he nodded at his car and two henchmen emerged, both with guns ready. One of the first henchmen glanced at them. "You have the same issue?"

The henchman sneered and smiled. "Standard procedure."

After moving away from their car, the henchmen positioned themselves in strategic positions, ready for attack, the first two men doing likewise. The unarmed man walked to the trunk and opened it, the opposing henchmen lifting their guns in readiness, uneasy about what was going on out of view. After grabbing a briefcase, he strolled to the front and placed the case on the hood. He stared into the interior of the other car and raised his eyebrows in anticipation.

The right rear door opened. A tall thin man emerged, glaring with distrust. He held a briefcase and carried it to the front of his car. He placed it on the hood, and used his thumbs to flick open the latches, revealing the contents. Donato couldn't see what was inside but thought it must be valuable to have so much security.

The obese man opened his briefcase.

The thin man produced a flick-knife from his pocket, extracted a plastic package from his case and cut it open. He removed a minute quantity of white powder, letting it sit in the palm of his hand, and put the package back in the case. He walked over and held the powder in front of the obese man who moistened his finger and placed it in the pile, small particles sticking to his finger as he pulled it away. He placed his finger in his mouth and looked at the man. "Tastes okay, but let's give it an actual test." He nodded to one of his henchmen, who walked over to him.

The man pulled a small kit from his jacket pocket and set it on the hood. For the next 10 minutes he prepared a syringe, filling it with a liquid form of the powder. He went to the trunk and pulled out a man, his hands and feet tied up and duct tape covering his mouth, dumping him onto the ground before dragging him to the front of the car. The man pulled up the hostage's sleeve and tied a tourniquet around his upper arm. The hostage's eyes bulged when he saw the syringe, and he struggled and tried to scream through the duct tape. "Hold still," he said with emotionless indifference. He pinned his arm to the ground and injected the liquid, releasing the tourniquet afterwards. The hostage continued to struggle, but after a few moments he stopped. The henchman pulled back the hostage's eyelids and felt his neck, searching for a pulse. He glanced up and nodded.

"That settles it," the dealmaker said.

He lifted his briefcase and took it to the man at the other car, showing him the contents. The man grabbed two wads of notes and inspected them, then replaced them. He closed his briefcase and handed it over, taking the case of money. "Nice doing business with you." He glanced at the dead man. "Take that with you."

"Likewise, and we will."

Chapter 43

Kidnapping

Donato wanted his Papa. Papa would keep him safe. Light illuminated the warehouse as the sun rose. Confident he was alone in the vast expanse, Donato walked to where the cars had been parked the night before. All evidence of what happened had vanished. After telling himself to forget the terrible men, he returned to the office and made some plans. He pulled the money from his pocket and placed it on the desk. He should have enough for a week if he didn't waste it. After placing the money back into his pocket, he sat on the desk, swaying his legs as he contemplated. He wanted to see Vovo again. He felt safe with him.

Donato left the warehouse and strolled back to the park. He skirted around the spot where the gang attacked him and arrived at the port's shopping district. The port had the familiarity of home, but Donato knew he needed to continue upriver, when he found a better means of transport. Vovo might help him work out a plan.

As he rounded the corner of the park, Donato searched for Vovo but couldn't find him. He crossed the park and sat on the bench seat, content to watch people pass by, as they lived their busy lives. Bored and hungry, he hopped off the seat and searched for a place to buy food. He shivered when recalling the incident at the shop yesterday, so he looked for a different shop. He found another grocery store across the road but a street vendor who had just set up caught his attention. The cooking aroma wafted past Donato, making his mouth salivate and his stomach grumble. He scampered over to the vendor instead.

"Want something to eat, young man?"

"Yes, I do, but I'm not a young man."

"You appear to be a young man to me."

"I'm a boy."

"Boys are with their mother or father. Young men are strong and brave and on their own."

"Oh well, I'm a young man then." Donato said, standing up straighter and smiling. "What are you cooking?"

"There's Pão de Queijo in the oven and I'm making Coxinhas."

"That sounds delicious."

"It is. You want a sample?"

"Yes, please."

"You'll just have to wait a few minutes. The Pão should be ready in 10 minutes."

"I can wait. Do you have water?"

"Yes." The vendor lifted the deep fry basket from the oil and peered at the contents. He nodded and deposited the cooked Coxinhas in a tray, leveraging the basket on the edge of the fry pan. Once he wiped his hands, he moved over to a cupboard and pulled out a bottle of water, giving it to Donato. "You won't run away before you pay?"

"Oh no sir, I can pay."

"That's alright, let's wait till you get the rest. Where's

your parents?" The vendor leaned on the counter, resting his head in his palm.

"Mama is dead."

"Sorry to hear that. And your father?"

"Papa is home, but I got washed away and I'm trying to walk back there. It's taking longer than I expected."

"Where is home?"

"Vila Feliz."

"Wow, you're a long way from home. You get involved in that dam disaster?"

"Yes, and the river swept me away, much further downriver."

"Hmm, that accident was a few weeks ago now. And you've been walking your way back?"

"I haven't walked the whole way. I rode in a truck part of the way. But now that I'm here, I'm stuck here. I can't catch a boat. They don't stop at the right spot, and I don't know how to catch the right ride."

The vendor looked at his watch. "The Pão should be ready." He stood straight and shuffled to the oven, peering inside. "Perfect." He put his left hand in a heatproof mitt and removed the tray, placing it on the stainless-steel counter. He grabbed a paper bag and placed two of the Pão's inside, then he placed two Coxinhas in another bag, giving both to Donato. "Here you go."

"How much is that, sir?"

"Since you have been so patient, these are free."

"Oh, no sir, I can pay, look," Donato said as he pulled out a note.

"Put it away. You may need it."

"Thank you, sir." Donato put the money back in his pocket and grabbed the two bags, the aroma of the bread teasing his tastebuds. He picked one from the bag and tested it for temperature before taking a cautious bite and blew over it until it cooled enough to swallow. "You cook delicious food."

"Why, thank you." The vendor parked himself on the counter again as he watched Donato eat.

Customers arrived at the stall while he ate, so he moved aside while they made their purchases. As the vendor busied himself making fresh batches, Donato thanked him again and returned to the park. "Thank you very much for the food, sir."

"Okay, young man. Come back whenever you want."

With delicious food in his stomach and a rekindled trust in humanity in his spirit, Donato walked with confidence to the bench seat but Vovo still wasn't there. Midday passed with no hint of the old man anywhere.

A teenage girl, about 17 years old, came along the path. She was slim with a curvaceous figure and long black hair falling to her waist. She wore a short blue and white check-ered dress and carried a backpack over one shoulder as she sauntered along the track. Donato watched her pass by, and she eyed him with a sullen expression, chewing gum.

A van idled nearby. Two men jumped out, opening the sliding door as the girl approached. Donato saw that it was empty. The men rushed both sides of the girl and grabbed her. She screamed, yelling at the top of her lungs, struggling to get free, her dress bunching up above her waist, but the men held her firm. They pushed her into the van as one man injected her with a syringe. The girl's eyes bulged in desperation, as the drug took rapid effect and the van sped off along the road. The entire episode took about 20 seconds and any bystanders stood confused, trying to process what had happened.

Donato's mouth was agape as he took in what he

witnessed. He shook with rage at the men's audacity. He couldn't blame anyone for not trying to help her. Everything happened too fast. He started crying for the girl.

Vovo sat beside him. "What's the problem, son? You look in the dumps. A little boy should be happy. Only old men get sad, because they've seen the world's problems. So, tell me what the problem is."

Donato looked at the old man as he wiped away his tears. "If only you were here. Men drugged a girl and drove her away in a van. You could have stopped them. I know you could have."

Vovo looked alarmed. "Where did they go?"

Donato pointed in the van's direction.

"Describe the van."

"White with black windows."

"And the men?"

"I don't know. It happened too fast. They were big and mean looking."

Vovo rubbed his stubble in thought. Hundreds of vans fit Donato's description, and it was far away by now. A fierce anger took hold of him. "Will we never get rid of the vermin?" he asked no one in particular. He calmed and looked at Donato, sadness replacing anger. "These are dangerous times. Be careful where you go and who you meet. I think I'm growing fond of you, little boy. I don't want anything to happen to you."

"Why are there so many mean people in the world? Every second person I meet is mean and wants to hurt me. I've never seen so many mean people."

The old man sighed and placed his hand on the boy's shoulder. "I wish the world was different, but it's not. More good people exist, but you're attracting the worst of them at the moment."

"Mean people came to the warehouse. One lot sold something to the others."

Vovo's interest piqued at the fresh information. "Did you see it?"

"Bags of powder. One of them sampled it, and then he heated it and put it in a syringe. And then they pulled a man from a car and injected him. He was tied up and had a gag over his mouth. He stopped moving after a while. Then he got paid, and they left."

"I think I should see this warehouse of yours." Vovo peered at Donato with concern. "Do you want to show me?"

"Can you help the girl?"

"I'm afraid there's nothing I can do for her."

"But she was so scared," Donato said, crying again.

The old man patted and rubbed Donato on the shoulder, comforting him as he gazed into the distance, busy with his own thoughts, the abyss of retribution blackening his eyes.

Donato stopped crying and wiped the tears away, sniffling. "Let's go then."

"Where?"

"To the warehouse."

"Oh, of course. How foolish of me to forget. Old men always forget things you know. Always have to remind them, and then they forget again."

Donato laughed. "You didn't forget. You're just making it up."

"Oh, no. I forgot, I did."

"Are you coming?" Donato asked, hopping off the seat.

"Where are we going?"

Donato laughed again. "You know."

The old man smiled. "Maybe I do," he said, as he patted

Donato on the shoulder. He stood and followed Donato to the warehouse.

It took half an hour to walk the distance, as Vovo asked Donato many questions about the warehouse and what else he had seen. Donato showed Vovo the gap in the wall where he had squeezed through and Vovo managed it after a few attempts. Donato showed Vovo where the drug exchange had taken place and the old man examined the scene carefully.

"Where do you sleep?" Vovo asked.

"Over in the office," Donato said, as he led the way.

"Hmm, a good hidey-hole. Make sure no one follows you here."

"I will."

"I had better go."

"Will I see you tomorrow?"

"I should be somewhere."

"Thank you for coming today. I was so scared after that girl got taken."

"Not a problem. Old men are excellent at helping scared little boys when their Papa's gone."

Chapter 44

Felicity

Roland woke early the next day, lying in a bed. He tried opening his eyes, but the task was impossible before daggers of pain stabbed at him. A bare sliver of light passed between his eyelids, revealing a hospital room. How did I get here? What happened? He remembered going to a park, but everything after that was blank.

Voices came to him, louder and clearer, along with footsteps.

"... He may still be unconscious. We've been monitoring him, and he is stable at present."

"I'll just be a moment then. I can talk to him if he's awake? We have notified his wife, and she's flying in. I'm not sure of her flight details yet."

The door opened and Roland heard footsteps come closer. He stirred and tried opening his eyes again.

"Oh good. You are conscious. I'll tell the doctor, and he can examine you. You can talk to him, but he's still weak."

"Okay. I'll keep it short."

Footsteps left the room.

"Roland? Can you hear me?" a familiar voice said.

"Who is it? What happened?" he said, a dazed slur in his voice.

"It's Felicity."

"Oh Felicity, that's right." Roland's anxiety eased.

"You were beaten up and you're in hospital in Porta Plata."

"That explains why everything hurts."

"You're lucky you don't have more injuries, from what the doctor told me."

Roland settled back in his bed, trying to remember. "Yes, there was a few of them. A group of men recognized me. They thought I needed to be taught a lesson."

"They did a proper job there. But what were you doing wandering around the port?"

"I was searching for the boy. I thought he might've gone there, and I was right. A shopkeeper recognized him. But then this happened."

"You're lucky to be alive. An old man stopped the bashing and called an ambulance."

"I won't be going anywhere soon, and I'll lose the boy's trail."

"Well, Deborah will be here tomorrow."

Roland groaned.

"Don't you want her here?"

"Yes I do, but she'll tell me 'I told you so'."

Felicity chuckled. "Maybe that's what you need. You might be more careful." They sat in silence for a moment, Felicity realizing how close her boss had come to finding Donato. "You say a shopkeeper identified the boy?"

"Yes."

"Where was the shop?"

Roland struggled to remember the port and the name of

the streets. He shook his head in frustration. "Bring me a map and I can show you."

Felicity pulled out her phone and zoomed in on the port, showing the screen to Roland.

Roland opened his eyes as far as he could manage and gazed at the screen. "Near the river. Runs next to the river. Lots of shops."

Felicity rotated the phone and adjusted the position and zoom. "How's that?"

Roland looked again. "Yes, that one along the river."

Felicity looked at the map. "Rio Esplanade." She looked at Roland and back at the screen, considering her options. "Tell you what, I'm staying here until Deborah arrives so I might do more digging for you. I'll organize security to take with me though."

Roland sighed. "I'd appreciate that."

"Well, the nurse said I shouldn't keep you talking, so I'll go. I'll return later today."

"Thank you."

Felicity rose from her seat. The nurse and doctor entered as she reached the door.

"Ah, you're leaving. Good, he needs to rest," the doctor said.

"Yes, can I return later today?" Felicity asked.

"That shouldn't be a problem. Call first, just to make sure."

Felicity drove into the center of the city and booked into the Plata Continental hotel, on the Carlos City Office worker's advice. She located the local branch of the security company the business used and hired two minders for the rest of the day. The quick change in routine that Felicity's job entailed was one thing she enjoyed. You could work through your normal activities, and without warning something happens, turning everything on its head, and you're doing something different. Still, searching for a boy was a new entry for her journal. She changed clothes and freshened up before returning to the lobby to wait for the security detail, sipping a cup of coffee. They came soon after and they left for the port.

They parked along Rio Esplanade and started walking along the footpath, the minders either side of Felicity. She felt self-conscious but she'd prefer having them there than not. As she came to a shop meeting Roland's description, she entered and approached the counter where the shopkeeper stood scrutinizing the two minders at the door with apprehension. She showed him the picture of Donato. "A friend tells me you've seen this boy."

"Yes," the shopkeeper said, his voice shaky as he stared at the minders. "He was in the other day."

Felicity glanced over to where he looked. "Don't mind them. They're here to protect me, not intimidate you."

"Oh, but someone else was in here yesterday asking the same question."

"Yes, I know. He ended up getting beaten up yesterday. The boy hasn't been back?"

"No."

"Did he buy anything?"

"He came in twice, about midday and later in the afternoon. He was buying for two when he first came in, but he just bought chips and a few other things later."

"Enough for the rest of the day?"

"Probably."

"Oh... interesting. Where could he have gone then?"

Felicity bought a packet of chips and a drink. "Thanks for your time."

Felicity walked out the shop with her minders in tow and looked around they strolled along the esplanade. A street vendor further along the street caught her eye, so she wandered over to the stall.

"Hello, young lady. May I help you?"

The minders smirked, which Felicity noticed. "Hey, I'm allowed to get compliments," she smiled.

"Sorry, Miss," one of them said.

Felicity turned to the vendor. "I'm not sure of the 'young' bit, but you can help me." She retrieved the picture of Donato and showed the vendor. "Have you seen this boy?"

The vendor looked and without hesitation said, "He was here this morning. Lovely little boy, I gave him food, although he had money. You police?"

"No, we're just trying to get him back to his father."

"Yes, he mentioned he came from Vila Feliz."

"Did you see where he went?"

"No, I was busy serving others when he left."

"Okay, thanks for the information." Felicity inhaled the aroma from the vendor's cooking. "That smells delicious. Can I have a few?"

"Of course."

"And you two, you want any?"

They shook their heads, although she could see them yearning for one.

"No eating on the job?"

"Job description," one of them said.

"I'll have three Pão," Felicity said to the vendor.

He placed three balls in a bag and gave it to her. Felicity paid him and turned to leave as she pulled out a Pão.

A loud woman's scream came to them from further along the street as the minders formed defensive positions around Felicity. They couldn't see any disturbance and heard no more noises. *Thank God I've got minders*, Felicity thought.

Chapter 45

The Reporter

Life as a reporter involved a good deal of luck so, when his source in the police force contacted Juan, telling him the CEO of Zagreus Minerals had been bashed, he rubbed his hands in glee. He identified the hospital where Roland was admitted and prepared to confront him with a barrage of questions. Even though the assault had only occurred yesterday, it astounded Juan that it had taken so long for the information to filter through to him, but he couldn't chastise his informant too much without losing his valuable asset.

Juan entered the hospital after two in the afternoon during visiting hours to provide a suitable cover. Although the hospital knew him — he visited the place often enough — he sometimes displeased the doctors and staff. He hoped this wasn't one of those times. After navigating to the general ward, he approached the nurse's station. "Is Mr Roland Cavendish in this ward?"

The nurse glared at Juan. "What's your business with him if he is?"

"I just want to ask him a few questions."

"No one is to disturb him at the moment."

"But it's visitor's hours."

"I don't care if you have a president's order, you will not disturb him."

Juan stared at the nurse, frustrated, but knew argument was futile. At least he knew Roland Cavendish was in the ward. He'd tackle the problem from another angle. "I hope you have a pleasant day."

The nurse looked after him with contempt. Running the ward was hard enough without reporters nosing around, even if she had no respect for the patient.

Juan veered off towards a fire escape and opened the door, ascending to the next floor. Traversing the floor, he located the other fire stairwell and went down one flight. It was a practice he used often when he encountered obstinate people blocking his path to a story. He peered out the doorway and searched for nursing staff in the corridor. No one was visible. He walked out acting as if he belonged in the ward, checking room by room for Roland. He checked the private rooms first, finding Roland's room after half a dozen failed inspections. As he checked for nurses, he slipped into the room with a satisfied smile.

Roland lay on his side gazing out the window, with little but his present predicament on his mind. He heard the door open and close but, presuming it to be a nurse, he continued staring at nothing.

"Good afternoon, Mr Cavendish," Juan said.

Roland tensed, as the unexpected and unknown male voice greeted him. He rolled onto his back and turned his head. "Who are you?"

"Hi, I am Juan Salvador of the Porta Plata Gazette. I was wondering if I could ask you a few questions?" Juan said with a pleasant smile.

Roland looked at him with a tired expression, in no mood for the press. "No, you may not."

"Why is that, Sir? Do you have something to hide?"

"No, I do not." Roland said, keeping his cool, despite the accusation.

"I understand a group of men assaulted you yesterday. What caused the altercation?"

"No comment."

"Did it involve the disaster at Vermelho Mine?"

"No comment."

"Have you determined the cause of the dyke wall collapse yet?"

"No comment."

"Is it because of cost cutting in the dam's construction, as several parties have alleged?"

"I wish you to leave."

"Can you please answer my questions? The public has a right to know what cowboy organization you run. There's no consideration for the safety of either your workers or the public. Do you accept responsibility for the collapse?"

Roland couldn't take the accusations any longer. "Will you get out of this room now or do I call the police?" he shouted at the top of his lungs with a blood-engorged face of rage, lifting his upper torso off the bed, before clutching his bruised ribs in agonizing pain.

Juan took a step backwards, as he heard running in the corridor. "No need to get abusive. I just want you to answer my questions."

The head nurse poked her head around the door. "You!

I told you not to disturb Mr Cavendish. How did you get in here? Now get out before I call security."

"Okay, okay. I'm leaving. Any last comment Mr Cavendish?"

Roland said nothing as he looked at Juan with utter contempt.

Juan stood, pulled a tiny microphone from his pocket and stuck it on the side of a cabinet, out of view. With his hands raised in surrender, he walked out, followed by the nurse.

Another nurse came into Roland's room. "Are you okay, Mr Cavendish?"

Roland heaved, both from the physical effort and the anger roiling inside of him. "I'm okay. I need a minute to calm myself."

"Your pulse is racing," she said, smiling. "Thought it might be because of me."

Roland looked at her sideways, wondering if she was serious, but then laughed, clutching his side in pain. "Maybe. You better keep your distance and please don't make me laugh again."

The nurse fluttered her eyelashes, mocking him, before returning to the serious business of nursing. "I won't. Bruised ribs are very painful."

"You won't keep your distance, or you won't make me laugh?"

The nurse giggled. "I won't make you laugh. I still have to do my duties, which might mean getting close and personal, but I assure you I will be professional."

Roland smiled, but remained silent. The nurse checked a few things. "Something I can get you?"

"No, I'm fine, thank you."

The nurse left, leaving Roland in peace again, except

for the turmoil of thoughts twirling around his mind. He couldn't get the reporter's accusations out of his head. Was he responsible? Had they taken shortcuts with the design and construction? Did the lives of these people matter less to him than those in his own country? He had no answer as he searched his heart. He prided himself on treating everyone equally, regardless of who they are. Was he deluding himself so he could sleep at night? He remembered seeing the proposals for the dam and asking about safety features several times. His staff had reassured him they had taken it into account, and the dam met the required regulations of the country, as per company policy. Was that good enough? Should he have demanded best practice design regardless of where they operated? A niggling pointed finger in his head kept accusing him as he stared out the window, desperately uncertain as thoughts swirled through his mind. The entire episode with the reporter disturbed him more than he realized.

Chapter 46

Movie Making

Donato's despondency and disillusionment with humanity was growing by the day, and he was seeing evil people everywhere. He experienced kind people, but the bad outweighed the good. As he sat up in his cubbyhole, he looked at his teddy bear sadly while he rubbed sleep from his eyes. He despaired of seeing Papa again. The world was too big and too bad. Papa would tell him off, though, for quitting. When Donato gave up on an arduous task, Papa always encouraged him to try again, and not cave into failure, until he had exhausted all his options. He sighed, held his teddy bear tight and warmed to the continuous smile from his half-blind companion. *You've got a bung eye, but you're still happy.* The bear's cheer brightened Donato's spirits.

He strolled to the water tap he discovered the day before and washed himself. His exploration of the office uncovered a working toilet, too. Refreshed, he left the warehouse and headed for the food vendor.

"Hello young man," the vendor said.

"Hello, sir. May I have more Pão and Coxinha, please?"

"Yes, you can. It's ready soon." The vendor busied himself cooking until he had supplies of both and handed Donato a serve of each. "There you go."

"Thank you, sir. How much is that?"

"The same as yesterday."

"But you gave it to me for free yesterday."

"Then that is how much I will charge you today."

"You are a kind man, sir."

"A woman came searching for you yesterday."

"She did? Who was she?"

The vendor scratched his head. "You know, I don't know. I didn't ask her name. But she was looking for you. She had a photo of you."

Donato's spirits soared with the news. She might return him to Papa. A smile spread across Donato's face at the prospect. "How do I contact her?"

"I don't know. She didn't leave a phone number. We heard a scream while we were talking, and her security men whisked her off before she could give it to me."

"That was when they kidnapped the young woman."

"Kidnapped, you say."

"Yes. I was sitting in the park. Men jumped out of a van and kidnapped her and drove her away."

The vendor frowned. "That's terrible. There's too much crime and violence."

Donato said nothing, as he started eating a cooling Pão. He finished eating the bread and licked his fingers. "Thank you, sir. I think I'll walk to the park."

"Okay. Goodbye young man."

Donato walked to the park and sat on Vovo's bench. The dreary sky darkened, and spots of rain landed on the concrete path. With no shelter, Donato ran to a tree but the rain was so heavy, he couldn't see more than a few meters away. Other people braved the weather with raincoats and umbrellas. He shivered at the prospect of being in the storm unprotected. The storm eased after 15 minutes and the rain stopped, but the sky remained overcast and gloomy. He decided to return to the warehouse in case another storm hit. As he rounded a corner, he came to a stop, seeing the gang of boys walking towards him in the distance.

"There's that little runt we saw the other day," one boy yelled.

"Let's get him!" another shouted, as they started running.

Donato started running too. He rushed along roads and alleys for what seemed like ages, not realizing the gang had given up the chase long ago. Exhausted, he came to a stop and slumped, puffing to regain his breath. Nothing looked familiar. Brick buildings surrounded him, but they looked derelict. As he walked further, searching for something recognizable, the rain started again. He sheltered in a building with several smashed windows and a door that hung loose off its hinges. Male voices met him as he entered the gloom, so he hid down the side.

The conversation was unintelligible in the distance, so Donato crept up the hallway until he was close enough to smell their cigarette smoke.

"She's an excellent performer. Better than others we've had," one man said.

"Yeah, she'll get us a mass of hits when we post our material," the other said.

"The guy's good, too. Very obedient," the first man said, chuckling.

"Still. You think they might be past their use by dates?"

"I think so. The climax'll get the viewers talking with these two."

"Okay. Let's get set up then."

They stamped out their cigarettes and went into a room. Donato crept around a corner and heard noises coming from a room up ahead. He snuck into the room next door. Noticing a small hole in the wall, he peered through. The two men busied themselves setting up a bed with surrounding scenery, lighting, cameras and recording equipment. One man glanced in Donato's direction and he jerked his head aside, even though he knew it was impossible for anyone to see him.

"What do you think?" one man said.

"We're ready," the other replied.

"Okay, let's get the guy and talk to him."

A very young man with shoulder-length black hair, clean shaven and a strong body entered the room minutes later. He wore a loose-fitting shirt and pants around his hips.

"Sergio, a brilliant performance this time and you can leave."

Sergio nodded.

"We want you to do something special for this one."

"What?"

The man glanced at the other one. "As you reach orgasm, we want you to choke the girl around the neck until she stops moving."

Sergio gulped in shock. "What? Kill her?"

"No, she'll revive afterwards. Look, we've done this act hundreds of times. It's safe."

"Okay then. If you're sure it won't kill her."

"She's an outstanding performer, isn't she?"

"Sure is. I'm lucky you found her."

"Yeah, well, get yourself set up and we'll bring the girl. You took the pill?"

"I'm ready to go," Sergio said, smiling as he grabbed his crotch.

"Okay." The man left, coming back two minutes later with a female teenager.

Donato gasped as he saw the girl from the park.

The woman shuffled in a drugged gait. "Now, you remember what I said? You do this shoot well, and you'll be free."

The woman nodded. She wore make-up and a bikini.

Sergio stood at the base of the bed, waiting. The woman moved over and flopped.

"Ready?" the man at the camera console asked.

The two nodded. The girl stood up and walked a few steps away.

"Okay, action."

"It's too hot at the beach," the woman droned as she approached Sergio. "So, I thought I'd come inside and play."

"I've been waiting for you," Sergio replied. "Me and my handle you enjoy so much."

The woman squealed. She squatted and caressed his crotch, "He is eager."

Once she undid Sergio's pants, she let them fall and grabbed his penis, licking and sucking it. Sergio moaned with pleasure. He pulled the girl up and undid the strings of her bikini top, caressing her breasts as he pulled the fabric away. She threw her head back in ecstasy. He pushed her backwards onto the bed and pulled off her bikini bottom, proceeding to kiss and suck her vagina, getting groans and moans from her as she wriggled with pleasure. He crept forward on top of her and penetrated her, getting a gasp as his shaft slid in and started pumping in rhythmic motion. The tempo increased as both their passions rose. Sergio glanced at the man, who nodded, so Sergio placed his hand around the woman's throat and squeezed as he kept thrusting. The woman panicked, struggling and writhing to escape, as life slipped away until she jerked her final death throes to the ecstatic orgasm of the man. The woman slumped to staring stillness. Sergio took his hand away, fear creeping into him as he realized the man had lied to him. He was turning his head when the man yanked it back, a knife slitting his throat from ear to ear, with blood spurting and pulsing over the woman and the bed as Sergio fell on top of her, life bleeding from him.

Donato turned from the peephole, placing his hand over his mouth to silence any noise he might make, as he gagged and gasped. He couldn't believe what he had seen. He couldn't believe the depravity to which people resorted.

"That's a take," one man said. "Excellent work. We should get a premium for that one when it's edited."

Chapter 47

Felicity And Deborah

Felicity returned to visit Roland the next morning. He was staring out the window, withdrawn, when she arrived. "What's the matter?" Felicity asked as she sat down.

"Nothing, just dark thoughts swirling around my head."

"Well, Deborah will be here today."

"You know how to cheer someone up," Roland said sarcastically.

"Don't you want her here?"

"Of course I do, it's just she's going to fuss."

Felicity laughed. "That might be what you need. Now, I checked out your storekeeper again, and I asked around other places too. The boy was at a street vendor yesterday morning. He's still staying in the port."

"That's promising," Roland said, his spirits improving.

"I couldn't ask around more. We heard a scream and my minders insisted I leave. I hope to return today sometime and see if I can find out more."

"Do you think we cut corners with the dam?"

Felicity raised her brow at the sudden change of topic.

She studied Roland's face to judge his mood. "I've been here from the start of the mine development, so I suppose it's a fair question to ask me. I can't say whether there were problems with the design, I'm not an engineer, but the relevant departments signed off and no brown paper bags changed hands, to my knowledge. There were design changes for unexpected conditions, but the authorities signed off on them. Santos kept a close watch on the construction, and I know he made the contractor redo things because they weren't done to his satisfaction. So, to the best of my knowledge, no, we didn't cut corners. What brought this on, then?"

"I had a reporter barge in here yesterday after you left. He shouldn't have been here."

"You said nothing, I hope?" Felicity said, alarmed.

"No, but I lost my cool when he kept badgering me on the dam and whether we were negligent."

"I'll have his balls. Who was it?"

"Don't do that. It'll just confirm his belief that we're covering up something. Besides, I can't remember who it was."

"He had no right though."

"The staff kicked him out him when they caught him in the room. It got me thinking, though. Did I do everything I could have done to make sure we built a safe dam? Is building to the country's engineering standards good enough, when we could've done better?"

"You can torture yourself with those questions forever and you still won't be satisfied. Do you think I haven't asked the same questions? Did we cut corners to reduce cost? No. Were we negligent in our duty? No. Did we do everything to the best of our ability? For myself, I can answer yes, and I'm sure you can, too."

Roland sighed, "I suppose you're right. We knew that wall had problems, though."

"And we kept monitoring it and advising the authorities. Everyone agreed it was safe and didn't need any remedial work."

Roland looked at Felicity and smiled. "I'm lucky to have you running things, and as a confidante."

"Everyone needs someone to confide in now and then."

The door opened, "Knock, knock," Deborah said, poking her tired head in, the effects of travel and lack of proper sleep clouding her face. "Can I come in?"

Roland's face lit up, "Only if you're good looking."

"That must be a yes, then."

They laughed, Roland still very subdued from his bruised ribs.

"Good to see you, Mrs Cavendish," Felicity said.

"Call me Deborah," she said, looking at Felicity and then at Roland, "Has he been behaving himself?"

"Well, good morning, I'm fine, happy to see you, too," Roland said.

Felicity smiled. "That's a question for the nurses, but he's been behaving himself in front of me."

"Oh, honey." Deborah strolled to the bed and gave Roland a quick peck. She stroked the only patch on his face without a bruise. "Of course I'm happy to see you and worried sick. How on earth did you end up in hospital?"

"I should go," Felicity said, feeling uncomfortable.

"Don't go on my account. I'm not getting into bed with him in his condition."

Felicity smiled at Deborah's earthiness. "True, but there are intimacies in a relationship that others need not hear. I have a few things to do." She turned to Roland. "I'll find out if anyone else has seen Donato."

"Good, and thanks," Roland said.

"Nice meeting you, Deborah."

"Nice to meet you, too. We must have dinner when this settles."

"That'd be good. I'm still here for another day. We could have dinner tonight if you're free. Here's my card."

"That's an excellent idea. I can't stay around this grump too long."

"Hello. I'm still here."

"Oh, you know what I mean, honey. Where are you staying Felicity?"

"The Plata Continental."

"That's where I'm staying," Roland blurted.

"Oh, I can use your room then. Perfect," Deborah said, looking pleased she had sorted out her accommodation. "I'll call you later."

"Okay. Catch you. See you too, Roland." Felicity left the room.

Deborah glanced back at Roland when the door closed, concerned. "How on earth did you get here?"

"Got bashed up by a gang who recognized me."

"Didn't you have protection?"

"No, I didn't think I needed any."

"Oh, Roland..." She sat on the chair and kept looking at him. She picked up his hand and patted it. "It sent shivers through my spine when Felicity called me. I was expecting the worst. You don't look beat up apart from the bruises and scratches. Is that it?"

"Pretty much. I've got a few bruised ribs that are killing me, but nothing's broken. Got knocked unconscious."

Deborah nodded. "Hope you'll be more careful now."

"I will."

As Deborah retrieved Roland's hotel key from the

bedside cabinet, she noticed a device stuck to the side. "What's this?"

"What?" Roland asked, turning his head. He frowned. "No idea. Could be hospital equipment."

"Could be a bug. I'll send a nurse in to check."

She kissed Roland on the lips and left.

A nurse arrived. "How can I help?"

"That thing stuck to the cabinet, is that hospital equipment?"

"Not to my knowledge." She pulled it off the cabinet and examined it. "No, nothing to do with us. I'll get security to check it."

Chapter 48

Rosita's Visit

S anchez inhaled the smell of perfume. The rose scent was familiar, but he couldn't place it. He turned over from his side onto his back, puffing from the meager but painful effort, and saw Rosita sitting in the chair beside his bed, reading a magazine. "What are you doing here?" he asked, disoriented by the unexpected intrusion into his sedentary life.

Rosita looked up and smiled, making Sanchez's heart monitor spike. "I thought you'd never wake up. The bell for the end of visiting hours will chime soon," she said. "Looks as if you're pleased I came, though." She pointed to the increased heart rate on display.

"That's not fair," Sanchez said, feigning indignation. "But you still haven't answered my question."

"I had spare time. Thought you might want company." A rosiness appeared on Rosita's cheeks. "You want to sit up?"

"Umm... yeah, wait a minute. They showed me." Sanchez fumbled for the bed's controls and found the button to lift his backrest after much trial and error. "How's that?"

"I can see you better now." Rosita studied Sanchez's face and looked deeply into his eyes. "You gave everyone a terrible scare."

"I don't have anyone though."

"There are people who care," Rosita said, her mouth quivering.

On realizing his gaffe, Sanchez said, "I know. People have more friends than they realize sometimes."

Mollified, Rosita said, "Even closer sometimes."

Sanchez gazed at Rosita, trying to find the deeper meaning in what she said.

"What happened?"

"Didn't Raf tell you?"

"I'm asking you."

"I was driving back from Vila Feliz, minding my business, when a car coming the other way pushed me off the road, and I lost control and rolled."

"Why were you in Vila Feliz? Do you want to move back there?"

"The opposite, I want to move to El Grieta. I picked up a few belongings and was driving back."

A sparkle of excitement appeared in Rosita's eyes. "Oh? Any idea where you might live?"

"Not yet, I need to find a place to rent, but I'm stuck here."

They sat in silence.

"I saw Catina," Sanchez said.

"That's impossible."

"When I was unconscious, she was in a meadow." Joy colored Sanchez's face before sadness returned. "She told me to come back. It wasn't my time. She said Donato is still alive. Could that be true?"

Rosita sat studying Sanchez and frowned. "I don't know. There's always a chance, but I don't want to raise your hopes, and dash them again."

"But where is he then? No one has found him, not even that Zagreus guy. At least not that anyone's told me."

"But they haven't said he's dead either."

"Yeah." Sanchez glanced over at Rosita, pondering a thought. "Did Raf tell you to visit me?"

Rosita reddened. "He may have suggested it, but I wanted to come."

"I'm glad you did." A current of happiness flowed between them. "How bad is my pick-up?"

The spell broken, Rosita blinked. "I don't know. Where is it?"

"Worry over that when I leave here, I suppose."

"Which is when?"

"No idea, when I can walk and take care of myself, I suppose."

"It'll be forever if we have to wait til you can take care of yourself." A cheeky grin spread across Rosita's face.

"Someone might have to take care of me then," Sanchez replied in riposte.

"Be careful what you wish for, Sanchez."

He sighed, growing tired of the banter, and returned to the misery of his life as he descended into self-pity, his face looking glum.

"What's the matter?" Rosita asked with tenderness.

"Nothing, nothing that anyone can fix. My life's a mess, and I have no idea what to do sometimes. When I think I'm moving ahead, this happens, crushing me and my miserable life. I'm just doomed to suffer."

"We are a depressed one then," Rosita said, studying

Sanchez, her caring nature clashing with the condescending tone of her voice.

"Well, how can I convince myself otherwise?"

"You'll continue feeling defeated, and behave defeated, while you think that way. You've had it rough, and I can't imagine the pain you've been through, but you'll only move on when you accept what's happened and put it behind you."

Sanchez wondered if Rosita's wisdom came from experience or was something she had learned. "How can it be any different? My life has been ripped apart with nothing to replace it. The emptiness is crushing." Sanchez jerked his gaze away, unable to tolerate Rosita's scrutiny.

"Don't friends count? Friends who want to help you."

"What friends?"

"Does everything Raf's done for you count for nothing?"

Sanchez looked back to Rosita. Shock gripped him as he saw how hurt she looked. He realized what he had said, and how ungrateful it must sound to her. "I'm sorry. I don't know what gets into me sometimes. Raf is a good friend and you are, too."

"I was hoping you'd say that. I hope we might be more than friends, but I don't want to rush it."

"Maybe I can't see what's in front of me."

"Is there something I can help you with while you're cooped up here? Search for a place for you?"

"That'd be good. Find out where my pick-up is, and what happened to my belongings."

"I can do that."

A chime rang through the building, signalling the end of visiting hours. "I'll go now."

"Can you visit again, please?"

"If you want me to come."

"I do."

Rosita smiled with joy. "I'll see you then."

"Soon, I hope."

With an extra spring in her step, Rosita left. Sanchez gazed after her, wondering where their relationship might lead.

Chapter 49

Thief!

A ring of people circled Donato, menacing smiles on their faces, as they crept closer to him, holding out their hands, trying to be the first to grab hold of him. Donato sat frightened, his teddy bear in his hands, as he crawled one way, and then another, to get away from the evil creeping towards him. No sooner had he eluded one monstrous tendril than he came within the clutches of another. He screamed for someone to help him, but no one came. The torment continued, endless, as he was always just outside his assailants' reach. His bear came to life, released itself for his arms, rising above his head. It started spinning faster and faster until it created a whirling wind with Donato at the center. The rushing air tore at the hair of the assailants, those who had hair, and it whipped at their faces, stinging them. They leaned forward as the wind grew stronger, the bear a rotating mass of color, trying to continue forward towards Donato, until the wind became so strong that one and then another flew away, flailing like rag dolls. Everyone flew away, and only Donato remained. The bear's rotation slowed, the wind died. It stopped and lowered itself into Donato's arms again, beaming its ever-present contented smile, as its loose button of an eye flopped around a few times like it was winking at him. "Thank you, teddy bear." *"You're welcome."*

Donato woke with a start. He felt scared and frightened by the dream. As he saw his teddy bear sitting where he placed it the night before, he sat it on his lap as he sat against the desk. He gazed at the bear, earnest as it looked back at him, one black eye reflecting a sparkle of light as the other dangled, and the small brown nose above its mouth highlighting a generous smile. Nothing could faze it. With a look into the bear's eyes, Donato said, "You will protect me, won't you?"

The bear sat mute but Donato imagined it saying, "Of course I will. I am invincible. I'll always be by your side."

Donato smiled and lifted the bear, hugging it to his chest, as he swayed from side to side with his cheek against the soft fur of the fabric, absorbing comfort. He held the bear at arm's length. "There're terrible people in the world. I won't let them hurt you, ever. Why are there so many terrible people? Where are the good ones? Vovo is good, and the food man... and the truck driver." He sighed. "There must be others somewhere. Otherwise, the entire world would be evil. Maybe it is, and our village was the last good place on earth. And now that's gone too, because the rotten people destroyed it."

He tucked the bear into his pants and made his way to the street vendor. The sky was fine with the sun heating the day.

"Hi, little man. Ready for food?" the vendor asked.

"Yes, I'm starving. I didn't eat last night."

"Oh, why was that?" the vendor asked as he placed Donato's food into paper bags.

"The bully boys chased me after the storm, and I had to run, and I got lost, and I found a brick building, and I saw the kidnapped girl, and..."

"Whoa, slow down there, little man. You did a lot of things yesterday." The vendor stopped his work and looked at Donato. "You say you spotted the girl who got kidnapped in the brick building?"

"Yes."

"What was she doing there?"

"She was sleepy, and she and a man started doing grown-up things."

"How do you know about grown-up things?"

Donato gave a sheepish smile and a guilty look. "I once heard Mama and Papa making noises and I sneaked a peek at what they were doing and they were doing grown-up things, but they were happy. The girl looked scared."

The vendor chuckled at Donato's confession, but returned to what Donato had seen. "What happened after that?"

"They were making a movie. Two other men were there with cameras. Then the man started choking her while they did grown-up things. She tried getting away but couldn't, and she stopped moving. Then another man cut the man's throat, and blood sprayed everywhere, and then I ran."

The vendor's eyes bulged from what Donato had seen. His expression turned to concern. "No one should experience such things, especially a little boy."

"Why are there so many terrible people in the world?"

"I don't know. There just are."

"But why?"

The vendor sighed and looked at Donato, fishing for an adequate answer. "Well, people sometimes get greedy, and when they get greedy, they sometimes do bad things to make money. You're a magnet for them at the moment."

"What's a magnet?"

"A bar of metal that attracts other metal... hmm." The man searched for one close by, but he didn't have one.

"Oh, a compass?"

"Yes, a compass. A compass has a magnet."

Donato nodded.

"Well, that's enough talking. Let's get you fed." The vendor selected two Pão, two Coxinhas and half a dozen Aipim fritos, placing them in three bags and giving them to Donato. "There you go, little man. That should keep you happy. And here's a bottle of water."

Donato struggled to carry so many bags and the bottle. "It's so much. I'll burst."

The vendor laughed. "You don't have to eat everything at once."

"How much is it?"

"The same as yesterday."

"But I have to give you something."

"No, you don't."

"Thank you very much, Sir."

"Your good manners is all the payment I need. Go somewhere and eat, little man."

Donato nodded and left, heading for the park. Fewer people were on the street than normal, but he didn't know why.

"Hi son. You're sitting on my seat, I see. It's not really my seat, but I sit here."

"Oh hi, I was letting my breakfast settle."

"Ahh... it's good to let your food settle." Vovo sat and looked at Donato. "And what have we been doing?"

Donato related the previous day's event to Vovo, as he had told the street vendor.

"That's no good, no good at all," Vovo said, frowning in disgust. "Not the thing a boy should see. Not a thing people should do, but the world is a terrible place. You should be more careful, you know. Someone will catch you one day."

"I try to keep out of trouble, but it follows me."

Vovo scratched his bristly chin. "Do you think you could find the brick building again?"

"I don't think so. I lost my way. It's far from the river. It took me a long time to walk back afterwards."

"How long?"

Donato shrugged. "I don't know."

"Ah well, that's enough of that. We'll watch the world go by."

Donato sat with Vovo for several hours, content to sit in silence. Few people walked through the park and Donato wondered why, but kept his thoughts to himself.

"Can you buy me some food from the shop?" Vovo asked. "Here's the money."

"Sure," Donato said, as he jumped off the seat and ran to the shop. He returned in half an hour, sharing the food with Vovo, keeping the rest for himself. As he sat back on the seat, he ate in unison with Vovo. Anyone walking past might have thought they were twins, despite the age gap.

Donato got bored after lunch. "I think I'll go now."

"Okay, Donato. Take care of yourself and keep out of trouble. I should get along too."

Vovo walked through the park and Donato returned to the shop for more groceries.

He bought his supplies and left, dawdling along the

footpath, swinging the plastic bag with the groceries back and forth in his hand, daydreaming and staring at his feet.

"Thief! Stop him," Donato heard behind him, before being knocked to the ground by a boy as he rushed past. He grazed his knee as he fell and sat up, rubbing it.

"Got you, you little thief," a woman said, as she grabbed Donato by the arm, lifting him up. "Now give back my purse."

"But I don't have your purse."

"Yes, you do. I saw the other boy give it to you. He put it in that bag."

Donato looked bewildered. He realized the bag felt heavier. When he gazed inside the bag, he spotted a maroon purse sitting on top of the other items. "But I didn't take it. I don't know that boy. He bumped into me."

"You can save your excuses for the police. See, here they come."

Two police officers walking the beat had seen the incident. They came up to the pair. "Can we help you?" one of them asked.

"This boy took my purse. I caught him before he could scoot off with the other one. See, it's in his bag."

One police officer grabbed the bag from Donato and peered inside, removing the purse. "Is this yours?"

"Yes, my ID is in it."

The other officer grabbed Donato by the arm while the first one opened the purse, checked the woman's ID and handed the purse back. "Explain yourself, boy."

"But I did nothing, and let me go, you're hurting me."

"Petty theft is prevalent here," the officer said. "A few gangs wander the streets. You're lucky they didn't get away this time."

"Thank you. I hope the thief gets everything he

deserves." The woman walked away, relieved she had regained her possessions.

"Now you little shit. You're coming with us."

"But I did nothing. And give me back my bag."

"We can discuss that at the station," the police officer holding Donato said.

"I'm not going anywhere." Donato struggled to get away but couldn't release himself from the man's grip. He resorted to biting the man on his hand.

"Ow..."

The officer's grip loosened enough for Donato to escape. He snatched his bag, which had dropped to the ground, and dashed away.

"Hey, come back here, you little shit," the police officer yelled as both of them started chasing him.

Donato ran into an alleyway at the first intersection and continued running, hearing the police behind him. He veered off to another alley, and another, but came to a sudden stop when a chain wire fence blocked his path. His shoulders sagged in defeat as he gasped for breath until he noticed a small opening in the fence's corner large enough for him to squeeze through. Taking his chance, he dashed over and crawled through as the police officers closed in on him.

"Come back here," one police officer said as they stopped by the fence, just short of catching him. Both officers heaved for breath.

Donato glanced back but continued running, shooting around the corner and out of sight. He didn't stop running until he was back under the desk at the warehouse with his teddy bear. He heaved as he regained his breath, miserable but relieved as he recalled his lucky escape.

Chapter 50

Execution

It's just not fair, Donato thought as he sat by the desk the next morning, nibbling on his snacks. He relived yesterday's events in his mind. How did the boy drop the purse into my bag? He must have needed a diversion when he realized the woman had caught him in the act. She thought I was part of the gang, and it was a ploy to create confusion. And now I'm wanted by the police, it's not fair. Donato looked at his teddy bear, wondering if he had any words of wisdom for him, but he just sat with his eye dangling, smiling his teddy bear smile at him.

He was hungry, but the police were looking for him, so he stayed hidden. He had bought enough to keep his stomach happy. After extracting the money left from his pocket, he noted little remained. He didn't have any plan for when it ran out. Donato sighed. He still didn't know how he would get back to his Papa.

Boredom set in, so he wandered around the warehouse and discovered an external door. When he poked his head out, he noticed another building a few meters away. Donato tried opening the door, but it held shut and locked. He looked around to check no one was watching and skirted the wall and noticing a loose sheet of iron, he pulled at it. The gap opened just enough for him to squeeze through.

Unlike his warehouse, this one held stacks of pallets piled with things he couldn't name. Shelves stacked with boxes from floor to roof stood along one wall and Donato wondered what they were, as he couldn't understood the writing on the labels. When he reached the end of the rows of pallets, he found an office cloaked in darkness. He realized the place was still in use as the desks were covered in paperwork. A clock ticked away on the far wall, and a water cooler stood in a corner. He returned to the pallets and discovered one of the boxes was slightly ripped, a colored plastic bag catching his eye. He tore at the box and made a hole large enough to pull a bag out. It contained Salgadinhos, one of Donato's favorite snacks. His mouth watered as he grabbed for the chips and started eating. He realized he was stealing and felt guilty. *They won't miss one,* he thought. He finished licking the salt from his fingers and plucked out another packet for later. He stopped in front of another pallet when he spotted boxes of Passatempos. Despite the guilt, he opened a box, pulling two packets of Passatempos to take back with him.

Donato spent the rest of the day exploring his warehouse, although he knew every inch. The light started fading as night time approached, so he went back to his cubby, placed the teddy bear in its night time position and ate the Passatempos before retiring for sleep, which eluded him as he kept thinking of the police and how he would get home. The noise of motor vehicles approached, growing louder. Moments later the doors of the warehouse slid open, and the vehicles drove inside, lights flashing across the walls. Donato crouched in front of his spy hole to see what was happening.

Headlights faced each other, illuminating the space between them. Doors opened and people got out. One man placed a plastic sheet on the floor in the light and another placed two folding chairs on it. From the second vehicle, they dragged a restrained, gagged and blindfolded man and woman who staggered to the chairs. They pushed them into the seats and tied them around their chests. Men stood behind each captive.

The rear door of one vehicle opened, and a well-dressed man alighted. He was middle-aged and balding and carried too much weight. While lighting a cigarette, he stood between the two captives, but to the side. Donato spied him gazing at both as he drew on the cigarette, pacing away and returning. He dropped the cigarette and stubbed it with his shoe, nodding to the two men.

They pulled the blindfolds off the captives, who looked terrified as they stared at each other, fear radiating through the warehouse like over-bright rays of sunlight. Their faces were swollen and covered in blood. The man tried shouting through his gag, but only a muffled sound came out.

"Now, are you ready to tell me your story?" the well-dressed man asked. He motioned to the men standing behind them. They removed the gags. The man shouted for help, but his minder rapped him on the head, silencing him. The woman stared at the man, shaking. "There is no point shouting. No one can hear you." The boss hissed. "Who's your contact?"

"I told you. I haven't said anything to anyone," the captive man said.

The boss sighed. "I wish you weren't so stubborn. It only makes it worse for you. Who are you feeding?"

"No one."

"Shall we play with your wife then, a gigga-gigga maybe?" The boss made thrusting movements as he gave a sinister smile. The two men sniggered. "Can she work three at a time? You want to find out?"

The captive man pleaded with his eyes. "I know nothing. I told you, you've got the wrong person."

The boss was annoyed at the lack of progress. He walked over to the woman and ripped open her blouse, revealing her breasts. He put his hand in his pocket, pulling out a flick knife and cut off her bra. The woman gaped at the boss, pleading for mercy as she sobbed. "Hmm, exquisite shape. Be a pity to damage them," the boss said as he flicked one of her nipples with the knife blade. "What do you think?" he said, taking two steps over to the male captive.

"Please. Leave her be. She knows nothing," the man sobbed.

The boss paced away, tapping the blade of the knife to his forehead. "Now, you said, 'she knows nothing'. That must mean that you do, yes?"

"I told you, I've told no one anything."

"You are trying my patience. What might convince you to talk?"

He nodded.

A shot rang out through the building and the woman's head slumped forward.

"No!" the captive man yelled in anguish.

Donato gasped but quickly put his hand over his mouth.

"Did you hear something?" the boss asked the two accomplices.

"No boss," one said, as the other shook his head while they listened.

"Must have been the wind or something. Now, where were we? Oh, yeah, are you ready to talk now."

"I'm telling you, I know nothing." Total despair showed on the captive man's face.

The boss sighed, shaking his head from side to side. "We're getting nowhere here." He nodded, and another shot rang out, a bullet piercing the captive's head. "If he was telling the truth, we'll never know." The boss shrugged his shoulders. "Clean up and let's get going."

Donato had an irresistible need to sneeze. He tried covering his mouth and nose to stop it but failed and a sneeze echoed out of the office towards the men.

"What was that? I thought I heard a noise before," the boss said. "Go check it out. We can't have any witnesses but bring them to me if you can."

Donato's eyes bulged and he realized he had to escape. As he snatched his teddy bear, he headed to the office door closest to the wall of the warehouse where he entered the building. He burst out of the office and towards the hole in the wall.

"There he is. It's only a boy," one man said.

"Get him," the boss said.

The two men started running towards Donato, but they were too far away to catch him before he darted through the hole. They stopped at the hole and peered out. The men couldn't push through the child-sized hole.

"Go find him, quick, before he gets away."

"He's long gone before we get around," one man said.

"Go look anyway."

The men disappeared out the doorway. They came

walking back 15 minutes later. "He's disappeared," one of them said.

"Where did he come from?"

"Out of the office. I'll go check." He walked over, returning moments later. "He was using the office as a home. There're empty bags and stuff on the floor."

"Let's clean up this mess and get out of here." The boss frowned.

The two men untied the bodies from their chairs and they slumped to the plastic sheeting. They packed the chairs away and one man opened the other vehicle's trunk, while the other wrapped the plastic sheeting over the bodies into a tight bundle. Both men lifted the bodies and deposited them in the trunk. They had a quick search around the warehouse and nodded to the boss.

"We must find the boy. You saw his face, didn't you?"

"Yeah," both men said.

Chapter 51

On The Run

Donato ran to the adjacent warehouse, fear driving him forward. He scrambled to find the loose sheet and crawled through the opening, hiding behind a pallet, his breath ragged from exertion and dread. He sat against the boxes, letting his head rest against them, as he closed his eyes in despair. *Why is this happening to me? I just want to go home to Papa.* He strained to hear any sound of his pursuers in the warehouse, waiting hours, but no one came. Feeling more relaxed, he ventured to the loose sheeting and peered out. Everything looked quiet, so he crawled outside again, but fear prevented him from returning to his cubby. Not knowing what to do, he returned to the warehouse, grabbed a packet of Passatempos, sat in a corner and ate them until he fell asleep.

He woke the next morning with a start. Voices came from inside the warehouse; workers opening the place to start the day. After snatching what remained of the Passatempos, he creeped to the loose sheeting and squeezed out into the fresh air. Donato felt glum and desperate. He lost the place he called home and terrible people and the police were looking for him. What else could go wrong? The sky above threatened rain and a few minutes later a storm broke, saturating Donato and chilling him to misery as he looked for somewhere to shelter, waiting for the storm to pass.

As he shivered in his rain-soaked clothes, Donato found only one solution to his problems. He had to leave the city and continue his trek upriver on foot, his only solution to escaping the people searching for him. Good people couldn't find him either, but at least he was away from harm, despite his concern about food. After finding a hiding place near the warehouse, waiting out the rain, he hid until the cover of nightfall. The location had a view of the warehouse and several vehicles with darkened windows coasted past, speeding up again afterwards. His clothes dried in the heat of the day.

The sun set and Donato crept from the shadows. His stomach growled for food, but the warehouse was out of bounds. As he drifted towards the port, and the street he frequented, he kept to the shadows as much as possible, running across roads after checking for prying eyes. The park beckoned him, streetlights highlighting the gloomy landscape. In the park, he moved to the shrubs and trees, watching people walk back and forth on the street. How he wished to join them and buy food, but it wasn't possible. He settled behind a tree and waited.

The chill of the night woke him. On realizing he had fallen asleep, he looked around. People had deserted the street. He crept from his cover and looked in nearby bins for any discarded food. He found scraps and devoured them, after swiping ants away. As he crept through the park, he headed to the river and found an alley leading there. He looked upriver when he reached the bank but grunted in disappointment as the port stood in his way and he needed to find a route around to continue his journey upstream. He started walking in the upstream direction along the road he knew well, although he hadn't ventured that way before.

Despite taking precautions, from behind him Donato heard, "That's him. Get him."

The two men from the night before ran towards him. He ran too, following the road at first, but detouring to a side street, weaving through alleys until he believed he lost them. After finding a small hole, he ducked in and sat still, listening for the chase to catch up with him. But the only sound was his breathing.

Moments later, the sound of footsteps filtered through to him. "I could have sworn he came this way," said a man from above, his legs all that Donato could see.

"Well, he's gone now."

"Slippery little rat."

"He'll show up again. We just have to be patient."

"Hope the boss'll wait that long."

Not daring to move, Donato took the teddy bear from his trousers and hugged it as he fell into a restless sleep.

Chapter 52

Discharged

Two days after Deborah arrived, Roland hobbled from the hospital with her at his side. His face was still bruised, although the swelling had subsided, and he had sight in both eyes. Pain speared through his side every time he put any pressure onto his chest, and he winced.

"You coping okay?" Deborah asked with concern and a hint of mock sympathy, as a slight smile lit her face.

"I'll live." His face soured as he saw her sardonic smile but she said nothing more.

They reached the car park and Roland eased himself into the rear passenger seat of the vehicle he had hired in Carlos City. Deborah hopped into the other side, as a driver Deborah had hired sat at the wheel.

"Back to the hotel, please," Deborah said to the driver.

"Is he a driver or a minder?" Roland asked as he inspected the driver. The tall, muscle-bound man looked intimidating in his dark sunglasses. He saw the man shuffle to look at Roland in the rear-view mirror, but said nothing, and his facial expression didn't move.

"A bit of both. You can't look after yourself, so I arranged things for you."

Roland scowled at his wife's implied reprimand. They drove in silence for a time. "Did Felicity return to Carlos City last night?"

"Yes, she did. I can look after you now."

Roland's foul mood intensified, but he said nothing that would lead to an argument, as he knew his chances of winning. "She visited me in the afternoon to update me on Donato. There were several more sightings of him."

"He must be in the port, then. I wonder what he's doing to survive?"

"Good question, although he stole money from a woman in Vila Rio Dobrar."

"That won't last forever though."

"No."

They drove the rest of the way back to the hotel in silence, which suited Roland fine with his mood. They had dinner in the hotel and retired to bed.

"... honey... wake up, honey," Deborah said, as she shook Roland's shoulder.

"Huh... huh," Roland said, as he woke from his sleep. "What's happening?" Perspiration glistened on his forehead, reflected in the bedside light, his nightshirt wet with perspiration.

"You were having a nightmare. You were mumbling you couldn't escape."

Roland sat up and rubbed his eyes, trying to recall his dream. "I was in the woods and I heard a sound behind me. When I looked around, I saw two bears following me, but when I ran, they started chasing me. I couldn't escape them, but they couldn't catch me either. But I dreamed something else before that. It was something terrible I had seen, something terrifying, but I can't remember what it was."

"That sounds weird. Why dream that?"

"I don't know. I could be just remembering my experience, and how its emotions are playing out."

"Maybe."

Roland rose and went to the toilet. Deborah did the same. He lay on his uninjured side and closed his eyes. Moments later, Deborah returned, got into bed, switched off the light and snuggled in behind him. They both fell asleep again, a smile on Roland's face as he felt Deborah's warmth and bumpiness behind him.

They both woke up late the next morning. He rose to a sitting position with his feet dangling over the side of the bed. His muscles protested the exercise, and he grimaced.

"Morning honey," Deborah said, as she leaned over to kiss him, having come out of the bathroom rubbing the towel through her hair. She stood in front of him naked, to Roland's pleasure and consternation, as he knew he was in no condition to carry through with what played in his mind.

"Morning."

"I left you sleeping. You needed it."

"Thanks. I'm still sore. I hope exercise will take the aches away."

"Well, get changed and we'll go grab breakfast."

"Okay." Roland rose out of the bed and used the bathroom to shower.

Half an hour later they left their room and descended downstairs to the restaurant. Once seating at a table, they looked at the menu.

"Do you want à la carte or the buffet, honey?"

"À la carte this morning. I don't have the energy for buffet."

"I will too then."

Roland ordered fried bacon and eggs with roasted tomatoes and mushrooms, and Deborah had a muesli dish with fruit. They both ordered a juice and coffee.

"How can you eat that and stay slim, honey? I'd bloat out in no time."

"I've been exercising."

They both sat sipping their coffee.

"Mr Cavendish?"

Roland stopped mid-sip and stiffened in anticipation, as he knew the voice. He turned his head and saw Juan Salvador standing beside him. He glared at the man. "What do you want?"

"I was wondering if we could finish our brief talk from the other day." Juan grabbed a chair from the next table and, presuming it okay, sat between Roland and Deborah.

Deborah stared in amazement at the intrusion.

"There's nothing further to say. Now, I wish to finish my breakfast in peace."

"This will only take a moment. We may've had a misunderstanding, and I apologize for that, but you must have a comment on the unfortunate dam collapse disaster."

"You saw the media statement I made?"

"Yes, I did."

"You have everything I wish to say then. I have a boy to find." Roland cringed after he let his purpose slip, as he didn't want anyone to know his reason for being in Porta Plata.

Juan's ears pricked up as he sensed a scoop. "What boy?"

Roland looked at Deborah, pleading for her to help him escape his predicament.

"Roland is still recovering from his injuries," she told

Juan. "Even you can leave an injured person in peace, can't you?" She started getting annoyed with the man too.

"But this will only take a moment. What of this boy then? Who is he? Why are you searching for him?"

"No comment."

"Is he a victim of your company's negligence?"

Roland's temperature rose as he bristled at the question. Deborah threw her napkin on the table and left, leaving Roland to fend for himself. He looked at her back in horror. "I have nothing to say."

"So, you admit that there may be a case of negligence against the company."

"No, I do not," Roland said, raising his voice louder than he intended. People at nearby tables turned and Roland blushed. "I do not appreciate this line of questioning."

"Why Mr Cavendish? Do you have something to hide...?"

An enormous hand grabbed the reporter by the shoulder. "I think it's time you left," Deborah's minder said to Juan, as he clamped his shoulder harder and started lifting him. Deborah stood behind.

Juan, one side of his body lifting from the chair, said, "But I'm not causing any trouble."

"You're upsetting my client. That is trouble." The minder had Juan standing, wincing in pain.

"I'll have you for assault if you don't let go."

"I can make your assault claim worthwhile."

Juan's eyes dilated at the threat. Realizing persistence was useless, he said, "Okay, I'll go."

Juan tidied his ruffled clothes. "Good day, Mr Cavendish. I suggest that you read tomorrow's paper." He walked out.

"Sorry, Sir. He got past me."

"That's fine, thanks." Roland calmed down from his flustered state.

The minder sidestepped but remained by the table as Deborah returned to her seat.

Roland, self-conscious, glanced at the minder. "Are you going to stay there?"

"Yes, Sir."

"It's very uncomfortable. Could you please go somewhere less conspicuous?"

The man glanced at Deborah and she nodded.

"Where were we?" Deborah asked.

Chapter 53

The Old Man

Roland woke from a deep sleep feeling warm. The sun shone through the curtains as he opened his eyes to another day. With an attempted stretch, he winced at the pain in his chest, as the bruised ribs announced their continued presence. His wounds' pains had subsided through the night. He donned a dressing gown and ambled to the room's door. A newspaper lay by the door, so he picked it up and started reading it. The reporter's words rang out in his mind and he breathed a sigh of relief when no mention of him appeared on the front page. He strolled to the small table and chair by the window and sat. A slit of light, filtering through the gap between the blind and the window frame, allowed him to read the print, while Deborah continued to sleep. He turned the page and froze. The headline at the top of page three read,

CEO IN PORTA PLATA — WHY?
'The CEO of Zagreus Minerals, Roland Cavendish, is visiting Porta Plata for undisclosed business. When asked

his purpose for visiting the city, he refused to give a reason apart from admitting that he was looking for a boy. He refused to offer further details of who the boy is, or why he seeks him, and whether there was any relationship to the recent disaster at Vermelho Mine. Could Mr. Cavendish better use his energy in rectifying the consequences of the alleged disaster cause by the company's negligence — his company? He alleges being attacked and hospitalized while in Porta Plata.'

The story detailed other mundane information on the disaster and the cleanup measures. Roland's temperature rose as he read the reporter's allegations and accusations. As he breathed deep, he calmed himself, knowing he could do nothing.

Deborah stirred and opened her eyes.

"Good morning, sweetie," Roland said as he walked over and gave her a kiss.

"Good morning, honey," Deborah said as she smiled up at him. "You're up early."

"I want to return to the port and ask if anyone's sighted Donato."

Deborah looked worried. "Are you ready to do that?"

"Don't worry, I'll take your minder with me."

"Okay then. Let's at least have breakfast together."

"You had better hurry," Roland said, even though he hadn't gotten dressed himself yet.

They both prepared for breakfast and descended. The minder stood waiting for them at the restaurant's entrance, ensuring that his slip-up did not recur. They had breakfast and prepared to part their ways forty-five minutes later.

"What will you do?" Roland asked Deborah.

"Just relax by the pool. I might go shopping later. Will you be back for dinner?"

"Yes, I will. See you then."

They gave each other a kiss and Roland started to the hotel entrance, his minder in tow. They reached the port an hour later.

Roland went back to the shop of his earlier visit. "Hi, remember me?"

"Oh, you again, you were here last week," the shop-keeper said.

"Yeah, I was just wondering if you had seen that boy again."

"There's a lot of interest in the boy. What's he done?"

"Nothing. I just want to find him."

"He was in here two days ago, but I haven't seen him since then."

"Oh, okay, thanks." Roland bought candy out of curtesy and walked out. He wandered the street as the day's business started bustling. Not knowing what else to do, he strolled over to the park despite the lingering memories. He had his minder with him this time, who walked two paces behind him, on constant alert for trouble.

Roland sat on the park bench and pulled a candy from the packet, a piteco fruit, placed it in his mouth and sucked on it as he sat thinking, his minder standing behind him and to the right, out of the way to give Roland privacy. Roland offered him a piteco, but he refused.

An old man came along ten minutes later. "Ahh, you are sitting on my seat, you are. It's not really my seat, but I like to think it is," he said, as he came and sat beside Roland. The minder became more alert for a moment, returning to his prior stance when he saw Roland in no imminent danger.

"Hello. Sorry, am I sitting on your seat?"

"No... no, I sit on the seat, but anyone can sit there. You're the man I helped the other day, aren't you? I see that you have mended."

"Yes, I'm still sore, but I'll survive. Thank you for helping. I didn't realize it was you."

"That is alright. You were preoccupied."

"Do you want a piteco?" Roland held out the packet.

"Don't mind if I do." The old man took one and placed it in his mouth. Roland did the same. They sat on the bench for a moment, each sucking on their piteco.

Roland showed the man the photo of Donato. "Have you seen him?"

"Donato? Sure. We have sat on my seat, where I sit, many times."

"Do you know where he is?"

The man frowned. "What's your relationship to him?"

"I am trying to return him to his father."

"Oh, no, I don't know where he is. He comes and goes, as do I. He's taken up residence in the warehouse district, but I don't know if he's still there."

"Oh... pity." Roland put the photo away, wondering what to do next.

"The boy's seen terrible things, things no boy should experience. He tells me of them. Maybe he'll come today, although he should be here, if he were coming."

"How do I find him?"

The old man rubbed his chin, thinking. "I could ask. See if anyone has seen him, people who stay out of sight." He glanced at Roland. "You could come with me, just in case I find him."

"I'd appreciate that. I'd be lose otherwise." Roland

picked a piteco from the packet and offered the old man one too. "Why are you here?" Roland asked, curious.

"Ahh, that story is too involved and boring to tell. We have more important things to do. Now... come, and we will start our search for the elusive Donato."

The old man and Roland stood, and they strolled out of the park, Roland following the direction the old man took, his minder following close behind them. The old man stopped. "Is he with you?"

"Yes. My wife hired him to protect me, after my unfortunate incident."

"That might make things harder. People won't want to talk very much with him with us. Looks too ganger."

"Ganger?"

"A minder in a gang around here. They might start thinking you're a boss."

Roland looked at the minder, uncertain what he should do. His getting rid of him would upset Deborah, and he was helpful with the reporter. With Roland's procrastination, the old man strolled to the minder and whispered in his ear. They had a whispered discussion before the minder came to Roland. "The guy reckons you're safe with him. I'll stay here and wait for you."

Roland looked surprised at the arrangement. He wondered what the man had said to convince him he could protect Roland. "You're satisfied it won't get you into trouble?"

"I am satisfied."

"Okay." Roland glanced back at the man. "Let's go then." Roland and the old man continued walking off, leaving the minder in the park.

Chapter 54

Rosita Again

S anchez looked at the world outside the window as he lay in his hospital bed. Boredom dominated his day as he wrestled with trying to find things to occupy himself. The doctors said his recovery went well, and they wanted him to exercise to stop atrophy taking hold of his leg muscles. He couldn't get back on his feet quickly enough, although apprehension gripped him as the time neared. The hospital staff encouraged him to dangle his legs over the side of the bed yesterday. They wanted to get the stiffness out of his good joints with leg raises. To his surprise, he started puffing after just a few cycles. The nurse reassured him the reaction was normal.

The weather outside was miserable, overcast and windy, rain splattering the window. It was as miserable as Sanchez felt. An image of Rosita flashed into his head, and he smiled as he remembered her face, eager for her next visit. But he presumed he bored her and didn't expect her to visit again. He considered it strange that he should think of her, since he didn't know her well, but they were growing closer. He sensed something with her, and he wondered what Catina would think. Would she resent him for forgetting her so fast, moving on with his life, or misunderstand, knowing her presence in his life was fading into a memory? She was always in his memory. Their attachment had been too strong. Maybe she was making space for another in Sanchez's heart. He sighed as a nurse entered.

"What's with Mr Grumpy?" the nurse said, trying to cheer him. "Today is a big day. We'll see you walking again. Now let's see you sit on the bed."

Sanchez groaned but did as the nurse ordered, sitting and rotating to dangle his legs.

"Have you been doing your exercises?"

"Yes," Sanchez said, like a recalcitrant child being asked if he'd done his homework.

The nurse stood straight with her fists on her hips. "Don't you want to walk again?"

"Of course, I do. I was just daydreaming."

"Well, we'll get you into a wheelchair first and wheel you to rehab for a physiotherapist to give you a workout. The chair's only temporary. Now, let me help you. Grab my shoulder and put weight on your good leg while you get into the chair."

Sanchez took the nurse's shoulder and he slid from the bed until his good foot touched the floor and he could balance his body.

"One, two, three," the nurse said as she pulled up, encouraging Sanchez to stand.

With weight on his foot, he wobbled with unexpected strain as he positioned himself and fell back into the wheel-chair. The effort made him break out in perspiration.

"Well done." The nurse, positioned his feet on the footrests.

She pushed him to the rehabilitation section, where the

physiotherapist worked with him for an hour, including walking a few steps with the support of parallel bars while he got used to walking on one leg. He returned to his room, tired and sweaty from the exertion. Once lunch had passed, he was alone again.

The clouds cleared away after lunch and sunlight filtered through the gaps. The wind ceased, and people walked in the enclosed garden. A soft knock rapped the doorframe, and he turned his head. His face burst into a smile as he saw Rosita standing in the doorway, a fresh floral colored dress clung to her, her hair tied into a ponytail and she wore minimal makeup, enough to highlight her features.

"May I come in?"

"Sure, please. I thought you mightn't come again."

Rosita's stilettos announced each step as she walked to the chair next to the bed.

"Are you going somewhere?" Sanchez asked, jealous.

"No... why?"

"You have high heels on, as if you're meeting someone."

Rosita blushed. "I put them on for you." She lowered her head as she confessed.

Sanchez raised his brow at the admission. "Well, you got my attention."

Rosita looked up again and smiled. "Good."

He smiled back at her.

"Oh... I forgot. I brought you something." She pulled a bag of fruit from her carry bag.

Sanchez swivelled around so he could see her better. "Sorry with the way I look. I'd have put on my best clothes, if I knew you were coming. Thanks." He only had his hospital gown on, which didn't complement anyone. He placed the bag of fruit on the table.

Rosita giggled. "You look okay with what you're wearing." She blushed again.

They sat in silence, each reluctant to engage the other, as if they were two teenagers broaching an intimate conversation.

"I started walking today."

"Oh. That's good. They'll release you soon then."

"I don't know. I suppose it depends on how soon I can walk unaided. My other wounds have healed well. But my ribs hurt, and I'll have the cast on my arm for a while."

"I suppose. Where will you go?"

"I don't know. I don't want to burden Raf in my condition, even though he'll protest, and I don't have a place of my own except at Vila Feliz."

"You can't return there," Rosita said with a hint of panic.

"I know. It's not practical. And I left there when I packed. I don't want to go back except to remove my belongings."

Rosita reddened. "There's a spare apartment in my building and it's on the ground floor. I could see if it's available."

"That'd be convenient," he said.

"Oh, I wasn't meaning you had to take it because it's in the same building."

"I wasn't thinking that. I meant there'd be no stairs to climb. What did you think I meant?"

"Nothing." Rosita blushed bright red.

Sanchez wanted to laugh but pitied her and her misunderstanding. He wanted to reach out to comfort her. They sat in silence for a while.

"Sanchez, I..." "Rosita, I..." they both said at the same time. Rosita giggled, and Sanchez sniggered.

"Sorry, you go ahead," Sanchez said.

"No, you go first."

"Well, I was wondering what will happen with us. Do we have something?"

Rosita giggled as she lowered her gaze. "I wanted to ask you the same question."

"Well?"

"I sense something. I hope I sense something, but I'm too afraid."

"Afraid of what?"

"Afraid that you'll reject me and afraid of my poor record with men."

Sanchez laughed. "So you think I'm the same as the others."

"No... that's not what I meant. You're different to the others. I can see it in your eyes. I'm afraid that I will drive you away because you're different."

Sanchez turned red, embarrassed by the complement. "Thanks."

"What do you think, then?"

He glanced sideways, not daring to face her, and said, "I sense something, but I'm scared too." He looked at Rosita, wanting to see her reaction. "I'm scared that it's too soon, and I'll forget Catina, and I don't want to forget her. I'm scared that Catina will come between us. But then I hear her voice in my head telling me it's okay, that she'll be happy for me, and I need to move on, and you're a fantastic person."

Rosita lowered her gaze. "I can't replace Catina."

"And you never will. I shouldn't make you. You're different to her."

"What makes me different?"

"... it's hard to say."

After a moment, Rosita said, "I'm willing to explore, if you are," as her eyes met his.

The gaze dazzled him for a moment, leaving him speechless. Eventually he said, "So am I."

Rosita broke the spell first and looked away. "Well, nothing'll happen while you're stuck here."

He laughed at her practicality. "I don't know. You can push me around in the wheelchair."

"You can push yourself around," she said, a challenge in her voice.

"Then be prepared for me to chase you!"

"You wouldn't!"

"Why not? It'll help strengthen my muscles."

"Men always thinking of their muscles."

"You're lucky I can't get off this bed."

"Or what?" she said, a cheeky grin on her face.

"Or nothing," he said, unwilling to go any further.

The banter abated, and they sat in silence again. Rosita jumped up, rushed over to Sanchez and kissed him on the lips. He resisted in shock for a moment, but then responded. They parted, and he placed his fingers on his lips, feeling the pleasant lingering tingle. He looked at Rosita, an intimacy he hadn't felt since Catina died returning to him. The perfume Rosita wore still tantalizing his smell with its sensuality. He cleared his throat. "That was a pleasant surprise."

"I couldn't hold back. I hope it was alright."

"It was more than alright."

Rosita came close. They embraced each other and kissed again for much longer.

Chapter 55

Homeless

D onato's eyes darted, scouring for a hiding spot from the chasing gangsters. No sooner had he crept into one spot than one of them saw him and gave chase.

"There he is," one gangster said. "Come here, you slippery little eel." He started running after Donato. The other gangsters did likewise.

"I've lost him again," the gangster said as he stopped running and started a thorough inspection.

Seconds later Donato darted around the corner of an alleyway and ran straight into an old scruffy man, winding him and knocking him backwards onto his rear. The man looked straight at Donato, confusion in his eyes. "Please help me," Donato pleaded. He saw the man was reluctant but could hear the gangsters coming closer.

"Quick, come with me," the man urged. He got off the ground and led Donato to a stormwater drain by the road. "Crawl through the grating and hide. I'll call you when it's safe to come out."

Donato crawled through the gap between the gutter

and the steel grating. It was a tight fit, but he squeezed through, lowering himself to the base. He stood up straight in the drain. Light from above filtered into the piping, and Donato saw a few mounds of rubbish still not dislodged by recent storms. Strange squeaking noises came from further up the pipe, but Donato kept those thoughts out of his mind.

He heard footsteps and the sound of someone rummaging through garbage and he cringed in fear. His pursuers came upon Donato's savior, who had been waiting for them, feigned fear in his eyes.

"Have you seen a boy come up the alley?" one gangster asked.

"No, it's just been me here."

"Are you sure?"

"It isn't a big alley and you can see I'm the only one here. I would have seen a boy coming in and trying to steal my things."

Both gangsters looked at him, as if they didn't believe him. One of them stepped nearer, cowering the old man. "Are you sure you don't need us to jog your memory?" he threatened.

"Yes, I'm sure, I'm sure, sir."

The gangsters glanced at each other and shrugged. "Well, tell us if you see him, okay?"

"Yeah, okay."

The gangsters started tossing things aside, looking for the boy, but they soon tired of their futile effort. "He must have gone further along," one of them said.

"Yeah, let's keep looking further along the road. He'll be sorry when we catch him. Pity the boss wants him in one piece," the other one said.

Donato waited in the drain as the men continued

searching through rubbish before they disappeared out the end of the alley. Soon he heard footsteps and then a man's voice from above. "You can come out now."

Donato was fearful the man might lead him into a trap, but he was alone, so Donato wrapped his hands around one of the grating rungs and lifted himself up into the gap, wriggling through moments later. He sat on the kerb, dejected, with his chin cupped in his hands.

The man stood over him, and then sat next to him. "What's your name, little boy?"

"Donato."

"Well, they're gone now, for the time being, Donato."

Donato started crying. "I just want to get home to my Papa," he said between sobs.

The man stared at him and frowned. "And where is your Papa?"

"In Vila Feliz."

"Can't say I've heard of it."

"It's upriver."

"Oh... how did you end up here?"

"There was a flood, and I got washed downriver, and it's red, and Mama is dead, and I've been trying to get home to Papa."

"Oh... the dam disaster."

"Yes."

The man scanned the alley. "We need to hide you. They might come back. Come with me."

Donato was reluctant to move, wiping tears from his eyes. The man looked okay, but so did the others, and they all had bad intentions. "How do I know I can trust you?"

Caught by surprise, the man looked back at him. "I suppose you can't, except I hid you from those men, and it's your choice to either come with me or wait for them to come back."

Considering his options, Donato said, "I don't have a choice. I don't want to get caught."

The man held out his hand, and Donato took it, as natural as a father out for a stroll with his young son. The man looked both ways before entering the next street. They threaded their way back to his residence. "This is my home. I'll make a spot for you to rest. You need to stay here until things settle. I don't trust people around here. I don't trust you either. You might steal something. I'll make an exception this time. Suppose trust works both ways sometimes. You got any money on your head? If you do, and they find out, they're likely to sell you."

Donato surveyed the place. An alley extended out before him with junk littering the ground everywhere he looked. The man lived here. Others lived here too, amongst the garbage and junk considered treasure. There were plenty of spots to hide from gangsters. "I'll keep hidden, sir."

"Don't call me sir. I hate it."

"Okay. What do I call you then?"

"Casimiro, Cas. Call me Cas."

"Okay, Cas. I'll stay hidden, but I'm hungry. Can I go buy food?"

"What do you mean 'buy food'? You got money?"

"Maybe. It's almost gone."

"Give it to me. Consider it rent."

"But then I won't have any to get home."

"You won't be going anywhere if those men get you. I mean, you need to hide, I don't mean to scare you. I'll buy food for you, if you give me the money. That way you can stay here."

Donato still didn't trust the man, but it was the logical thing to do. He fumbled in his pocket and pulled out some money, making sure he kept some in reserve. "Here," he said as he held it towards Casimiro.

He snatched it from his hand. "I'll be back soon." He walked away, disappearing around a corner.

Donato felt sure Casimiro would run off with his money but waited. To his surprise, Cas returned with a bag of food, and two clinking bottles in a brown bag that he hid from Donato. Whatever they were, Casimiro kept them well away from him.

Late afternoon turned into evening, and other occupants of the ghetto started returning. Casimiro eyed them with suspicion as they walked to their homes. Donato made sure he stayed hidden, as he had been instructed. Casimiro brought out a bottle and took a long swig. The smell of tequila wafted to Donato's nose. *No wonder he doesn't want me near it*, he thought. His Papa kept the alcohol he brought home away from Donato too, saying that it wasn't good for boys to have. He and Mama shared a bottle of whatever it was now and then. Mama got the giggles, and they often retired to the bedroom afterwards.

"What have you got there?" someone asked Casimiro, as he took another sip of tequila.

He wiped his mouth, sealed the bottle and put it under his chair. "None of your business."

"You got grog, haven't you? How did you get it? Did you steal it or something? Why don't you share?"

"You stay away, you worthless bastard. Go earn your own stuff."

"Earn?" the man said. "You haven't earned a Real in your life. Where did you get it?" He came closer to Casimiro.

"I'm warning you, stay away from my things or you'll be sorry."

"Come on," the man pleaded. "Just a mouthful."

"Stay away," Casimiro said as he swayed to his feet.

The man came nearer still. In a flash, Casimiro produced a knife and pointed it at the man. "Stay away."

The man's eyes bulged when he saw the blade. "Okay... okay, keep your damned drink, you selfish bastard!"

Casimiro continued to drink the contents of the bottle, as he sat glaring at the world around him. Donato left him undisturbed and settled on cardboard out of sight for the night. He slipped into sleep.

A commotion bolted Donato awake, ready to run. He poked his head from his hiding spot and saw Casimiro fighting the other man in a drunken state. He fought well, given his state of intoxication. The man had Casimiro's arms pinned but couldn't keep hold of him in the struggle. The man's eye wandered and he spotted Donato. He pulled back, puffing from the exertion.

"Who's he?" the man asked, confused.

"Mind your own business."

Donato, realizing his mistake, ducked back inside.

"Why are you hiding a boy? Is that where you got the money? He needs to share it with the rest of us."

"I'm warning you. Keep away from here or you're dead.

"Okay, okay. Don't get too excited. I'm going."

Casimiro poked his head into where Donato hid, a powerful stench of alcohol on his breath. "You shouldn't have done that. Everyone will know you're here now. Can't help it now. Go to sleep."

Chapter 56

Your New Home

Sanchez considered himself lucky to be able to leave hospital three days after Rosita's visit. He was recovering well, according to the doctor, and his physiotherapy exercises had strengthened him enough to use crutches. He still had no home or transport. He called Raf last night, asking if he could pick him up from the hospital. Raf had promised to arrange something. Ten in the morning came and Raf still hadn't arrived. Sanchez, tired of the hospital's sterile atmosphere, wanted to start his life again, albeit without Catina and Donato. The prospect depressed him. The flood swept away everything he loved in a moment, and yet something to treasure remained deep inside. The knowledge that Catina wanted him to continue warmed his heart, but the doubts about Donato's survival dogged his conscience.

"You ready to go home?" a familiar voice called out to him from the doorway.

He was greeted by Rosita's cheerful face, fresh and sparkling, as if she had just blossomed from a flower bud.

He smiled. "I was ready a long time ago, but I thought Raf was coming."

Rosita lowered her gaze, self-conscious. "Something came up. He asked me if I could do it."

Sanchez looked at her, knowing there was more to the story, but left it at that. Being picked up by Rosita instead of Raf made him happy. "We had better go, then. I don't have much to take with me. The medication on the table there, that's it."

"Oh, there's a change of destination too. I leased the unit I mentioned. You can move in there. I've moved your things from Raf's place."

Sanchez stared at Rosita in shock. "But... but I don't know if I can afford it. I can't even look after myself."

"Raf rang Zagreus Minerals and they've paid the first year's rent."

"They have?"

"Uh-huh, and I'll be close by when you need something." She blushed.

"I don't know what to say."

"Say thank you. Let's get you home." She found a bag for Sanchez's pills and his few other things. She brushed against him at one stage and they both glanced at each other, the incident a lingering memory of promise. "That's it, shall we?"

Sanchez grabbed his crutches and placed them under his armpits. "Let's."

When they arrived at the unit, they both gazed out the passenger window. "That's it there," Rosita said.

"Looks simple enough." The unit occupied part of the ground floor of a three-story building. The curtains flashed bright red with green and yellow diamonds. "Did you pick the curtains?"

"Yes. Do you like them?" Rosita asked nervously.

"Yeah, I do." He turned and smiled.

"Let's get you settled then." Rosita got out of the car and gave Sanchez his crutches.

He eased himself into a standing position and started walking to his new home, Rosita behind him. He stopped in front of the door and Rosita stepped forward with the key. Her scent teased Sanchez until he couldn't resist and put an arm around her waist, pulling her towards him. She didn't resist and drew her back up to his body, resting her head on his shoulder. She closed her eyes with pleasure. "What will the neighbors think?" she asked, with an 'I don't care' smile. Sanchez said nothing, as he enjoyed her warmth against him. When they let go, Rosita stood aside for Sanchez to enter. She followed and waited for Sanchez to respond to her choice of furnishings and decorations.

The place was immaculate and set up with everything Sanchez needed. He felt sure they had leased the property a few days ago, and he wondered whether they had set the wheels in motion even before Rosita's visit. The smell of freshly cut flowers floated over from a vase sitting on the kitchen table. He hobbled over and lowered himself onto a seat, surveying his domain. To his left, a living space projected into an alcove with a lounge and coffee table. Further on, two doors led off a short hallway, presumably bedrooms. A bathroom was on the opposite side. He stared in awe at the unit, as Rosita returned with his belongings. He looked at her with the hint of tears in his eyes, "Thank you."

"You're welcome," Rosita said, a pleased smile on her face.

"Come here."

Rosita raised an eyebrow but complied. She moved over

to him. He cupped the back of her head and pulled her to him, bringing her mouth to his as they kissed.

Chapter 57

Captured

A ruckus buffeted Donato's ears as he roused from a restless sleep. Confused by the noise, he cowered, protected by Casimiro's hoarded junk. It sounded as if the place was being pulled apart. He found an opening in the piled trash and peered out.

"There, Sir," Casimiro's opponent from last night said gloatingly to someone Donato couldn't see.

"Go away," Casimiro said. "You have no business here."

Donato froze with dread as he glimpsed the same sinister, grumpy face from yesterday, intolerant of impertinence or obstruction. "Where's the boy?"

"No boy here," Casimiro said.

"He's in that pile of rubbish."

The gangster glanced in the direction the homeless person pointed. "Here?"

"Yeah, there."

"You hiding someone?" the gangster asked Casimiro. "Don't lie if you know what's good for you."

"I'm not hiding anyone. He's had too much to drink." Casimiro glared at his nemesis.

Donato saw the other gangster appear. He tore and tossed the piles, searching to see what lay underneath. Donato turned away from his spy hole and sat with his back hard against the wall. He was hyperventilating. They would discover him if he stayed in his spot, but he knew he couldn't escape. The men would catch him as soon as he tried to run. Despite Donato's distrust of Casimiro, he had helped him and hid him, so he felt obliged to protect him from the gangsters. He heard trash being removed from the pile above and realized it was only a matter of time before they discovered him, but he couldn't move. He was frozen in terror.

"I can't see anything."

"He's in there, I promise."

The gangster kept tearing away layers of junk, trying to get to the end.

"Hey, that's my home you're ruining. Leave it alone," Casimiro said, shuffling up to the gangster, trying to get him to stop.

"Nobody wants this stuff. Stay out of our way," the gangster said, giving Casimiro a backhanded slap across the face, sending him floundering backwards over the garbage, toppling him onto his back and knocking the wind out of him.

The man tore a hole, allowing daylight to shine into the cavity. He poked his head in and smiled straight at Donato. "Hey, I found him."

Donato kicked him in the face and made his nose bleed.

"Ow, you little shit."

Donato kicked again as the gangster couldn't fit his arms through the hole and Donato was safe from retribution. His foot connected with the man's eye socket. Donato didn't have anything to lose. They would soon capture him, so he may as well have fun.

"Ow... stop it."

Donato kicked again and hit under the man's nose.

"Ow, you'll be sorry when I get hold of you." The man's angry face retreated from the hole.

The other gangster laughed. "Beaten up by a kid. Sure you can handle him?"

"Shut up," the gangster said, drying his bloodied nose with a napkin. "He keeps kicking." He looked at the pile angrily. "I'll fix him." He started ripping away the rubbish with abandon, increasing the size of the hole.

"The boss doesn't want him hurt, remember."

"Oh, I won't leave any marks."

"You traitor," Casimiro said to his fellow tramp, glaring at him in disgust, and spitting on the ground towards him. "You dishonored the code."

"Hey, they were offering good money for him," the tramp said with a smug smile.

"Traitor." Casimiro still lay on the ground. It was the best place for him to stay.

The gangster managed a large enough hole to gain access to the cavity beneath, Donato still frozen in fear. He leaned his upper torso into the cavity and grabbed at Donato. Donato grabbed his hand and bit hard before the man jerked it back. He flicked his hand to subdue the pain, "Stop that." He reached in towards Donato again, but when Donato tried to bite, the gangster grabbed his arm and yanked him away from the wall and out of the hole. Donato struggled and kicked at the man to no avail, as he grabbed his other arm, holding both of them behind his back and pulling them tight until his shoulders started hurting. "Stay still. You can't get away now."

The other gangster paced up to Donato. "You're a slippery little eel, aren't you? I don't know what the boss wants with you for, but you're lucky he doesn't want you hurt." He glanced at his compatriot with a sniggering smile, "Let's go then."

Donato continued to struggle, trying to get away, but he tired, and the movement reduced to a token effort once he realized his futility.

"Hey, where's my reward?" the tramp yelled, fearful the gangster was reneging on the promise.

The gangster stopped, ordered the other to continue to the car, and walked back. "Yeah, we said you wouldn't have to worry for the rest of your life, didn't we?"

"Yeah, you did," the man said, a satisfied grin on his face.

The gangster patted the tramp on the shoulder, grabbed his chin and wagged his head. His other hand flashed up, both hands wrapping around the tramp's head, and he twisted, with a loud snap. "Can't trust snitches."

Casimiro fled in the other direction but the gangster didn't bother following him.

"Where's the boy?" he asked when he returned to the car.

"In the trunk, I tied him up and gagged him."

Donato tried kicking the top of the trunk, but his fettered legs were useless.

"Let's get back to real work, instead of this child-minding shit."

They drove into a warehouse and pulled the boy out of the trunk, untying him and tossing him into a cage. Donato sat alone except for his teddy bear, which had stayed in his trousers throughout the ordeal. He screamed for help but no-one could hear him.

Chapter 58

Despair

A man Donato didn't recognize came into the warehouse towards evening and gave him food and water.

"Can I use the bathroom?" Donato asked.

The man opened the cage and shackled Donato's legs together. He grabbed him by the shoulder and led him to a toilet in an office. He allowed Donato to enter alone, knowing there wasn't any way of escape. The man led him back to the cage, unshackled him, and locked it again.

Donato grinned as he devoured the food. He gazed at the bear. "The man didn't check if I stole anything." He pulled a scrap of wire from his pocket. When he finished eating, he bent the wire into shape and inserted it into the padlock. He tried for a long time and became frustrated. "It looks so easy when they do it on TV." He gave up after an hour. The warehouse faded into darkness. Donato grabbed his bear from the side of the cage and cuddled him, as he lay on the floor trying to go to sleep. He wondered what his fate was now. Who had captured him, and why did they want him alive? Why did they want him undamaged? His head was heavy, but sleep eluded him until he nodded into a light sleep, waking up with a jerk at the slightest of sounds.

The first light of dawn shone into the warehouse as Donato lay on the floor, half sleeping. He felt frozen and miserable. As he woke with the morning, he sat, placed teddy bear against the cage's side and attempted unlocking the padlock again. An hour later, he heard a click as he manipulated the wire. The padlock fell open. As he basked in his success, he removed the padlock and opened the cage. Just in case, he found a small hole in one of the cage support struts and slipped the wire into it, leaving the barest of wire poking out. He grabbed teddy bear and crawled out of the cage.

With a dash to the warehouse door, he pushed at it, but it didn't budge. He grunted in frustration. He strolled around the perimeter of the warehouse, searching for another exit. There were open windows, but they towered above out of his reach, and he couldn't find anything to use as a ladder or pile up. He searched the office but there was no way out.

They would know he was in the warehouse somewhere when they returned to feed him or fetch him, so Donato tried to think of an escape plan. His best chance was to surprise them when they opened the door and run past them.

He didn't have to wait long. Donato heard a vehicle approach the door and stop. The motor cut and a door opened and slammed closed again. Another door opened and closed, and moments later footsteps approached the warehouse door. Donato braced himself to run as soon as the door opened. It did and he raced past the man.

"Hey," the man yelled in surprise. He dropped what he was carrying and ran after Donato.

Donato searched for an exit, but a fence surrounded the warehouse compound except for a locked gate, and the fence was too high for him to climb. After running along the entire perimeter, he realized his escape had failed. He stopped running, slumped to the ground and cried.

The man ran up to Donato, puffing. He bent to regain his breath and glanced at Donato. "I could have told you there's no escape. Could have saved us both the bother. How did you get out of the cage? I know I locked it. You a locksmith as well?" He grabbed Donato's arm and pulled him up, making him walk back to the warehouse. "Give me your leg," he said as he produced a pair of handcuffs from his pocket. He placed one cuff around Donato's ankle and the other around a bar on the cage. "You brought this on yourself. I can't afford for you to escape again."

Donato tugged at the cuffs but knew it was pointless trying to get loose. The man strolled out and returned with Donato's breakfast. "The food's squashed thanks to you, but you can still eat it. Eat that or starve." He locked the cage door and left the warehouse, careful to lock that door, and drove away.

Donato picked at the food, no longer hungry in his despair. He sat trapped and caged like an animal, never to see Papa again. Whatever his fate, it was far from Papa, and the safety of his past life. He sat against the side of the cage, crying in self-pity. His misery exhausted, he tried pulling the cuff over his foot, but it was wrapped too tight and soon hurt with the strain of trying. He retrieved the wire and tried picking the lock. *I'm improving,* he thought, as the mechanism clicked and the cuff ratchet opened. He did the same with the cage lock soon after. After opening the door, the futility of his actions hit him. He had no escape. At least I can play in the warehouse.

The day passed, and Donato filled the time with games. The man would return soon to give him his evening meal. He considered locking himself in the cage, or whether he'd give the man another surprise. Escape was impossible but perhaps his captor would let him roam free knowing he couldn't be caged. Donato locked himself back in the cage in case an opportunity presented itself, although he thought his stay there was ending. They would either move him or kill him, like the other people he had seen murdered.

A vehicle arrived, and he looked up as the light started fading. It sounded different to the last one. As he listened, he realized at least two vehicles approached. His heart raced, expecting what was to come. A sedan and a four-wheel drive coasted into the warehouse. The man from that morning strolled over to Donato in his cage, pulling his key ring from his pocket and unlocking the cage.

"Decide to stay put this time," he said, for conversation instead of cynicism.

Donato said nothing as he watched him and eyed the vehicles. Released from the handcuffs, the man grasped his arm and pulled him from the cage. Donato didn't resist, as he knew it was pointless.

When they were five meters away, two men hopped out the vehicles and surrounded Donato. He didn't recognize either of them.

Donato glanced up at his captor and said, "Am I that dangerous?"

The man smiled, but remained silent, and they waited.

The four-wheel drive's rear window cracked open. "You are an elusive one," a male voice said from inside. Donato thought he recognized the voice, but he couldn't place him. The door opened, and the man emerged.

Donato's jaw dropped. The man from the cafe who negotiated to buy him from grandma stood in front of him.

"So, you remember me," the man said. "That old woman pissed me off for letting you escape before I could collect you. You saved me six thousand dollars, though. So I shouldn't complain too much. I didn't realize until now it was you they'd caught. Thought it was one of the other urchins from the streets. So, you made it here. I wonder how? Not to worry. It's not important. I have the witness to the execution, and I can make money from it." The man laughed sinisterly.

As he understood his circumstances, Donato was crushed in total defeat. He didn't have the energy to fight any more. His shoulders slumped, and his head hung low. He wondered if he should try running, and maybe they would shoot him to end his misery. The alternative didn't sound promising. "I won't go with you," he said in a mumble.

"Oh, you don't have a choice."

Donato stared at the man, tears dripping to the floor. "You're a monster."

The man laughed harder. "You hear that, guys? The kid said I'm a monster. He might be right, I suppose."

The men stood silent.

"Not to worry. You'll be out of my hair soon. Let's go."

The man who chased Donato moved forward to grab the boy. Donato struggled with his last ounce of energy. "Let me go... let me go!" he pleaded.

Chapter 59

Rescue

"I think I've found him, I have. I have found him."

"You have?" Roland said, straightening up in bed, alert, as he recognized the old man's voice. "Where?"

"We still have searching, we do, but we have a trail. Come and we will follow it together."

"Sure, where do I meet you?"

"Come to the park. We will start the hunt from there."

"Okay." Roland looked at the clock. It was nine in the morning. He could dress and grab a bite to eat in transit or when he arrived. "Give me an hour."

"I'll be waiting." The old man hung up.

"Who was that?" Deborah asked as she roused from sleep.

"The old man. He thinks he's found the boy. I have to go meet him."

"Not on your own, you're not."

"You can't come with me."

"Of course not. Promise you'll take Sergio with you this time. Not like the other times."

Roland had mentioned that the old man preferred searching without the minder, and she hit the roof. He knew he wouldn't get away with it a third time. "Okay, I'll persuade the old man to bring him with us today."

Deborah sat up in bed, not happy, but relieved. "What's his name, anyway?"

"I don't know. He just says to call him 'the old man'. I better get ready." He jumped out of bed and into the shower. Ten minutes later he leaned over Deborah, who was lying in bed, watching him. He kissed her. "I'll call you later, when I know something."

Deborah responded to the kiss and then said, "Promise?"

"Yes, I'll keep Sergio with me."

Roland and Sergio arrived at the park later than expected, but the old man sat waiting, watching life pass by with complete serenity. He looked towards Roland and the minder. "Ah, there you are."

"I'm sorry we're late."

"Never mind. Let's be on our way."

"I have to bring Sergio with us today," Roland said.

After glancing at Sergio, the old man said, "He'll be handy." They entered a more squalid and dilapidated part of Porta Plata and Roland soon lost direction, as they walked through narrower and more sinister looking alleys and side streets. He glanced at Sergio a few times, but Sergio just kept following the old man as if he knew their destination. After an hour's walk, Roland felt frustrated. "Where're we going?"

The old man kept his steady pace. "I heard a report of a murder in a ghetto yesterday. A whisper said a boy was there. We are just about there."

Fifteen minutes later, they arrived at an alley, the path

filled with the remnants of society, stacked up along the walls on either side.

"Do people live in this?" Roland asked.

"Of course. When there's nothing else and no one else, this becomes your home. Now stay quiet." The old man pottered his way into the alley's depths, poking at the piled rubbish as he shuffled. He stirred up a rustle of boxes.

A head poked out. "What do you want?"

"Now Casimiro, you know I rarely come looking for you."

Casimiro emerged from his boxed home and scanned his surroundings. He spied Roland and Sergio at the end of the alley. "Who are they?"

"Friends."

"They don't look like friends, especially that tall guy with muscles. You sure they're not trouble?"

"No, I'm helping them," the old man said, waving for Roland to come over.

Casimiro looked at him with distrust, and then at Sergio, and grunted. He returned to the old man. "What do you want then?"

"We're..." Roland started but the old man raised a hand.

"I hear you had trouble yesterday," the old man said.

Casimiro shuffled his feet. "You could say that. I found a boy hiding from a gang. Felt sorry for him, so I brought him back here. Stupid jackass, who sticks his nose into everything, saw him, and snitched. He heard there was a reward for the boy. They came and took him. They gave the idiot his reward alright. A loose neck. I'd have one too, if I hadn't vamoosed out of here."

"You got that picture?" the old man asked Roland, extending his hand.

Roland's heart started pounding. He fumbled through his wallet and handed over the picture.

"This the boy?" The old man showed the creased photo to Casimiro.

"Yeah, that's him. Said he was trying to get back to his Pa."

"He is."

"What's he to you?" Casimiro asked Vovo.

"We met at the park by the port. I've taken a fondness to the boy. Felt sorry for him. Roland here wants to take him back to his father. The other guy is just making sure Roland stays out of trouble."

"Oh. Well, I felt sorry for the boy. Guess he grew on me too." Casimiro looked at Sergio, still not trusting him.

"You know where they might have taken him?"

"No. I suspect one of the old warehouses in the old part. You can work there out of sight. It's a gang and they want him unharmed."

"You know why they're chasing him?"

"He told me he saw an execution, and they saw him watching."

"Hmm," the old man said, scratching his bristly chin. "They might want to sell him. That's the only reason for them wanting him unharmed."

"That's what I thought. He's lost to us now."

Roland's hopes plummeted.

"He-hem…" Sergio cleared his throat.

Everyone looked at him.

Sergio whispered in the old man's ear.

"You think so?"

Sergio shrugged. "I can make a few calls."

"Go ahead."

The bodyguard phoned a few contacts and came up

with a lead. "I might have something. One of my contacts says there's been action in a warehouse out in the old industrial precinct, it's a favorite for the Francosas. They're known for human trafficking. It's nice and quiet. It's driving distance, though."

Roland's hope soared at the news, and the renewed prospect of finding Donato at last. "Let's," he said.

The old man gazed at Roland. "Don't get too excited. Even if he's there, we don't know his condition." He looked at Sergio, thinking.

"You got a better idea?" Sergio asked.

"No, I don't. Okay, go get the car. We'll wait here."

Sergio looked at Roland, who nodded his approval.

"Thank you very much," Roland said to Casimiro, as they prepared to leave.

Casimiro shrugged. "I hope you find the kid. He deserves a break."

Roland opened his wallet and took out some money. "Here have this," he said.

Casimiro hesitated. "You know I'll spend it on drink."

"I hope you don't. Take it."

Casimiro accepted the money. "Thanks."

Delayed by frequent traffic jams, the drive to the warehouse took three hours. The vehicle's cabin was soured by the old man's body odor and Roland cracked the window, attempting to dilute the smell. The day approached evening as they arrived at Sergio's tip-off.

As the vehicle coasted to a stop one hundred meters from the back of the warehouse, Sergio assessed the streets. "Looks quiet here. There might be someone keeping watch in the front yard if someone's there."

"I'll peek," Vovo said, opening the door. "No one will notice a scruffy old man pottering around the street."

Sergio nodded. The old man slipped out and shuffled along the road, disappearing around the corner. Roland sat waiting, nervous, not used to taking part in clandestine operations.

The old man returned ten minutes later. "There's a guard in the front yard so someone's inside the warehouse. He's having a nap so we can go have a look."

Roland glanced at the old man, unsure what 'the guard having a nap' meant, but decided against asking. They jumped from the vehicle and walked to the warehouse in silence. The guard slumped against the fence without moving, oblivious. The warehouse door stood ajar, so they could peer through the gap, but the old man waved back Roland and Sergio as he saw danger on the other side. A man led Donato towards two vehicles. Two other men jumped from the vehicles and surrounded him. A third man also appeared. Vovo watched for a few more seconds before stepping away and beckoning Roland and Sergio to follow him.

"Donato is in there," the old man whispered.

"Well, let's get him," Roland said, taking a step towards the warehouse.

"Hold it. There are four men guarding him. They just arrived and are ready to start their business with Donato, whatever that might be. I dare say at least two are armed."

Roland's shoulders sagged at the revelation. "So what can we do?"

Sergio opened his jacket and revealed a hidden pistol in a shoulder holster. "I can use this if I need to."

"Let's hope not. Donato's in enough danger without bullets flying," the old man said. He thought for a moment. "I have an idea. I'll go in as if I'm just being inquisitive. If I can get close, I'll see if I can jump at least one of them. I'll leave the door open so you can cover me, Sergio. You stay where you are, Roland. This might get dangerous and it won't do for you to get hurt."

"I can't ask you to do this for me. I wanted to find him and I can't ask you to put your lives at risk."

"Point is, he's grown on me too," the old man said, a wistful smile crossing his face.

"I'm here to protect you," Sergio said with a sardonic smile. "Besides, I hate these people."

Roland surrendered to the two and let them run the show. They crept back to the door. The old man shrugged his coat into position and prepared for his performance. When he pulled open the door Donato was being dragged in a handgrip and they were preparing to leave. They glanced at the old man, bent and doddery, as he wandered inside the building.

"Hey, what are you doing, old tramp? Get out," one henchman said, as he walked over to him.

"I saw the door open, I did. I have a peek to find a bed and some comfort. Can't say no to an old tramp wanting shelter, can you?"

"You're not staying here."

The man holding Donato pulled him towards a vehicle.

Roland's phone started ringing, the noise reverberating through the silent evening. Startled, he tried switching it off, but his nervousness made it worse. Knowing the ruse over, Vovo lunged at the henchman, knocking him off balance. He jumped on top of him and pummelled him unconscious. The boss man took shelter near his car and the other two henchmen pulled out pistols. One of them roamed free from the group, scouting the darkness, while the second henchman held Donato with one hand and his pistol in the other and scanned the door. The old man rolled off his victim and used him for protection. He patted the man's torso and found a revolver. He cocked it, ready for use. Sergio became alert, arming his pistol. He pushed Roland away from harm. Roland complied.

Donato, realizing Vovo had come to save him, bit his captor's hand hard. The grip loosened, and Donato wriggled free, running to a vehicle for cover.

"Surrender the boy," the old man shouted in a commanding voice.

"That'll be difficult," the boss said. "if we don't have him. I can find him and we can come to an arrangement."

"Stay where you are. The boy can come out when he's ready."

Inching back to where Donato was hiding, the boss attempted to gain leverage. The old man fired a shot above his head. The two henchmen started shooting back to protect him. Sergio came into the fray and shot one man in the shoulder who fired back, hitting him in the chest. Outnumbered three to one, the old man shot the other henchman, removing him from the battle.

The boss had maneuvered himself to the rear of the vehicle and cornered Donato, grabbing him around the shoulders and lifting him off the ground. He took a gun from his holster and held it to Donato's head. "Stop or the boy dies," he shouted. The old man stopped shooting.

"Throw away your gun."

Vovo threw it towards the others, knowing he had failed.

"Stand."

The old man stood, staring at Donato, defeated. The boss relaxed the gun held to Donato and pointed it away. He dropped him to the floor but kept him close. The injured henchman nursed his shoulder wound.

A shot reported through the door, surprising everyone.

The bullet hit the henchman, dropping him to the ground. The boss aimed his gun at the old man and fired, hitting him in the hip. Donato broke free and ran away. Another shot came from the door, hitting the boss in the chest. Vovo quickly picked up the boss's gun before confiscating both henchmen's weapons. He looked towards the door, confused over who fired the shots. Sergio lay on the ground in no condition.

"Is it alright to come in now?" Roland asked.

Surprised, the old man said, "Of course." He held his hip as blood seeped through his clothes and the pain started outdoing the adrenaline.

Roland crept into the warehouse, expecting to get attacked at any minute. He walked over to the old man. "How bad are you hurt?"

"I'll live." The old man looked around. "You can come out now, Donato," he said, raising his voice.

Donato crept out from his hiding place, but when he saw the old man, he ran up to him, "You're hurt."

"Just a scratch," Vovo said, wincing as Donato's encircling arms nudged his injury. He looked over to Sergio. "Is he alive?" he asked Roland.

Roland felt for a pulse. "He's still alive. We should call an ambulance."

The old man considered his options. "I can't afford that. Go get the car. We'll load him into that and go to someone I know."

"Why not call an ambulance?"

"Long story."

"Who are you?"

"That is something I can't tell you. Where did you learn to shoot?"

"I was a marksman in the army when I was younger. I'd better go." Roland disappeared.

Donato clung to the old man, looking for comfort.

"It's okay now, Donato. You're safe and you can go home now."

Donato looked confused. "How?"

"That man will return you to your Papa."

"He will? Who is he?"

"Someone who promised to find you."

Roland returned in the rescue party's vehicle.

"Are you taking me to Papa?"

Roland smiled, despite the stress of the situation. "Yes, I am. As soon as we sort this out."

"Thank you."

"Let's get Sergio fixed." He maneuvered him onto the back seat.

The old man scrounged around the vehicle's glove box and found a first-aid kit with gauze, which he used to wrap his wound. "I'll drive," he announced. Roland got in the front seat and Donato sat on his lap. They sped off looking for help, leaving the others for someone else to find.

Chapter 60

Reunion

Roland and Donato arrived back at the hotel late in the evening, Donato falling asleep as they drove. They had left Vovo and Sergio at a hospice trusted for privacy. Roland realized that Vovo was more than he pretended to be, but he couldn't extract any information from him when pressed. Vovo had reassured Roland that Sergio would get expert medical treatment. Roland looked over at the sleeping Donato as they neared the hotel. His head slumped to one side and his chest rose and fell in slumber. His face relaxed. He wondered how long it had been since Donato had relaxed. Roland felt privileged that the boy felt at ease in his presence. They drove into the hotel basement carpark, and Roland picked him up out of the seat in his arms. He noticed a teddy bear tucked in his pants and smiled.

After taking the elevator to his floor, he fumbled for the key without wanting to wake Donato. The door opened as he aimed for the keyhole. Deborah, about to spray anger at her tired husband, noticed the sleeping boy in his arms and relented. She stepped away to let them enter and Roland placed Donato on the bed.

"He looks so peaceful," Deborah said as she gazed at Donato.

"Yes, he does."

"Where shall we put him?"

"We'll get a trolley bed set up." Roland picked up the phone and conveyed his request to reception. Room Service set up the bed and Roland had Donato tucked in half an hour later, still fast asleep, with the grime of his experiences still on his face and clothes. Roland drew the teddy bear from his trousers and placed it in his arms. Donato by reflex wrapped him tight.

A tear trickled down Deborah's cheek.

"What's wrong, sweetie?"

She wiped the tear away. "It just makes me sad we couldn't have a child of our own."

Roland walked over and hugged her in his arms. "It's been a long eventful day," he said, as the tension started unwinding, tiredness flooding in.

"Is there something you want?"

"A bite to eat and a good bottle of red wine would be nice."

Deborah ordered Room Service, and they sat sipping their wine after the meal, Roland relating the events of the day. He showered and fell into bed after that, plunging asleep.

He woke the next morning to his arm being shaken. He opened his eyes and saw Donato standing by the bed. "Morning, Donato."

"I need to use the bathroom."

"Of course. It's right through there."

Donato scampered into the bathroom, closing the door behind him.

Deborah stirred from her sleep beside Roland. "What's happening?"

"Nothing. Donato just wanted to use the bathroom."

"Oh. What's the time?"

He looked. "Just after seven."

"Ahhh..." Deborah complained.

As Donato averted his eyes from the sleeping woman, he stood next to the bed, uncertain what he should do. "Donato, I want you to meet my wife, Deborah," said Roland, laughing.

"Hello Mrs Deborah."

Roused from her sleep, Deborah hoisted herself up onto her elbows and smiled. "Hello Donato. You can call me Deborah."

"Hello Deborah." He stood waiting for any new instructions.

After a pregnant pause, Roland asked, "Are you hungry?"

Donato gave an exaggerated nod.

"Well, let's get you cleaned up and we'll go have breakfast."

"He needs new clothes," Deborah said.

"Nothing'll be open this early."

"I'll go to reception and get their help." Deborah hopped out of bed, strolled into the bathroom and freshened her face, before returning and getting dressed. She left as Roland led Donato into the bathroom.

"You want a bath or a shower?"

Donato gazed at the spa bath and then the shower next to it. "Bath," he said.

"Okay. Let's get it filled with warm water and you can

hop in." Roland turned on the taps and adjusted the water to the right temperature, filling the bath to half full. "That should do. Do you want help bathing?"

"I can do it myself."

"Okay. I'll leave you to it then. Just call out if you need anything." Roland left the door ajar and heard Donato splashing around, giggling. He collected the newspaper and sat on the bed, reading while he waited.

Deborah came back 45 minutes later with a bag in her hands. "It took persuading, but I got the owner of a children's clothes shop to open for me with the hotel manager's help. Hope these fit him," she said as she raised the bag.

"They'll be fine." Roland walked to the bathroom door. "How are you going in there? Ready to come out?"

"Yes, sir." A splashing sound echoed as Donato climbed out of the bath. "I can't reach the towel, sir."

"Can I come into the bathroom?"

"Yes."

Roland entered the bathroom and grabbed a towel for him. Donato dried himself. "We bought new clothes for you. We hope that you like them." He got them from Deborah and gave them to him, leaving the bathroom for him to dress. Donato came out dressed in the fresh clothes a few minutes later, clean and considering his new look.

"Do you like them?" Deborah asked.

He nodded.

"I'll get ready, and we can have breakfast," Roland said.

Donato ran over to his bed and grabbed his teddy bear, tucking it into the elasticized belt of his new pants. Roland and Deborah smiled. Donato reached up and held Roland's hand by instinct as they descended in the elevator, bringing a lump to Roland's throat. Ushered to a table, they had a buffet breakfast. Donato kept getting up and helping himself to more food to fill his plate. Roland looked on, amazed, wondering where it went.

Donato started crying.

"What's wrong?" Roland asked, concerned.

He looked up at Roland. "Why are people so mean?"

Roland turned to Deborah, stumped. "Not everyone is evil. Most people are good. We sometimes do things that upset others because we don't realize that we are hurting people by doing so. You've experienced so many terrible things over the past few weeks, you think everyone is bad. You will recover."

"I will never trust anyone again." The raw sadness that weighed on Donato's face showed how his childhood had been completed destroyed over the past weeks.

It filled Roland with grief, devastated that someone so young should have his innocence ripped from him before he could enjoy the carefree days of his childhood, never to regain what he had. "Not even us?"

"When am I going home to Papa?"

"As soon as we finish here and pack up," Roland said. "We have to drive to El Grieta first. That's a long way. We'll find Papa when we get there."

"Okay, thank you."

They started the journey an hour afterwards, with the prospect of a four-hour drive ahead of them. They stopped at a few places along the way for fuel and refreshments. As they reached the outskirts of El Grieta in mid-afternoon, they stopped at a cafe, going inside for coffees for themselves and a drink for Donato.

Roland phoned Sanchez. "Hello, is that Sanchez Barbosa?"

"Yes," a wary voice answered.

"It's Roland Cavendish. We met at your wife's funeral."

"Oh, yes, I remember you."

"I was wondering if we could meet."

"Okay, but you will have to come to my home. I can't travel at present."

"That's okay. Where do you live?"

Roland consulted a map. "It's twenty minutes from here."

"Why didn't you tell him you had Donato?" Deborah probed.

Roland shrugged. "Wanted to surprise him, I suppose."

At Sanchez's unit, Roland knocked on the door, butterflies in his stomach. He glanced at Deborah and saw she was nervous too. Donato kept shuffling from foot to foot in anticipation. A woman opened the door.

"Oh, we must have the wrong place," Roland said.

"Who are you looking for?"

"Sanchez Barbosa."

"This is his place."

"Oh, good. I'm Roland Cavendish. Is he here?"

The woman stared at Donato open-mouthed. She couldn't speak. Shaking herself out of her trance, she said, "Yes," and opened the door wider. Sanchez sat at the kitchen table.

"Papa!" Donato shouted as he ran to his father, arms held wide.

Sanchez looked shocked and broke into tears as he wrapped Donato in his arms and kissed his head repeatedly. "My dear Donato... Donato..." He looked up at Roland and Deborah, tears flowing from his face. "Thank you."

The End

About the Author

John Wegener grew up in the Adelaide Hills of South Australia. He has decided to express his imaginative dreams and start engaging in writing after a 34-year career as a Chemical Engineer in the steel industry, which has taken him to many countries and allowed him to experience many cultures. John currently lives in Wollongong, Australia with his wife and children.